INFECTION

A Pandemic Survival Novel

M.P. MCDONALD

D0381322

MPMcD Publishing

Join MP McDonald's Newsletter list and get a free copy of Mark Taylor: Genesis (The Mark Taylor Series: Prequel)

❀ Created with Vellum

For my beautiful, sweet, kind and talented daughter, Maggie. Happy Sweet 16th Birthday.

Also by M.P. McDonald

The Mark Taylor Series

Mark Taylor: Genesis

No Good Deed: Book One

March Into Hell: Book Two

Deeds of Mercy: Book Three

March Into Madness: Book Four

CJ Sheridan Thrillers

Shoot: Book One

Capture: Book Two

Suspense

Seeking Vengeance

Sympatico Syndrome Series

Infection: A Post-Apocalyptic Survival Novel (Book One)

Isolation: A Post-Apocalyptic Survival Novel (Book Two)

Invasion: A Post-Apocalyptic Survival Novel (Book Three)

Contents

Chapter One

"Cole, you need to put on the news."

Cole Evans dropped his spoon into his bowl of cereal and strode to the living room, phone pressed to his ear. He didn't bother asking why he needed to watch the news. If Elly Jackson told him he had to watch the news, then that is what he had to do. Unflappable Elly never panicked, and if her tone wasn't quite panic stricken, it was teetering on the edge and close to plunging over.

He shifted the phone to his other ear and reached for the remote on the coffee table. Clicking from the all sports network over to a morning national news show, he stopped on a station known for national news. The program was showing a split screen with the news anchor on the left and a correspondent on location on the right side of his screen.

"Okay. It's on. Any specific channel?"

The last few days there had been mentions on the news about an outbreak of 'flu' on Aislado Island, but most media outlets played it down. They said the rash of deaths was limited to those who had been in poor health anyway, but Cole had felt uneasy about the explanation. He feared Elly was going to confirm his worst suspicions.

"The WHO has issued a travel advisory to the Aislado Islands. It's just a precaution, but this virus, Sympatico Syndrome, named for the unusual

socially outgoing behavior displayed by victims, has already killed more than a dozen young sailors stationed here."

"What do you mean by 'socially outgoing behavior'?"

The correspondent held his hand to his ear, adjusting the feed. "Good question. I asked the same thing. In most cases, when people become ill, they take to their bed, but in this case, the virus does something one of the scientists explained takes place in the brain on a chemical level. The victims actually feel great. Their brains are flooded with feel-good chemicals that induce a euphoric state."

"So they die happy?" The anchor smirked, then looked off-camera, the smirk vanishing as he put a serious face back on. "I'm sorry to make light of the situation, it just seems like it's not such a bad disease if it makes you feel good."

"If it wasn't deadly, it might not be a bad thing, but with the mortality rate, currently sitting around ninety-eight percent, this disease can't be taken lightly."

The anchorman gave a quick nod. "Absolutely." His expression turned grim as he watched the feed from a tropical beach. "Jim, how have the locals been taking it? Have you noticed anyone panicking?"

Jim shrugged and glanced over his shoulder. The camera panned to a beach dotted with people stretched out on towels, kids shrieking as they played in the surf, and sailboats in the distance. His serious demeanor cracked as he took in the benign scene. "No, Bob, most consider it a problem confined to the naval base. And, as you can imagine, this isn't exactly a bad place to be stranded."

Bob chuckled. "No, I guess not. Thank you for the update, Jim. We'll check back with you at the top of the hour."

"Will do. And maybe I'll check out the local food until then." Jim grinned and added, "It's a tough job…"

His gut churning, Cole switched to another station—then another. With each channel, his stomach twisted tighter and tighter. Each program showed similar news. Ordinary people probably wouldn't be too worried. After the Ebola threat and the Zika virus, people had learned to tune out even the direst of reports. Yes, the diseases were real, but in faraway lands and too remote to worry over.

But most ordinary people weren't epidemiologists. Even the few who were hadn't worked on Aislado Island in the level four bio-labs.

Sure, it had been three years ago, but he had warned them not to mess with the virus. It was innocuous in its natural state, but when manipulated, it had properties which had provoked nightmares. He hadn't been in favor of biological warfare and cited Geneva Convention. He'd been assured it wasn't for that purpose. Intelligence hinted that some enemies of the U.S. may have it and if they didn't study it, they'd be in great danger. A vaccine or cure needed to be found and the project was fast-tracked. He understood the need but the risk posed by just having the virus around had him butting heads with his commanding officer.

If the illness being reported had started anywhere else, Cole wouldn't be worried yet, attributing it to so some exotic and isolated disease, but Aislado was the only bio-lab controlled by the U.S. that had the necessary security and facilities to study the virus. Only it wasn't as secure as everyone thought.

Was its release into the wild accidental? Or had there been an attack? Attack didn't seem likely because intentional dispersal of the virus would take place in an urban setting where the virus could spread quickly. It didn't make sense for the epicenter to be a remote island in the South Pacific. No matter how it started, it was out there, and unless they had come up with a vaccine or cure in the year since he'd left the Navy, then everyone was in grave danger.

He also knew how tight-lipped the government was, especially the military. If this was hitting the news media, chances were, it wasn't a new situation, just one that had finally escaped the stranglehold of information released to the public.

"Elly…is this what I think it is?" He'd worked closely with Elly before even though she worked for the CDC. They had been in West Africa together helping to contain the Ebola outbreak. He trusted her to tell him the truth. Cole's first worry was for his son. He had to get him back home if Elly's suspicions were accurate.

"I'm almost certain it's the same only they're calling it Sympatico Syndrome. I'm in Chicago right now trying to track down the people who flew in from Aislado over the last month. This is a hot spot because of the proximity of the naval base just north of here. We don't know how or when it escaped the containment lab, so not only am I searching for passengers who traveled from Aislado, but I'm also investigating unexplained deaths. So far, the news isn't good. The numbers the media has are probably only a small fraction of the actual deaths." She paused. "Do you remember how it killed the mice?"

Cole swallowed hard. "Yes." *So much blood.* Even for little mice. One minute they were running around in a frenzy in their cages, squeaking at each other through the glass, the next, they dropped dead, usually after vomiting a massive amount of blood. "It wasn't something I'd ever forget."

He knew the properties of the virus. It destroyed blood vessels from the inside out. Everything would be just fine until they suddenly burst throughout the body, causing instant death. Not that he'd seen it happen in a human, but he'd seen it in mice. It had made his blood run cold. Back then, the only mode of transmission had been blood and body fluids, but for it to spread so quickly, it had to have either been modified, or it mutated on its own. In all likelihood, it was now airborne. It was as if the Spanish Flu and Ebola virus had a baby and Sympatico Syndrome was the offspring.

"Me neither, but the difficulty I'm having in identifying cases is that doctors are attributing the cause of death as stroke and drug overdose. You know how festive this virus made the mice? Well, now plug that scenario into a twenty-year-old with access to drugs. Their urge to party skyrockets, so yes, they often do drugs just before death, but I would bet my last dollar that they aren't dying from a drug overdose."

Cole remembered the odd behavior of the rodents very well. The mice had practically been dancing in their cages. He tried to wrap his mind around the same behavior on a massive human scale. "What's the government doing to contain it?"

Elly sighed, her breath blowing over the mouthpiece and making it sound like she was in a wind tunnel for a moment. "That's why I'm here in Chicago. Some of my colleagues from the CDC are in San Diego, New York, Houston, Miami, L.A...I don't even know where all, but there aren't enough of us and the way this seems to be spreading." She paused, and he could picture her on the other end, her hand on top of her head, a fistful of hair pulled away from her face before she'd let it fall and sigh with frustration. "It's going to make it next to impossible to contain. Cole, I wanted to warn you. I know it's against protocol. I'm not supposed to tell anyone about this to prevent fear-mongering, but I think it's only a matter of days before we have a full-blown panic anyway. This thing is spreading faster than anything we've ever seen."

She didn't say she was afraid, but he heard the fear in her voice. "Thanks for the warning, Elly." Cole stood, but then immediately sat again, restless but with no direction yet.

"Hey, no thanks necessary. You'd do the same for me. I got your back here just like you had mine in Africa."

Cole didn't think what he'd done in Africa was a big deal. He'd merely sided with her when she'd refused to compromise on a proposal to cut some measures taken in regards to personal protective equipment. "You were right, they were wrong. It was easy to have your back in that one."

"Still, you stuck your neck out for me. We had each other's backs."

"We did." They had grown close during the humanitarian trip. "I owe you."

"Yeah. I hope I get a chance to collect on that debt someday." The doom in her voice drove the danger home. He had to make plans.

"I hope to god you do too. Listen, Elly…I have to call my son…" His mind raced as he wondered what to tell him.

"How's Hunter been doing?"

"He's good. Away at college now." He'd kept in touch with Elly via occasional emails, but she had a home in Atlanta, and he lived in southern Wisconsin. The spark of attraction they'd felt for each other on their trip to Africa had never had a chance to ignite. Any romantic feelings had to be stifled while there was still a chance one of them could have contracted the deadly Ebola virus, and then they had gone their separate ways. He'd thought about her often since then.

"Hey, Elly, if you need anything, let me know. I'm not that far away. I can be in Chicago in a couple of hours."

"Thanks. Right now, I'm working out of my hotel room, and I'm checking to see about catching a flight back to Atlanta. When the shit hits the fan, I want to be home. I have supplies stockpiled."

Cole rubbed his forehead with his thumb and first two fingers. "I don't. *Damn it.* I should have been prepared."

"There's still time if you hurry."

"Yeah. I'll get what I can. How long do you think we'll have to stay isolated?"

"I wish I knew. A month? Two? Maybe as many as six."

"Shit!" Cole paced his living room and peered out his front window at the neatly kept homes lining his street. "I need to warn my neighbors…" He spoke the thought aloud as he made a mental list of everyone he needed to inform.

"*No!* You can't tell *anyone!*"

"What?" Cole sank to the couch, circling the heel of his hand against his forehead as he tried to stave off the sharp stabs of a headache. "They'll need to prepare."

"Don't tell anyone until you have your own survival plan in place. Get supplies. Food, shelter, weapons. Whatever you can. If you tell anyone—even close neighbors— they'll tell others, and before you know it, the stores will be ransacked, and you can kiss your survival good-bye."

Cole understood her rationale, but it felt wrong. "But, there must be something I can do."

"What you need to do is save yourself and your son. Don't you have a brother?"

"Yes. Sean. He's married, and they have a boy and girl, both teenagers."

"Okay, well tell them. A small group will have a greater chance of surviving if this virus is the doomsday virus I think it is. You'll have to take extreme measures."

"Extreme measures? *Jesus, Elly.*" He knew what that meant, and he thought he might vomit. Cole couldn't imagine killing another person. His job had been to try to prevent as many deaths as possible, not contribute to mortality rates.

"You'll have to do what you have to do, Cole. Now, listen, my best estimate is you have a few days at most before all hell breaks loose. If you want to stay alive, you need to get supplies, and then go into seclusion. Don't interact with anyone for at least a month. By then, we'll know how bad it'll be, and you can adjust your plans, but I'm telling you, Cole. This could be *it*. This could be the infection that wipes mankind off the face of the earth."

Chapter Two

Where could they go? Elly said seclusion and he knew better than most the safety in proper isolation and quarantine, but he couldn't exactly stick a quarantine sign on his house and expect anyone to abide by it. If Elly's predictions came true and things got really bad, food could become scarce. How could he keep hungry people from breaking down the door and taking whatever they wanted?

He had one gun, but it was a hunting rifle which he'd had since he was a teenager. It had been a gift from his grandfather on his fourteenth birthday. He turned off the television—the news couldn't tell him anything more dire than what Elly had already revealed. He tossed the remote on the coffee table and scrubbed a hand down his face. "Shit." He needed a cup of coffee to get his brain working.

While he waited for it to brew, Cole stared from the kitchen into the living room. It was more of a great room, separated from the kitchen only by an island and a kitchen table.

The house was comfortable, but it wasn't a fortress. There was no hidden room in the basement, not that he could imagine living in one small room for at least a month. He and Hunter would probably be at each other's throats inside of a week.

Thinking of Hunter, his stomach twisted. How was he going to break the news to his son? How could he tell them that he had to leave college and get home as soon as he could? School was a thousand miles away. Hunter had never made the drive alone. Late last summer, Cole had driven with him and had then flown home. At Christmas break, Hunter had flown roundtrip. The weather was too unpredictable in January to risk driving, but now Hunter would have to do it alone. Cole thought briefly about flying him back, but the thought of his son cooped up on an aircraft with other passengers who could possibly infect him set Cole's heart racing.

Hunter would have to drive. Or maybe he should go get him? But by the time he drove there and they headed back, at least four or five days would pass. If Hunter got a few supplies and left tomorrow, he could drive it in a little over two days. The sooner he spoke to him about it, the better.

That still left the problem of what to do when Hunter arrived home. Would he be any safer here than in Colorado? In his mind's eye, he saw them trying to defend their home from a horde of diseased neighbors. Scenes from a popular television program popped into his mind. He shook his head. Dragging a hand down his face, he wiped the image of defending the house from zombies out of his mind. He needed to focus on what he could do to secure their safety, not conjure up far-fetched images of flesh-eating zombies.

Cole thought of his brother's family— Sean, Jenna, and their two children. They were the only family he had left since their Uncle John had died a few months ago. Sean's kids were Hunter's only cousins.

Brenda's family had been scattered, and it was possible his late wife's brother might have some children by now; Cole hadn't seen Kevin since Brenda's funeral, but he hadn't heard anything. Kevin had been only about twenty at the time of Brenda's death and hadn't been close to his sister.

Cole had never met Brenda's father as he'd died of cancer a few years before he'd met her, but her mother had lived until a couple of years ago. He and Hunter had attended the funeral, but Kevin hadn't been there. Cole couldn't recall the reason. Active duty maybe?

He poured a cup of coffee and took a sip, then made a face. Maybe one day he'd learn how to brew a decent cup. His cell phone buzzed on the counter, and he glanced at it. *Hunter*. Crap. He hadn't had time to decide how he was going to break the news. How could he tell his son that the world as he knew it could be coming to an end?

Cole decided he didn't have to blurt it all out right away. A warning would suffice—for now. He'd try to play it down until he had some kind of plan in the works.

He cleared his throat. "Hey, Hunter! How's it going?"

"Hi, Dad. Things are good."

They made small talk, caught up on how Hunter was doing in his classes, and Hunter let slip that he'd accidentally spilled a drink all over his laptop.

Cole's usual response would have been an annoyance. Today, he only said, "Oh. Well, we'll have to get you another one soon."

Hunter's silence let Cole know his reaction was unexpected. Well, there was nothing he could do about it now. A computer would probably be next to worthless in a month.

"Uh, okay, Dad. Did I tell you that I'm pulling a B in chemistry?"

"That's great." He had tried to force some cheer into his comment, but it was no use. He was too busy trying to figure out how to broach the subject of the disease. Hunter could have told him that he was failing every class, and it would have garnered the same response. His mind was so busy trying to form an escape plan that he responded with words that he hoped were appropriate.

"And, Dad, I wondered if I could take some friends up to that island this summer?"

"Island?" Had he missed some crucial part of the conversation? The last thing he remembered was Hunter saying something about hiking in the foothills.

"The island Uncle John left you. You said you were going to sell it, but I wondered if, before you do that, I could go there for a few days. A couple of the guys here were talking about coming for a visit, and there's nothing to do at our house. I thought it would be cool to camp out on the island. So? Could we?"

Cole couldn't speak for a moment as his thoughts raced. "Hunter, you're a freaking *genius*."

"Huh? Why?"

He yanked open the drawer where he'd stuck the large manila envelope with the information about the island, found it and dumped the contents on the counter. There they were—the deed and a ring of keys. Also included was a report from the lawyer who had handled

Uncle John's will. Another sheet of paper listed the buildings and a brief inventory of the contents, ending with miscellaneous. He pulled out two more sheets of paper that were titles to two boats. One a pontoon, the other some kind of fishing boat. He didn't recognize the make of it and made a mental note to do an internet search. He wondered if they were in working order. Had his uncle prepared them for winter?

"Hello? Dad? Are you still there?"

"Yes, hold on a minute. I'm looking at the information about the island."

"That's okay, you don't have to give me an answer right this minute. A week or so will be fine."

"I know, hang on a sec, okay? I'm trying to think something through."

"Do you want to call me back later?"

The island would be perfect. He'd received the paperwork around Christmas time, and he and Hunter had talked about a little camping excursion before he sold it, but now, instead of selling it, he could make it their refuge.

"Yeah, sure. I'll call you back soon. Keep your phone handy." He wondered if the buildings on the island were habitable. Cole pulled his mind from the island to the present and the disease, catching his son just before he hung up. "Wait! Hunter? Could you do me a big favor today?"

"Yeah, I guess so." He sounded puzzled.

"I've been seeing stories on the news about a new bug floating around and for the next day or two, think you can skip the socializing a bit?"

"Well, it's not like I'm mister popularity here, Dad. I spend most of my time studying anyway."

Cole sighed. He was a smart kid, but he found focusing on school-work difficult. "Are you still taking your meds?"

"Yeah, Dad."

The eye roll was practically audible over the phone, but Cole wanted to make sure Hunter was able to focus on what he was about to say next. "I'm serious, Hunter. I want you to stay in your room until I call you later today. I have some important things to do, but I'll get back to you today. Meanwhile, make sure everything is charged up and maybe pack your clothes and stuff."

"*Pack my clothes?* What the hell is going on, Dad? I have a class in an hour."

"I can't tell you until I know more, but I'll let you know as soon as possible. Just…just don't talk to anyone. And about your class today —skip it."

"You *want* me to skip my class? *Now* you're freaking me out."

HUNTER CLICKED off the phone but stared at the screen for a few moments as he tried to fathom his father's odd request. Stay away from everyone? But what about getting the computer? And why hadn't his dad given him grief over the broken computer?

He'd heard the spiel more times than he could count.

Be more careful, Hunter.

Take better care of your belongings, Hunter.

These things aren't free, Hunter.

He tried to be careful, but he wasn't programmed to be neat and tidy. His room was always a disaster, his notes a chaotic mess, and on a good day, he managed to find matching socks. He glanced down at his feet and wiggled his toes. Both socks were white but had different colored stripes on them. Close enough.

College had been both a relief and a nightmare. He no longer felt the constant pressure to keep his room ready for a surprise inspection —as his father used to call it—but on the other hand, without that pressure, he'd let things get out of control. He told his dad that a soda had spilled on the computer, which was bad enough, but the truth was, he'd stepped on the laptop by accident when it was buried under a pile of dirty clothes.

He glanced around his now neat room. Too little too late. He'd pay his dad back someday. If he ever graduated from college. That was a big if at this point. Even with all of the studying he did, he usually forgot some paper or did it, then forgot to turn it in.

Hunter flopped onto his bed and turned on the TV, flipping through channels. If he was going to be stuck here, at least he could find something to watch. He didn't mind skipping class, especially since his dad had sanctioned it, but he didn't want to be bored out of his mind either. With the laptop reduced to a big paperweight, there wasn't much to do in his dorm room. He eyed his books and briefly thought about studying, but only for a moment. He wasn't that bored yet.

He paused as he scanned channels. Some morning talk show was interviewing a celebrity who looked familiar but whose name he couldn't remember. It bugged him and he was hoping they'd flash the woman's name on the screen or say it, but the host never did. Instead, he practically cut the celeb off mid-sentence and switched to the anchorperson at the news desk.

Hunter zoned out for a moment as he thought about the trip to the island and why his dad had called him a genius. It didn't make sense, but he wasn't about to turn down praise even if he wasn't sure what he'd done to warrant it. He hoped he'd be able to go now that he'd already brought up the trip. His grade in calculus was borderline, and if he failed, he'd have to repeat the class in the summer. His fall schedule was already full.

The other problem would be paying for the class. His father paid for most of his college, but he had flat out stated that any classes he had to retake were not going to be on his dime. Hunter groaned. He loved his dad, but why did he have to be such a hard-ass at times? No way he'd tell his dad he'd flunked calculus. Again. He'd already taken it in the fall. What he'd hoped to do was squeeze it in some-where along the line, maybe take it as an online course over the summer, but then he'd stepped on his computer.

Shame made him squirm. It was so embarrassing. Most of his friends had taken the class in high school, and here he was taking it in college.

Would his dad ever get it through his head that he was too stupid to graduate from college? It had to be obvious by now that he hadn't inherited the brainiac gene.

Did he take after his mom? He often wondered. She was only a hazy memory, but what he remembered, he treasured. His clearest recollection was cuddling with her while she read him stories before bedtime. She'd feather his hair with one hand, and he'd turn the pages for her while she held the book with the other.

What would his life have been like if she hadn't driven to school that day when he was six to bring him the lunch that he'd forgotten? Logically, he knew it wasn't his fault. It was the fault of the drunk driver who had worked the night shift, went out after work at a local pub that opened early, and drank for a few hours before getting back behind the wheel.

She had gone to college, though, so she had to have been smarter than him. In fact, his dad always told him how brilliant she had been. So, if she was smart, and his dad was practically a genius, how come he was so stupid?

Hunter glanced over at his desk and the ruined laptop. He envisioned himself still taking classes when he was fifty, his hair gray or gone, as he tottered around campus, his back bent and twisted from lugging a bag of books for thirty years.

He had barely even been accepted to this school and had a feeling his dad had pulled some strings. How else to explain his acceptance at his father's alma mater when his grade point average had been a C-plus at best?

The only reason it was even that high was because of the shop classes he'd taken every year. He liked woodshop best and one time his class had volunteered a Saturday to work with Habitat for Humanity. That had been a fantastic day. Now that his dad had retired from the Navy and was buying houses, doing some work on them and flipping them for profit, why couldn't he just help with that? He was good at that kind of thing, and he liked it. He wouldn't need college for that.

"...and so what does that mean for us here in the U.S.? Is there any danger of the disease spreading beyond the island?"

Hunter focused on the television as the question cut through his thoughts. He turned the TV up and swung his feet off the bed, sitting on the edge.

"Not really, Barbara. As you know, there's a Navy base here, and they have everything buttoned down. All non-essential personnel are restricted to their quarters. MREs have been distributed, enough to last them at least a week, if need be, but the official word is that is all precautionary, and the

restrictions will probably be lifted in the next few days if cases don't increase."

A woman, apparently Barbara, occupied the left side of the split screen and the reporter she spoke to appeared on the right side. He was in front of a hotel. Palm trees framed the scene and so Hunter relaxed. Whatever was going on, it was a long way away from him.

"It seems the situation has deteriorated rather quickly. Are they telling you what is going on inside the base?"

Hunter cocked his head. The reporter was saying one thing, but his movements didn't jibe with his words. He looked nervous. Jumpy. Sweat trickled from his forehead as the reporter pulled a handkerchief from his pocket and swiped his face.

"How are you and the crew holding up, Roger?"

Roger shrugged and looked past the camera, presumably to his cameraman and whatever other crewmembers were out of camera shot. *"We're great. As soon as we're done with this report, we've been instructed to return to our hotel rooms until further notice."*

"Do you have to eat MREs too? You'll have to give us a review of them when this is over." Barbara smiled, but it looked forced.

"We actually haven't heard how we'll be eating. Most of the local shops have already closed down either by order or because of fear. We picked up a few items yesterday, so I guess we'll just have to raid the mini-bar. As long as the network is picking up the tab." He gave a weak smile.

"Okay, well, you all get to safety, and we'll check back with you later. I've learned that we have arranged to keep in contact via phone."

Roger nodded, already packing up his microphone as the feed cut off.

Hunter pulled his phone from his pocket to call his dad. This must have been what he'd been talking about. But it was way out in the middle of the Pacific. He didn't get why his dad was freaking out. Maybe he didn't know it was so far away. He really couldn't afford to miss a class. If he did, he'd never catch up.

Then he thought about his dad and about the disease on that island. There must be something else going on. His father had been concerned about Ebola long before it hit the national news. No. If anyone were up to date on this, it would be his dad. It was one thing to withhold the outcome of his calculus grade, but it was another to go against his advice about something like this. His dad wasn't prone to panic.

He reached under his bed and grabbed his suitcase and backpack and began packing.

Chapter Three

Sean Evans clicked through the tax forms. Damn taxes. He'd envisioned a relaxing Saturday watching basketball, but he had to get this done before the deadline.

"Jenna? Do you have a receipt for that donation we made to the soup kitchen? I really wish you'd be more organized about this stuff." As an electrician, he ran his own business, and most of the time, enjoyed it, but he hated tax time, and his accountant had called, said he was sick and wouldn't be able to do it this year. At least he'd let Sean know before he drove across town to deliver all the documents.

His wife appeared at the door to the office. "I put everything I had in the folder. If it's not there, I have no idea where it is."

"Jeez." Sean sorted through the tiny scraps of paper. Why didn't they make receipts full-sized? These sticky-note sizes were a pain in the ass to copy and fax, not to mention they fluttered all around the desktop. He spotted the one he was looking for. He sighed. A hundred bucks. It was hardly worth claiming.

He glanced up when he saw Jenna watching him, her arms crossed. "What?"

"No apology?"

"For what?"

She crossed her arms, her eyebrow arching.

"Listen. I'm sorry. I'm really stressed. You know how much I hate dealing with all this crap."

She approached the desk. "I know." She circled behind him and began kneading his shoulders. It felt wonderful.

He allowed himself a moment to enjoy her ministrations, then shrugged and turned, pressing a light kiss on the top of her hand. "Thanks, but I better get this done."

"You have a few days. The kids are watching a movie in the family room, and we could actually sneak upstairs..." She dropped to bring her head level with his, her arms loosely clasped across his chest. She played with the top button on his shirt. "I know something that'll relax you."

Sean was tempted. *So tempted.* Before he could answer, he heard the slam of a car door. "Who's that?"

Jenna straightened and peeked through the curtain to the driveway. "It's your brother." She sounded as surprised as he felt.

"Cole?"

Jenna turned and grinned. "You have another brother I don't know about?"

He shook his head with a smile. "Shut up, smart ass."

Cole knocked, and then he did something completely out of character. He walked right in, his voice echoing in the entrance hall. "Hello?"

Sean strode to him, grinning. "Hey, Cole. How's it going?" He held out his hand to shake and pull Cole in for a brief, manly hug like they normally did, but Cole ignored the hand and said, "Are the kids here?"

Jenna shot Sean a puzzled look, and he was sure his face mirrored hers. "Yeah, they're in the other room watching a movie. Some horror movie."

"Good. I'm glad they're home."

"I'll get them—"

"No!" Cole waved her off. "I have something I need to discuss with you two first."

Sean nodded. "Yeah. Sure. Why don't we go have a cup of coffee? I think we still have some cake leftover from last night's dessert." He looked over to Jenna, who nodded.

Cole gave a brief nod and headed to the back of the house, but when he got to the kitchen, he didn't sit at the table but leaned back against the counter, his jaw tense. Sean wondered if he was angry about something and if so, what did it have to do with him and his family?

"Have you guys been listening to the news today?"

Sean shrugged. "I saw sports scores. Been busy working. In fact, I was going to call you in the morning and invite you out to dinner tomorrow evening. To celebrate." Cole gave him a blank look. "Remember? I told you my company was in the running for the contract from the A&Y Builders for that new subdivision. Well, we got it!" He beamed and waited for the congratulations. When he'd told Cole about his bid for the contract, his brother had wished him well. Now, the expression that crossed his face was anything but happy.

Jenna glanced at Sean but then focused on Cole. "Are you talking about that thing going on out on Aislado Island?"

Sean tilted his head. Jenna kept better tabs on the news than he did. Most of it was just depressing stuff, and he didn't have time to waste on shitty news.

Cole looked from Jenna to Sean. His expression hit Sean in the gut. He'd only seen his brother wear it one other time. When he'd come over to tell them about Brenda's death. "Oh, Jesus. Cole...is Hunter okay?" If something happened to Hunter, Cole would fall apart.

Jenna gasped, covering her mouth. Already, Sean saw tears pooling in her eyes.

Cole's eyes widened, then he raised his hands, shaking off Jenna's question. "No...no. Hunter is doing well. I spoke to him only a few hours ago."

Sean heaved a sigh. "So then why the somber expression? You're scaring the crap out of us, bro."

Jenna crossed to Sean to stand beside him. She nodded agreement to his question.

"That disease they're talking about...it's spreading. *Fast*. I got word from one of my former colleagues who works for the CDC, and she said we need to disappear for a while. Get away from everyone.

That this virus is bad. And it spreads faster than anything they've ever seen."

Sean crossed his arms. "Get away? Where the hell would everyone go?"

"I'm not talking about everyone going somewhere. I'm talking about *us.*" He circled his hand, encompassing all of them, "and our kids. We need to go, and I have just the place."

"Hold on a second." Sean held up a hand. "We're not going anywhere. I have a big meeting with the other contractors next week, and I have to prepare. No way am I jeopardizing it because of some flu bug out on some island in the Pacific."

"You don't understand. This virus, *Sympatico Syndrome*, is going to have a *global impact*. In fact, it already has. It's killed over four hundred people in the U.S—"

"Four hundred people? Seriously? Out of three hundred and thirty million?" Sean chuckled. "Yeah. I'm scared of that. I think the reason you're worried is that it's your job to worry about diseases." Then he remembered Cole was retired from that job. "Or, well, it used to be your job."

Cole stabbed his hands through his hair. "Shit, Sean. Give me a little credit. Did I panic during the whole Ebola scare? No. I was the voice of reason. I remember you were worried that Jenna would catch it at work. Did I laugh at you?"

Sean shrugged. "So? I was right to be worried. Two other nurses caught it."

"And they were over a thousand miles away. I told you as long as she was cautious, the chance of her getting it was minuscule. Remember? Just coming into contact with someone who had the disease was improbable, but even if she had, with correct precautions, the risk could be minimized. I know. I dealt with the disease in West Africa."

Jenna nudged him with her elbow. "You called Cole about me?"

Sean slanted a look at his wife. "Hey, I was worried. I'll admit it."

Jenna rolled her eyes but turned her attention to Cole. "I've heard some rumors at work that there was some new virus, but we haven't had any official word on what's going on."

"Here's what's happening." Cole pulled out a kitchen chair and sat down. "Do you have a pen and paper?"

Sighing, Sean opened a kitchen drawer and pulled out a yellow legal pad and dug around for a pen that worked. He tossed both on the table in front of Cole. "Here you go."

"Thanks." He started drawing circles and labeling them. "This is the chain of infection. The top of the chain is the infectious disease itself. Could be a virus or bacteria, even a fungus, but in this case, it's a virus."

"So antibiotics won't kill it?" Sean felt stupid. This wasn't his realm at all.

"No." Jenna worried her bottom lip. She did that when she fretted, and now Sean was worried, too.

"Jenna's right. Antibiotics won't touch this. They might help with a secondary infection, but we don't know if that will be an issue." He tapped the next circle in a clock-wise rotation. "This is the reservoir where the virus sets up housekeeping before heading out to find other hosts. At this point, it's probably too late to worry about that right now. We need to worry about the next parts of the chain—portal of exit and mode of transmission. I'm guessing it's respiratory tract. It's the only thing that makes sense for such a rapid transmission." He jotted some words down, but Sean couldn't read them from where he stood.

Cole continued, "But, is it airborne? Droplet? What about contact? Does it require direct contact with an infected host? Or does it remain infectious for an extended period of time on surfaces?" He rapped on the tabletop. "Like furniture and doorknobs—that kind of thing. And it may also be blood borne although that has the least chance of spreading so it's not my concern right now. It's something to think about later when survivors are over the initial illness." He crossed out *blood borne*.

"What kind of precautions do you think we need to take?" Jenna moved closer to the table and peered at the diagram.

Cole pointed with the pen to what he'd written. "I would guess it's airborne for sure, and probably lingers in the air for quite a while. There's no other explanation for how it's spread so quickly. Regular masks won't keep it out. You'd have to wear an N95 mask." He pointed to Sean. "You probably have some of those in your work truck for keeping out fumes and such. I have some also, but we need a hell of a lot more to get through this. Jenna, do you have any around the house? Or could you get some from work? Time is of the essence. Once others realize what is going on, those masks will be hard to come by. It has to be our chief priority."

Jenna's eyes widened. "I suppose I could find some in the storage closet at work, but I could get fired for taking them."

Cole set his pen down and pinched the bridge of his nose then rubbed his eyes. He sighed and spread his hands. "I'm obviously not making this clear. This disease—*Sympatico Syndrome*—it's going to change the world. We're talking pandemic, possibly on a scale mankind has never seen. It'll make the Spanish Flu look like the common cold. The bubonic plague will be a footnote in history after this." He looked directly at Jenna. "Your job is gone. All of our jobs are gone. Right now, our only task is to survive, and I'm trying to draw up plans for that. But I think it would be better for you not to even go near the hospital. There's too big of a chance you could get exposed. We'll have to get masks at the drug stores. Once we get to the island, we shouldn't need them anymore."

Sean saw Jenna's eyes pool, tears escaping, and he crossed to the table, slamming his hand down. "*Stop it, Cole!* I don't know what the hell you're thinking, but I won't tolerate you coming in here with your doomsday disease and scaring the shit out of my wife!"

The television in the den, where the kids were, became quiet. Muted, probably, when one of them heard him yelling. Light foot-steps sounded in the hallway. *Piper.* Trent didn't tread lightly. At four-teen, he clomped around the house like an ungainly young colt.

"Mom? Dad? What's going on?" Piper came around the corner and stood in the threshold between the dining room and kitchen. She spotted Cole and broke into a grin. "Hi, Uncle Cole! What are you doing here?"

She tucked a few long strands of dark hair behind one ear and crossed to the table, giving Cole a quick hug. At least his brother managed a return smile. The first crack in his serious countenance since he'd arrive.

"Hey ya, Piper. I had some news I had to tell your parents."

Piper's eyes swept the room, landing on each of them, and frowned. "What was all the yelling about?"

Sean answered, "Nothing, sweetie. Me and Cole are having a disagreement. You know how we are...sometimes."

It was more than sometimes. Sean loved his brother, but Cole tended to try to take charge of everything. He was only a year older but sometimes acted like he was more Sean's father than an older brother. It probably had something to do with their dad dying while they were still kids. Their mom had been devastated, and it took her years to be able to deal with normal life again. If it hadn't been for Cole, Sean knew he probably would have ended up running with the bad crowd in school, so he guessed he had that to thank him for. Still, high school was more than two decades ago. He had a family and business now. Sure, he hadn't gotten advanced degrees and been a big shot in the Navy, but he'd built a good life all on his own.

"Oh. Okay." She opened the fridge and pulled out an apple and moved to stand by Sean. "The movie was stupid. That's the last time I'll let Trent choose. Mom, can we go shopping later?"

Jenna shot a look at Cole, then gave a vague reply. "We'll see. Why don't you go clean your room, then we can discuss it."

"Fine." Piper sighed, but then smiled at Cole. "Tell Hunter I said 'hi' next time you talk to him."

Sean held his breath, waiting for Cole to launch into his spiel about the disease, but he only nodded. "I will."

When Piper was safely out of earshot, Sean said, "What? You draw the line at frightening my kids?" He painted his words with sarcasm.

Cole gave him a long, steady, look. "I'm sorry you think I'd do something like that. I didn't come here to scare anyone, but I'll admit this disease—it scares the living hell out of me. Listen to me, Sean...I studied disease for a living. Not just diseases we have now, but killers from throughout recorded history, and I'm telling you, we've *never* seen one like this. Do you really want to know why it has me beyond worried?"

Jenna nodded, and Sean shrugged.

"For one thing, it delays symptoms, or somehow masks them."

Cole's eyebrow cocked as he jabbed his first two fingers on the table to emphasize his points. "Victims don't seem to know that they are even ill until only minutes before they die. It's like the virus floods the body with endorphins. Dopamine, oxytocin, vasopressin. All feel good hormones. The victims feel fantastic! They want to be around people. Mingle. Have a good time." He snapped his fingers. "Then they die. Like, drop dead, literally."

"Is that why it's spreading so fast? Can't we quarantine everyone who's come in contact with the virus?" Jenna—the voice of reason. Sean sent her a grateful look.

"They tried that. Did you see on the news how the sailors on the base on Aislado were confined to quarters? It didn't work. Not only didn't it work, but the virus has spread to all corners of the globe by now. What they should have done was close the airports at the very first sign of infection, and even then, that might not have helped. How do you screen for a disease that has few symptoms until the victim drops dead?"

Sean finally had something to offer. "Anyone who seems extremely chatty could be quarantined if that's the only sign."

Cole shook his head. "Too many false positives. Lots of people are chatty—especially when they're nervous."

"Okay, Cole, so you've given us an overview," Jenna waved at the diagram, which Cole had stopped working on, "but what kind of mortality rate are we looking at? Ten percent? Twenty?"

"I don't know for certain, but from what I learned, it's closer to ninety-eight."

"*Percent?*" Even Sean knew that was bad. Worse, it was awful.

Cole gave him a grim nod.

"Shouldn't you be doing something about it? Calling to see if you can help manage the crisis? Hell, Cole, I know you're not in the reserves anymore, but this is an emergency!"

Pain and guilt flashed in Cole's eyes. "I wanted to help. I told Elly that as soon as I saw that my family was safe, I'd call and do whatever they needed. She said it was too late, and basically, to save our own skin. That my job was to survive." A muscle jumped in Cole's jaw.

It was the pain and guilt that convinced Sean. One reason Cole had retired was he had felt useless as he'd watched so many people die in West Africa. One night, the two of them had gone out for drinks. It was the Saturday after Hunter had left for college and Cole had seemed a bit lost. They'd ended up getting hammered, and it was only then that Sean had learned the scope of what Cole had seen. He'd spoken of whole families wiped out by Ebola. He'd been haunted by the sight of children orphaned and then left to fend for themselves out of fear that they harbored the disease. Some villages deep in the forest had lost half of their population.

The free flow of alcohol that evening had weakened the barriers Cole erected to deal with his emotions. He'd blinked back tears as he'd confessed his feeling of helplessness in the face of such suffering. Not used to seeing his stoic brother so emotional, despite the several shots he'd downed, Sean knew he'd never forget the stricken expression in his brother's eyes. Cole wore the same look now, and it sent a bolt of pure fear straight through Sean.

"What do we need to do?"

Jenna gave Sean a look of surprise, and opened her mouth as if to question him, but as her eyes searched his face, she blanched and closed her mouth. With a deep breath, she nodded.

"Yes, Cole. Tell us what your plan is?" Jenna got another pad of paper from the drawer along with another pen. She sat down at the table, pen poised.

Sean slid onto a chair, his thoughts not nearly as organized as Jenna's. Fear for his family was foremost in his mind. Piper and Trent were only teenagers. He had to do whatever he could to keep them safe.

Cole looked at both of them for a moment as if judging whether they truly believed him, and then he began outlining his plan for using the island Uncle John had left him. Sean had remembered wondering what in the world Cole was going to do with an island in a lake in the middle of the Northwoods. Sure, it would be good for the occasional fishing trip, but maintaining it for an occasional fishing trip seemed like a huge expense. It would be cheaper to just take a fishing trip once or twice a year.

Sean had even felt guilty that he'd received the beautiful house in town and wondered why Uncle John hadn't given Cole the 'good' property—especially since Cole's new career was flipping houses. He would have loved fixing up Uncle John's house and selling it for a profit. It wasn't in bad shape, but could use some updating.

From Sean's fuzzy recollection of the island and the resort, he thought it might work, short term. The cabins had been pretty bare-bones even to a young kid. He couldn't imagine what they looked like now, over thirty years later. Were they even still standing?

He voiced his fears to Cole. "What if we get there and no buildings are habitable?"

Cole nodded. "I know. I was worried about that too so I dug out the information I received on the property. There's at least a main house that should be fine. Uncle John stayed there as recently as three months before he died, according to the electric bills, so it couldn't be that bad. As to the rest of the buildings, they're listed in the will they're still standing, but your guess is as good as mine as to what shape they're in. I guess we should include some building supplies to bring with us."

"I can take some lumber in my work truck. Jenna, you'll have to follow me in your car. We need to bring as much as we can."

Cole agreed. "Do you think Piper can drive my car? I'm going to get a rental truck to get as much as we can to the island. I'm heading out to get more supplies when I leave here. I don't think we'll be able to transport it all in our own vehicles."

"Just how much do you think we'll need?"

"I asked Elly how long we should plan for, and she wasn't sure. Anywhere from a month to six months." Cole leveled a look at Sean, his expression bleak. "I think we should be prepared to be on our own even longer."

"Jesus." Sean swiped a hand down his face as he tried to envision the world as Cole was predicting it. "I hope you're wrong, Cole."

"Me too." Cole took a deep breath. "But if I am wrong, and believe me, I hope I am, if you guys join Hunter and me on the island, you may end up losing your job." He looked at Jenna, then at Sean, "Or your business. While I would never intentionally mislead you, with such high stakes, you have to know that I can't see the future. I'm going by my colleague's advice and supplementing it with what I've learned from listening to the news. Even though there isn't nearly as much as there should be, I suspect what we're hearing on the news is just the tip of the iceberg. There's so much going on beneath the surface that either the media hasn't learned what's really going on yet, or they have, and they're making their own escape plans and not letting the general public in on it yet."

Chapter Four

"Now that we have a basic plan, I need to call Hunter back. I have him sitting tight in his dorm. I told him to pack, but who knows if he really did." Cole pulled out his cell phone and got up from the kitchen table. Sean and Jenna exchanged a look, and he knew they were thinking about their own kids and how to break the news to them.

"Hey, it's me." Cole dragged in a deep breath. "Remember when I said I had news to discuss with you?"

"Is it about that disease? Sympa—sym something?"

"Yes, Sympatico Syndrome. Remember Elly Jackson? From my Ebola mission?"

"Yeah. The one you had the hots for?"

"*The hots...?*" Cole shook his head. Now wasn't the time. "Anyway, she called me to give me some inside information. The situation is grave. The news isn't giving the whole truth, or maybe they don't know it, but Elly is confident this is going to be devastating and wants us to take precautions. That's why I said you were a genius. I didn't know where to go to isolate ourselves, but you gave me the idea of using the island. It's far enough out in the lake from what I recall that the only way to get to it is by boat."

"What about school? What if it turns out to be nothing? I have finals coming up, and I can't afford to miss them."

"Forget school. If Elly's wrong, we'll figure out where to go from there. Your safety and health are more important." Cole couldn't believe he was basically advising his son to drop out of school.

"Okay, but what should I do now? I packed like you told me. Am I flying home?" There was a hint of fear in Hunter's voice, as though he was trying to mask it.

"No. It's too dangerous. There's no way to know if the other passengers are contagious. You'll have to drive."

"Drive? Alone? Won't that take me days to get there?"

"Two days if you only stop to sleep and go to the bathroom."

"Okay." There was a pause, then Hunter asked, "Dad, what if I catch it?"

"Listen to me, Hunter. This is scary, but you'll be okay. I'm sure I'm just over-thinking this. It was my job to predict worse case scenarios, remember?" Cole spoke in his calmest voice and glanced at Sean and Jenna. They looked as worried as he felt.

"But, here's what I want you to do. Go to the nearest ATM and use the credit card I gave you for emergencies. Get a cash advance. Whatever the limit is. Then get yourself some supplies. Water, hand sanitizer, masks, gloves. Food you can eat in the car. That kind of thing. Be low-key. Don't act panicked. If you can, go to a few different drug stores for those items, buying gloves at one store and masks at another. Try a hardware store for masks. They carry respiratory masks that filter out pretty much everything. Forget about those flimsy paper masks." He paused. "Are you still there, Hunter?"

"Yeah, just writing it all down." He sounded scared but calm.

"Good. Don't freak out. I'm probably way over thinking this and next week we'll laugh over this."

Hunter chuckled. "I sure hope so."

"Hey, while you're at it, get some camping gear. Heavy duty stuff. Use the card. If there really is an epidemic, the safest place you can be is out in the country, some rural location away from other people. Do you have those portable battery chargers? I gave you one for Christmas."

"Yeah. Have it right here. I'll charge it up."

"Good. Get a couple more at least, to keep your phone charged. Hell, get a solar charger if you can find one."

"You know all of this is gonna cost a fortune, right? You're not going to get pissed off when the bill comes, are you?"

"No. It's okay. I'll deal with the bills later. Besides, we can always use the camping gear out on the island. There are woods set away from the lake and it would be fun to camp there." He tried to make it sound like that was the real reason he wanted the camping gear, but his mind was whirling. What if there was a panic before Hunter reached home? What if the trip became dangerous? He wanted his son to have some kind of protection and food in case of an unforeseen event.

"Is this all I should get?"

"Food. Get food. Stuff that doesn't spoil. Beef jerky, granola bars, water purification tablets. They'll have those at the same place you get the camping gear. Those packs of tuna. That kind of thing. Powdered milk. And a camp stove."

"You know you're kind of freaking me out. All of this for a two-day drive?"

"Like I said, I'm over-thinking. I want you to be prepared for anything, and we can always use the supplies on the island." Cole heard a faint beep on Hunter's end.

"Word must be getting out, Dad."

"Why, are others leaving too?"

"No, but this is the third 'End of the World' party I've been invited to."

Cole groaned. "Well, for god's sake, don't go."

"No, I won't, but it figures I finally don't have to study, and I still can't accept the invitations." He chuckled, and Cole heard his valiant attempt to act like he wasn't scared. Cole blinked hard and turned his back to Sean and Jenna. "Okay. Well, I'm going to head out and get some supplies too. If you have any trouble, call me. I'll text you directions on how to get to Uncle John's island."

"Okay, Dad. I'll see you soon."

———

COLE LEFT Sean's house and headed to a gun shop. He wanted a shotgun and another hunting rifle, plus as much ammunition for them that he could get. It had taken longer than he expected because the shop had been busy.

As Cole listened in on some of the conversations, and it sounded like most of the people there had the same idea he did—to bug out until the crisis was over. While he was glad people were taking precautions, it made him anxious that he could get enough food to last them for six months or longer. What if everyone was thinking the same way?

He called his brother when he finished getting the guns. "Hey, Sean, it seems like the word is leaking out somehow or people are reading between the lines. The gun shop was packed. I think we need to leave tomorrow. I'm heading to the store now to get as much food as I can, but I think it would be a good idea if either you or Jenna made a trip to the store. Probably Jenna. She'll know what we need."

"Yeah, she left for the warehouse store on the west side of town. We're packing stuff here."

"How did the kids take it?"

Sean sighed. "Trent is a little scared, but he thinks it's kind of cool too. Like we're going on a camping vacation. Piper was quieter, but she's pretty scared. She's up in her room packing clothes right now."

Cole stopped at a light as he waited to turn into the Walmart parking lot. He pinched the bridge of his nose. *Poor kids.* He didn't have any words of comfort so he told Sean to pack up as much as they could today, focusing on clothes, non-perishable food, kitchen items like pots, pans, and utensils—anything they had that didn't require electricity. He didn't know if the island had any right now. Even if the island was fully powered, if the infrastructure broke down, which it could if enough people died, the grids might go down. His first priority was to get several generators. He was hoping he'd be able to get fuel for them, but that was a problem for later.

"I'm at Walmart now. I'll call you later."

Cole sat in the parking lot, gauging the people going in and out of the store. After leaving the gun shop and driving across town, he'd listened to the news on the radio. The death toll had risen to over eight-hundred already, but it was confined, so far, to four cities—and it was confirmed that at least some of the initial victims had flown in from San Diego in the last few days. Unfortunately, one of the cities was Chicago.

Even though Cole was closer to Milwaukee, he knew that ninety miles separating the two cities were pretty much negligible. He debated wearing one of his painter's masks into the Walmart. He still wore the clothes he'd intended to wear to paint a house he was working on, but Elly's call had canceled those plans. He kept this pair specifically for painting in and few splotches of green paint decorated the old jeans. He reached into the back seat and found the box of masks, and slipped one on, but let it dangle around his neck for now. He could pull this off without causing too much of a stir.

As Cole walked towards the door of the store, he lifted the mask from his neck and started to settle it over his nose and mouth. This was Walmart, after all, and there were internet memes about the crazies who shopped there. Wearing a mask shouldn't even raise an eyebrow. But then he thought about it. They might take him for a robber, so he left the mask dangling again and used one of the anti-microbial wipes near the front door of the store to thoroughly wipe down his shopping cart.

While swabbing the handle, he created mental lists of what they'd need for an extended stay on the island. He prayed it wouldn't be more than a month or two, and even more, he prayed that he was wrong. If he were mistaken, Sean and Jenna would be out of jobs. His brother's business would likely be ruined, and Jenna would be fired from the hospital. Granted, as a nurse, she'd probably be able to find another job, but her references would be shot. He'd do whatever he could to build Sean's business back up, but it would be tough. The weight of the responsibility threatened to crush his resolve.

What if Elly was wrong? What if *his* hunches were garbage? Hunter was in college, and he'd probably fail since he'd miss the last three weeks, including finals. Cole pushed that from his mind. So, it was a wasted semester. They could deal with that and Hunter could make it up eventually.

As he pushed the cart through the store, he found that the crowd he'd expected wasn't there. Sure, there were other people, but fewer than on an average day at this time. Maybe people's first instincts were to just hunker down at home for a few days? If that was the case, he was grateful for it because it meant less chance of coming into contact with someone who might be harboring the virus. He found himself in the food area of the store and loaded flour and sugar, salt, spices, bags of cornmeal, quinoa, rice, and dried lentils to the cart. He added four large boxes of baking soda, baking powder, cornstarch, and vanilla, cleaned off the shelf of bags walnuts, peanuts, and pecans. He put gallons of cooking oil on the bottom of the cart, hoping they wouldn't fall off as he pushed the cart to another aisle.

He was glad for his great credit because he didn't have to worry about cost too much. He had a feeling the bills would never arrive. If they did, it would be a cause for celebration.

The food cart was brimming once he added cans of fruits, vegetables, and as much tuna and salmon as he could find. He parked it in an empty aisle near the underwear and socks, hoping it would remain untouched until he finished getting other supplies. Leaving the cart, he took his second one and headed towards the camping section.

He tallied the projected cost and gave a low whistle. He'd barely even begun and was already hundreds of dollars down.

What would people who didn't have cash on hand do? Or if they had crappy credit? Then he realized that most wouldn't be able to stock up on anything because once everyone realized what was happening, riots would break out and looting would run rampant. *Shit.* He stopped dead in the middle of the aisle as the gravity of the situation slammed into him, nearly buckling his knees. He gripped the blue handle of the cart, his knuckles blanching.

Fluffy towels in every color of the rainbow lay stacked on tables on one side of the aisle, and fragrant candles were displayed on endcaps on the other side. Cole swallowed hard and fought to make his legs work again. The soft clink of glass candle holders drew his gaze to an employee with a cart full of more candles. The young man arranged them on shelves as if it mattered. The scent of pine, vanilla, and some sweet flowery aroma warred with the taste of bile in the back of Cole's throat.

Had today been the last normal day of his life? Of *everyone's* lives? Every customer and employee he passed became a future casualty. He mourned them even as they chatted and laughed while they shopped or worked.

He shook his head. *Focus.* Cole pried his hands from the handle, gave them a shake, flexing his fingers, then re-gripped the handle, pushing his fear into the recesses of his mind, locking it away until safety and survival were secured. He didn't have time to give in to fear now. Not if he wanted to save his family. As he passed the shelf of candles, he piled candles of all colors and scents into the cart. The guy stocking them raised an eyebrow at Cole. He ignored him and added several boxes of tapers on top of the jar candles.

In the camping supply area, he selected tarps, most of the mosquito repellent on the shelf, and water purification tablets in case he couldn't get the well working if the power went out. At least they'd be surrounded by plenty of water in the lake. He added four of the best axes on the shelf. If they had to spend the winter there, they'd need plenty of wood. An assortment of utility knives went into the cart, ropes, stakes, netting, and then he came to the tents. The island had cabins, but he didn't know what kind of shape they were in. He might not get a chance to acquire a good tent, so he bought two. One for him and Hunter, and one for Sean's family.

After grabbing six lanterns, five flashlights, including a couple of crank varieties, extra bulbs, and batteries, he got kerosene for the lamps, Googled the supplies needed for a solar oven, then bought enough for three. His cart full, he found an empty cart in an aisle, and not seeing anyone around who seemed to be using it, claimed it for his own, dragging the full cart behind him as he filled the third cart.

Cole already had cast iron pans, but didn't know if Sean did, so he got several frying pans and a big Dutch oven. He went to the fishing aisle and added poles, lures, nets, and weights. He added a couple of filleting knives, and other items he thought might come in handy.

With the cart rapidly filling, he knew he'd have to check out soon, but he spied the inflatable rafts and realized how handy those could be. He could even tow some of the supplies out to the island in the rafts if he had to. He bought two, and an electric pump to inflate it. Thinking about a power issue, he found a hand pump too, and several patch kits, adding that to the mix. That made him think about duct tape, and soon, he had a dozen rolls, along with various tubes of glue and caulk.

Cole found his first cart, pushed it to the front of the store, hurried back for his other two, and pushed and pulled them to the front as well. He knew that he was forgetting things but hoped he'd still have time to get some necessities tomorrow.

At the checkout, he saw the sticks of beef jerky and dried meat sticks and put all of them on the conveyor belt. Looking at all the food he'd bought, he hoped it would be enough for six adults for at least three months. They could supplement with fish and maybe some hunting, but those were no guarantees. Of course, he figured Sean would also bring some food, but how much would he be able to get? He knew finances were stretched tight for Sean. The recession had hit his family especially hard. Sean had put a second mortgage on his home to pull his business through, and while things had improved in the last several years, Cole had a feeling they were still struggling. What if they hadn't had enough cash or credit to get the needed supplies? He should have asked them if they needed any money.

"Wow! Going camping?" The cashier eyed the three carts, her eyes huge. She called over a bagger to help her.

Cole snapped out of his musings and fumbled for a reply. "Uh, yeah. Kind of. It's an expedition for a...an extended stay." He longed to warn this young woman, but chances were, she'd never believe him and think he was a kook.

"Cool." She popped her gum and started scanning items.

Luckily, she chatted with the bagger while she rang up his items, and Cole paid, trying not to wince at the final tally. Money wasn't going to matter soon. And if it did, well, he could always earn more. He'd relish the chance.

Chapter Five

When Cole arrived home, he unloaded his purchases and stacked them in the garage until he got the rental truck, except for the guns—those he'd take into the house.

Hands on his hips, Cole caught his breath as he surveyed the bags of food and other goods. It looked like so much, but he knew it probably wouldn't last them more than three months. Shit. Why hadn't he thought to buy vegetable seeds? A year from now, there may not be any grocery stores—they'd have to grow most of their own food.

He wasn't much of a gardener, and it hadn't entered his mind. He took out his phone and sent a text to Jenna to bring whatever she had. He knew she usually planted an extensive garden and was always offering tomatoes, cucumbers, and zucchini to him in the late summer. He hoped she had some beans, peas, or corn too.

They'd definitely need the rental truck by the time he had clothes, blankets, towels and other essentials packed. While his SUV was good-sized, he kept the back filled with painting supplies and had a couple of ladders secured on top. It didn't leave a lot of room for much else. He reached in and cleared out all of the cans of paint and other painting supplies. Then he looked around the walls of the garage and started loading tools he thought he could use. Shovels, a hoe, rakes, a broom, a hack saw and some rope he'd used when he'd patched a few spots on his roof a few years ago to tide it over until he was able to get a new roof.

He bent at the waist, his hands on his knees. Even though he was in pretty good shape, he was running on fumes and knew he didn't have the luxury of sleeping for hours yet. This morning, it had seemed like it was still early enough in the disease process that getting a rental appeared to be a sure bet, but now he worried. He'd tried to call and reserve one, but the business was closed for the day. What if they didn't have one?

Cole had figured he had at least a few days before the general public caught on, and even then, most wouldn't comprehend the scale of the disease. Not at first. Hell, he could hardly believe it was going to get bad, and his whole career, his field of study, was making predictions about diseases.

He hoped the crowd at the gun shop was just the first wave of people preparing. Walmart hadn't seemed any busier than normal, so that had him breathing a little easier, but he didn't want to push their luck. They'd have to leave tomorrow.

Cole entered his kitchen through the garage door, grabbed a glass and filled it with water, mesmerized by the simple act of filling the glass from the tap. So many things he took for granted. There had to be at least one well on the island. He prayed it was in good shape. But if they didn't have power, how would the water pump? What would they need to make it pump? Could they rig something up? Maybe a windmill? Obviously, people had wells before electricity was invented, and he pictured a pump with a handle, but what went on below ground was a mystery. He took his glass to the other side of the counter, where his laptop rested on the breakfast bar.

Opening his browser, he was dismayed to see more news stories about Sympatico Syndrome, but they still were pretty far down on the list of trending stories. At the top was some celebrity who was getting a divorce. Cole shook his head in disgust at people's priorities. A second later, the disgust melted away as he realized he would gladly accept shallow priorities if it meant nobody had to worry about a global pandemic. Yes, society was spoiled and obsessing over the marital status of an actor was a luxury only afforded to those who didn't have to worry about where their next meal might come from.

When clean water and shelter were things you never had to think about, it was easy to get caught up in inconsequential worries. It was a first-world privilege, and he'd been as guilty as anyone. Sure, he didn't give a rat's ass about any celebrity marriage, but he obsessed over sports and what player his team should trade for, what a pitcher's ERA was, and whether his team had a chance to win the World Series that year. Hell, he'd been discussing that exact thing in a baseball chat room just last week. It was a privilege Cole hadn't ever acknowledged before. And now he feared that it was a privilege which would soon come to an end for everyone.

His stomach rumbled so he popped a frozen dinner in the microwave since it would soon go to waste if he didn't eat it. While it heated, he headed to his room and dug through his closet for appropriate clothing, pushing aside the suits and dress shirts, pulling out old camouflage he hadn't worn in years. He wasn't sure if he'd fit into it although he was still in good shape. He packed it anyway. It might fit Hunter or even Trent at some point. The clothes were thick and durable. As he looked for sweatshirts, he came across a box with old photos in it. He dragged it out beside the bed and lifted it to sit next to the half-full suitcases.

Cole wondered if they'd have room for the box, but decided he'd make room. He went into the living room and took the framed photos from the mantle above the fireplace, pausing at the picture of Hunter and Brenda. Mother and son both laughed as they looked into the camera. He wished he could remember what they had been laughing about, but was glad to have captured a carefee moment. He added the frames to the box and carted it out to the garage.

The remainder of the night, he went room to room, deciding what was needed and what would have to stay. Clothes all went—even old stuff with holes. Cloth could be repurposed into other uses. He should have picked up needles and thread. He had a small sewing kit he'd used once to sew a button onto a dress shirt, but it only contained three needles and a couple of spools of cheap thread. *Shit.* Why hadn't he thought of that?

He glanced at his watch. It was almost midnight, and he should be getting to bed, but he knew there was a Walmart on the other side of town that was open twenty-four hours.

Deciding he could sleep after they got safely to the island, he trudged to the garage and headed to the Walmart. Again.

As he pulled in, he was surprised at the number of vehicles in the lot. It was at least as many as this afternoon. He grabbed his facemask and donned it, not caring this time who saw him. Apparently, people were becoming alert to the situation. There were empty boxes of sanitizing wipes strewn on the floor by the automatic doors, but he was glad to see another container with one sticking out. He grabbed it and made a beeline for the lawn and garden section.

Surprisingly, this seemed to be overlooked by the crowd and Cole grabbed packets of seeds. Beans, peas, corn, carrots, and spinach were the first to go in, then he added cucumbers, squash, pumpkin, watermelon, and zucchini. He noted packs of herb seeds and took two of each on the rotating rack. Not only would they come in handy when their dried supply ran out, but he knew they had medicinal uses as well.

He went through the produce aisle section, this time, thinking of getting potatoes— not to eat, but to plant. Cole wasn't sure of the process but knew it had to do with cutting up the potatoes around the eyes, and planting them. It would have to be a priority if they wanted a harvest this year. How many plants could a twenty-pound bag of potatoes yield? He wasn't sure, so grabbed two of them. Most people seemed to be shunning the fresh food for canned stuff, so he took advantage of it and piled his cart with carrots, eggplant, jicama, onions, garlic, oranges, and apples. He looked longingly at the strawberries but decided they'd rot too quickly and didn't want to risk spoiling any of the other fruits they had.

He scoured the deli area, finding several rounds of hard cheese. Those would keep for a long time, so he scooped up all of them.

Next, Cole made a pass through the food aisles, getting more canned goods but the selection was limited and heavily picked through. He was able to get several large cans of sweet potatoes, squash and pumpkin, but he'd hoped to add more beans, peas, and carrots. He reached for a can of mushrooms at the same time another man did and got an elbow to the ribs for his efforts. Rubbing the sore spot, he glared at the guy. "What the hell are you doing?"

The man threw Cole a dirty look and shrugged. "I got it first."

Shaking his head, Cole turned to his cart but stopped when a pack of seeds slipped between the bars of the cart. Bending over, he snatched it and saw a gleam of metal way in the back of a shelf. Grinning in triumph, he went to his hands and knees and grabbed the two cans he saw. He didn't care what he came up with. He pulled out an industrial sized can of baked beans and another of tomatoes. He looked down the length of the aisle and spotted more overlooked vegetables pushed way back. Setting his finds in the cart, he headed for the end of the aisle, and almost ran into a woman pushing a nearly empty cart. Two kids clung to the side of it.

She took one look at the shelves and burst into tears.

Stunned at her sudden emotion, Cole stopped. "Are you okay?"

With a long, hiccupping sob, she shook her head. "I had to wait to shop until today. I've been watching the bank, waiting until my paycheck hit my account at midnight so I could get something for us to eat. But everything is gone, and one guy already stole my cart. Now I only have these." She waved her hand at a few boxes of lasagna noodles, and two cans of soup.

Cole tried to steel his emotions. It wasn't his problem. They weren't his problem, but guilt flooded him. He looked at her then to the children, a boy about seven and a little girl who appeared to be about four, and his resolve melted away. He reached into his cart and took the tomato sauce, beans, and a round of cheese and set them in her cart. In the long run, it probably wouldn't help them survive, but he couldn't walk away knowing that children were going hungry. *Damn.*

The woman's eyes opened wide, and she swiped at the tears on her cheeks. "Are you sure?"

Cole nodded. "If I didn't have others counting on me, I'd give you more. Listen, out in the garden section, there were still loads of seeds." He lifted a couple of the packets from his cart. "They might help you out in the long run. If you can, get out of town. Take the kids somewhere in the country."

"I can't. I have to stay with my mom. She can't take care of herself."

It was on the tip of his tongue to say that she was probably destined to be one of the first to go, either from disease or from lack of medical care, but he just nodded. "Well, keep it in mind. Grow a garden in the yard at least."

With that, he left her behind, heading to get the rest of the items he thought they might need.

COLE LEFT the items in the back of the SUV when he got home. Too tired to unpack, and figuring he could deal with it in the morning after he rented a truck, he trudged into the house. It was almost one a.m., and he had to get some sleep if he was going to drive tomorrow. He wondered how Hunter was doing but didn't want to wake him if he was sleeping. He sent him a quick text, giving him directions to the island. With luck, Hunter would arrive in a couple of days. Driving alone, he'd have to stop and take breaks sometimes.

Despite his exhaustion, his brain refused to shut down. There was so much he still needed to get ready. Clothes for all weather situations, towels, soaps, cleaning agents... The list went on and on, but he rolled over, punching his pillow. Should he have bought more guns? Possibly a handgun? He imagined things could get dangerous when actual panic set in, and he wanted to be able to protect the island.

Finally, he slept but dreamed of zombies breaking into the house and tearing the kitchen apart. They climbed the stairs and took Hunter from his room, dragging him with them as they left. Even in the dream, he wondered why Hunter wasn't at college, but dream logic kicked in, and he didn't question it too much.

He awoke with a start, bathed in sweat, and glanced at the clock. Six thirty-five. He flopped back in bed, wishing like hell that he could just pull the blankets up and go back to sleep. The sudden hope hit him that maybe the disease had been contained. Maybe he had just panicked yesterday. He got up and jumped in the shower. As he soaped up, he went over the news on the Sympatico Syndrome. He had to have over-reacted. That was it.

As he dressed, he grabbed the television remote from his nightstand and aimed it at the small TV mounted in the corner of the bedroom.

The story was getting bigger but seemed as if most of the panic was centered on the West Coast. He wasn't sure he was buying it. While last night's trip to the store hadn't been a brawl-fest like what he saw on the feeds from the West Coast, his ribs were still tender from the sharp jab he'd received.

Cole flicked through the channels, reading the crawl across the bottom of the screen that told of another nine hundred and eleven people who had died overnight. Most of the deaths were in California, but there was also several hundred in Texas, most on military bases. Chicago was reporting a hundred and eighteen deaths overnight.

His first thought was of Elly. Had she made it out okay? He hoped she had found a way to get back home to Atlanta.

That the disease was hitting the military made sense from his perspective. The disease had started on a military base. He wished he had access to passenger lists departing from Aislado.

Cole itched to hop on a plane and head to the source of the disease. It was too late now, but if he'd learned of it last week, maybe he could have made a difference. What if he hadn't retired? Would he have spotted the danger earlier? He liked to think he would have, but the truth of the matter was, he might have missed it too.

He wanted to dig into what had happened. Was it some dormant virus found only on some remote part of the island? Was it a virus that humans had never encountered before? He supposed that could be the case, and Aislado had only been inhabited for the last hundred years or so, but it didn't seem likely. It wasn't that big of an island. While it had some forest, it wasn't a jungle.

Only one other island in the world was as remote, but it didn't have a military base. In fact, one of the reasons the base had a level four bio-lab was due to the remoteness of the island. It was felt that in the event of a breach, the island could be locked down. He shook his head. Obviously, that hadn't worked. His gut instinct was that this disease wasn't naturally occurring. What if it was the result of biological weapons experiment? He'd bet a good number of the military personnel who had left Aislado in the last week had carried the disease with them. And, being military, once they got to San Diego, they would have scattered to various connecting flights, or stayed over a day or two before catching a flight to other parts of the country.

After dressing, he grabbed his phone and called Hunter. No answer. Dammit! He looked to see if his son had replied to the text he'd sent last night. Nothing. His stomach clenched. How could he leave for Uncle John's island if he didn't know where his son was?

Chapter Six

A knock on the window woke Hunter. He blinked, and bolted upright in the driver's seat. A police officer rapped his knuckles against the window a second time.

"Could you step out of the vehicle please?"

"Uh...yeah. Sure." He fumbled for the door handle and slowly opened it. "Is there a problem?" He looked around the parking lot. He had driven as far as he could last night, but had become too tired to drive anymore, but heeding his dad's warning, didn't want to stop at a motel or even a rest-stop. Instead, he had pulled into a church parking lot. It had seemed the safest place he could find. The church was located on the outskirts of a small town only a few hundred miles from his college. He'd hoped to get more miles in, but after getting as many of the supplies that his father had suggested, he'd only been able to drive a little over three hours before fatigue set in.

The cop eyed him but didn't get too close. "Show me your license."

Hunter reached for his wallet, conscious of the officer's tense posture. Slowly pulling his license from the billfold, he extended it to the cop. "I was just catching a few hours of sleep. I was driving," he gestured in the direction of the highway, "but got so tired, I thought I better pull off before I fell asleep at the wheel." He thought maybe the cop would give him credit for doing the smart thing, but instead, he just scowled at Hunter.

The cop glanced at the license and handed it back. "You're a long way from home."

"I go to school in Colorado, but I'm on my way back home."

The cop looked Hunter up and down, and then peered into the backseat of Hunter's car. "Well, if you're looking for the homeless shelter, this church only serves as an emergency shelter one night a week, and that's on Thursdays, so you'll have to leave."

Hunter put his license away. "Homeless shelter?"

The cop indicated the clothes piled high in the back of Hunter's car. "Living out of your vehicle?"

"Oh! No. I just told you—I go to school in Colorado at the university." He was glad he'd put most of his purchases in the trunk of the car. One of them had been an excellent crossbow along with two dozen arrows. He had taken archery classes when he was a kid and had been pretty good. He had even competed for a few years but gave it up when he started working a part-time job after school. Since all the guns—every single one—was sold out, it couldn't hurt to have a good bow. Since buying it, he'd been rehearsing how to tell his dad about the purchase. At close to five hundred dollars, not including the extra arrows, he knew his dad would have a fit when the bill came due. He'd have to figure out a way to pay for it, but last night, with the fear of an apocalypse looming in his mind, it had seemed like a logical purchase, but now in the light of day, he felt silly for the fear he'd felt last night.

The cop opened his mouth to say something, but his shoulder radio sounded, the dispatcher saying something about a fight at some store. The cop sighed and keyed in a reply. Afterward, he pointed at Hunter and circled his hand to encompass the car. "I'm going, to put it bluntly. Leave town. And here's some more advice—don't go into any other towns. Go straight to your destination. People are going a little crazy because of that Sympatico disease."

Hunter nodded. Maybe his dad hadn't been exaggerating his fears. "Yes, sir."

After returning to his car, he sat for a few minutes and checked his phone. *Shit*. It was dead. He rooted around in the center console for his charger. He had the extra power banks, but he'd tossed them in a backpack that was now buried under the pile of clothes. After plugging the phone into the car charger, he had to wait for it to get enough juice to power on.

He glanced in the rearview mirror when he heard raucous laughter. Curious, he watched a group of people at the far end of the street. Even from over a block away, he had no trouble hearing them. They seemed to be drunk, and he glanced at the dashboard clock. It was still early. Barely after seven a.m. He could understand a lone drunk staggering down a street, but a group of twenty? At this time of day? As he watched, a few men in the group darted off, dodging oncoming cars, making the drivers screech to a halt and blast their horn. The guys returned to the group, laughing hysterically. The sound of it sent a chill down Hunter's back. There was something off about them. Even the women were cackling like hyenas. Not waiting around for his phone to charge, he put the car in drive and tore out of the parking lot and made a beeline for the highway.

After driving for about ten miles, he finally eased back on his speed. He needed to look for a gas station in the next hour or so. He'd hoped to go through a fast-food restaurant connected to a gas station. That way he could get gas and go through the drive-up and have the least amount of contact with anyone, but was the disease spread through food handling? He wasn't sure and decided not to risk it.

According to his GPS, there were few towns in the next sixty miles and he could probably avoid any people if he went to some isolated filling station.

Hunter fished around in the bag of snacks he'd put on the front seat and found a cereal bar and tore one open, eating it as he drove. The bottle of water he had was warm, and he grimaced as he washed the cereal bar down.

He spotted a sign for a nature preserve, and the sign had the logo for restrooms, so he pulled off the highway. The park looked deserted which, given the beautiful day, made him pause. Where was everyone? Holed up at home or maybe this park was normally deserted at this time of day during the week. Either way, at least he wouldn't have to avoid anyone.

Hunter went into the bathroom, pausing to make sure it was

empty before taking care of business. As he washed his hands, he wished there was a shower available. Even in the rippled, dirty mirror, his hair stuck up in five different directions and stubble darkened his jaw. He didn't normally have to shave every day, but it had been about three days since the last time, and he was actually starting to grow a bit of a beard. No wonder the cop had thought he was homeless.

He pushed the button on the soap dispenser, happy to see a small pile of foam in his hand. Rubbing his hands together, he washed his face and scooped water over his head. He gave his head a shake, sending droplets flying. Feeling a little better, he returned to his car but paused with his hand on the door handle. Sirens sounded in the distance. Lots of sirens. He hadn't thought there were many towns around, but maybe there was an accident somewhere. Uneasy, and hoping the sirens were for some run of the mill accident or possibly a fire, he returned to the highway.

———

COLE DROVE to the local truck rental place and was relieved to find someone working. The news was full of dire reports of deaths, and the schools were closed for the rest of the week. There had even been a plane crash. The pilots had become giddy as they communicated with air traffic control and when the controller suggested an emergency landing at the nearest airport, the pilots had refused and instead, said they felt like attempting loop de loops. They had actually tried the maneuver—with a 747 full of passengers. All had died on impact.

He approached the rental counter, almost relieved to see that the clerk wore a surgical mask over his nose and mouth. Cole hadn't resorted to using his yet, but he probably would from now on. Nodding to the guy, he said, "Hi. I want to rent one of the twenty-footers."

"You got a reservation?"

"Uh, no." Cole didn't know he needed one. "Are they all reserved already?"

"Yeah, but I got a twenty-four footer if you want. Cost more, though."

Cole let out a breath. Whew. "That's fine." He pulled out his wallet and withdrew his credit card and driver's license. In short order, he had the truck secured but then wondered about his own vehicle. He should have picked up Sean first to come with him. He'd have to leave his car here and get Sean to come back with him to get it.

Driving through town, he noted a good number of cars being loaded as though the family was going on vacation. Lots of suitcases and bags. The parking lot as he passed the store was packed. He was glad he'd done most of his shopping last night. He hoped he had enough for Sean's family too. If only they could get some chickens or goats. At least they could supplement with eggs and milk then. A cow would be great, but he had no way of getting anything bigger than a goat to the island. At least, not until winter and they could walk over on the ice. Of course, by then the whole scare would be over.

Chapter Seven

Cole backed into Sean's driveway. Before he exited the truck, Sean was in the front yard.

He eyed the truck, his arms crossed as he shook his head. "Don't you think this is a bit of overkill, Cole?"

"I wanted a twenty-footer, but they didn't have any, and judging by the madhouse I saw in the parking lot of the grocery store, I think others are getting the idea of the severity of this disease."

Sean looked down, scuffing a toe in the grass. "You better be right about all of this. The kids are giving up so much. Piper had her heart set on prom. She already has a date, and she and Jenna were supposed to go out dress shopping this Saturday."

Cole had a soft spot for Piper. Not having a daughter of his own, he felt protective of his only niece. He wouldn't hurt her for the world. He rubbed the back of his neck and avoided Sean's gaze.

Sean continued, "And Trent has baseball starting up soon. If he misses tryouts for the travel team, he can forget about playing this year."

"Yeah. Sorry about that." Cole didn't know why he apologized because this wasn't his fault, but he was the one who planned their survival strategy. Maybe he was wrong. He saw the fear in Sean's eyes—fear that he covered with gruff annoyance.

"Well, we better start loading up the truck."

Jenna greeted Cole with a brief hug when he entered so at least not everyone was mad at him.

"Have you heard from Hunter today?"

Cole shook his head. "No. I tried to call first thing when I woke up, but the call wouldn't go through. Everyone is talking on their phones, I guess. I sent a text but haven't heard back yet. I'm going to keep trying to call too. In the meantime, why don't we get you packed up, head over to my place and get my stuff, then we can go?"

"I was up most of the night packing clothes and odds and ends. Blankets, sheets, towels—that kind of thing." She ran a hand through her hair, blowing a few strands that settled back over her face. "No matter what Sean says, Cole, we're glad you warned us when you did. Otherwise..." Jenna shook her head, worry pinching at her mouth. "I was too keyed up to sleep, so I went to the supermarket at six this morning and am I glad I got there when I did."

"I saw the parking lot on the way over here. Was it bad?"

"A complete zoo. The shelves were emptying fast, but most people were grabbing milk and bread, as though this was a winter storm instead of something bigger. I was able to get quite a bit of canned food, dried stuff like beans and fruits. Hope you like apricots because there were bags of them."

Cole smiled. "Sure. I guess."

Jenna gave him what he decided passed for a return smile, but tension bracketed her mouth. "Good. Oh, and I bought a bunch of salt, vinegar, bleach and I don't even know what all. I probably went overboard, but once there, I couldn't seem to stop. I kept thinking, what if this is the last time I get to shop at a regular grocery store? So bizarre to think about."

"I know. I couldn't help wondering about the employees I passed at the Walmart. Last night, there was no panic, and it was so normal." He shook his head, unable to finish the sentence.

Jenna reached out and gave his shoulder a brief squeeze before continuing, "Anyway, I charged it all and got some cash from the ATM, too. I wish I could have taken out more, but there was a limit on the machine. Plus, people were lining up behind me to get cash too. Oh, and since I'm not going into work, I couldn't get the masks you wanted, but I did hit the drugstore before I even went to the grocery store, and I got two boxes of masks, plus as much first aid stuff as I could get my hands on. If nothing else, our medicine cabinet will be stocked for the next year with pain relievers, cold and flu medicine, and antibiotic ointment."

Cole nodded, but his mind was on Hunter. Had he even received the directions to the lake? Maybe after he got Sean and his family settled on the island, he could come back and wait for Hunter. "We better get a move on."

It took them two hours to pack up everything. Cole eyed the blow dryer on top of one of the boxes Piper carried out to the truck. He picked it up. "Really?"

She stuck out her tongue at him and grinned. "There's no reason I have to face the apocalypse with bad hair."

"Yeah, whatever, but make sure to pack some warm clothes. Hats, coats, and gloves, and boots too. If you have hiking boots, pack those also. Those sneakers aren't going to last long."

Trent trudged to the bottom of the ramp with two boxes stacked one on top of the other. He set them in the back of the truck, and Cole moved them deeper in, along the wall. One was full of baseball gear. He was about to veto it but then thought better of it. It might help pass the time. He turned back to his nephew. "Hey, Trent. Do you guys have a Frisbee? How about a volleyball net and ball?" He remembered Sean stringing up a net a few years ago at a barbecue. They needed something fun to do to pass the time. While there would be a lot of work to do, they would have to take breaks now and then. "Also, grab your guitar and as many books as you can."

That reminded him. He wanted books on how to do stuff. Practical things like gardening, canning, curing meat and hides. There were so many necessary tasks they didn't know but might have to learn to survive. He decided that despite the time, as long as they had computer access, he was going to take a few minutes to print out some basic guides on those topics. He knew Jenna was a good gardener, so that was something. He pointed to the back of the truck when Piper came out with another box. "Stack that one over there. I have to go ask your mom something." And he wanted to remind Sean to pack his tools too. They could be invaluable in the coming days.

Cole hopped off the truck and trotted into the house. "Hey, Jenna—"

"I can't believe you spent this much, Jenna. We don't have that much! How are we going to pay the mortgage next month?"

Jenna stood in the kitchen, a box of dishes on the table in front of her. "Don't you get it, Sean? The mortgage isn't going to matter in a month."

"And you know that for sure? Or is this based on what Cole's been saying?"

Cole halted in the threshold between the living room and kitchen. Sean's tone didn't sit well with him. Not the doubt—he understood that. This whole situation was a lot to comprehend. It was the emphasis on his name, as though Sean was sneering as he said it. He looked between Jenna and Sean. Jenna's eyes darted to him, then she shook her head at Sean. "I have a lot to do still." She brushed past Cole on her way out of the room.

Cole watched her for a second, then turned to his brother. "What's going on?"

"I can't believe we're actually abandoning our home and jobs on your say so—that's what's going on."

He didn't respond. What was there to say that he hadn't already said? Instead, he turned away and saw Piper struggling down the hall with a plastic bin that looked heavy. He moved to help her. "Here, I'll take that." Cole grunted as he took the weight of the bin, wondering how the skinny teenager had managed to carry it as far as she had. "What do you have in here? Rocks?" he joked.

"Just some of my books."

Sean came into the hallway, craning a look over Cole's shoulder. "I told you not to bring all the books, Piper. They're not essential."

"It's okay, Sean. There's plenty of room, and the books will help pass the time. In fact, that's what I came in to discuss with you and Jenna. I thought that if you have any books that might come in handy, grab them. We may not have Internet and we'll have to look things up."

Piper bit her lip, glancing at her dad before looking at Cole. "I have some How-To books in my closet. I got them at a thrift store. I was going to glue them together and make a cool table out of them like I saw on Pinterest, but I guess I can still do that when we come back."

Sean's lips clamped together, and he gave Piper a curt nod. "Fine."

She spun and ran back to her room as Cole shifted the bin of books. He lifted an eyebrow when Sean remained in the hallway, blocking his way. "This box isn't getting any lighter, you know."

"Look, Cole—I get that you're trying to help us. And I respect your expertise in this area, but my family is *my* domain. You don't get to override my authority regarding my children."

Shocked, Cole simply nodded. "I apologize. I wasn't trying to—" He broke off and hiked the bin higher. "I'm worried we might be out there a long time, and the kids will need something to keep them occupied. That's all. I wasn't trying to make you look bad."

Sean blew out a deep breath, shaking his head. "Fine. This thing is freaking me out."

"Yeah. Me too." His fingers were going numb from the weight of the bin so he shouldered past Sean. He wanted to offer reassurance that everything would be all right, but he couldn't make that offer.

―――――

IT WAS noon before they had everything they felt they needed from Sean's house. The beds had been the last things to go into the truck. Most of the other furniture had to be left behind. A few chairs and some folding tables were added, but Cole hoped the cabins at the island still had some furnishings. They had been furnished at one time, but it could all be gone by now. He tried to remember what the papers from the will had stated. It was just something about the land and holdings, whatever that meant. He had received a ring of keys to the various buildings. He hoped one was to the boathouse on the shore.

Cole secured the back of the truck, and wiped his hands on his jeans, turning to Sean and Jenna, who were shoving last minute items into the back of their van. "I need someone to ride with me to get my vehicle at the truck rental place."

"I'll go." Sean tossed his keys to Jenna. "Are they going to follow us or meet us back at your place?"

Cole started to tell Jenna to meet him at his house but then changed his mind. He wanted to stick together. "You might as well follow us. My house key is on my keychain with the car keys and it's a pain to get off the ring." That was his excuse, and they seemed satisfied with it, but really, he just had a gut instinct. In the five or so hours he had been here, he'd caught glimpses of the news on the television in the kitchen. Panic was already starting to erupt in larger cities as deaths increased.

Cole pulled into the parking lot at the rental place. "Shit!" a guy stood beside Cole's car, a rock in his hand, poised to bash in the rear passenger window. He laid on the horn, which startled the man. But it didn't make him run. Instead, he raised the rock again.

Slamming to a stop, Cole leaped out of the truck, leaving it running. "Hey, what the hell are you doing? That's my car!"

The man turned on Cole, the rock now aimed at him. "The stores were empty, but you have a shitload of food. I need stuff for my family!"

"Sorry to hear it, but that doesn't give you the right to steal from my family and me."

"Yeah, well, just try to stop me!" He raised the rock. Whether he was going to throw it at Cole or take a few steps closer and try to crush his skull with it, Cole never found out.

"Drop the rock and step away." There was the click of a safety.

Cole watched Sean step up beside him, a gun in hand. His eyes widened. He hadn't known Sean even owned a handgun.

The man hesitated, but finally dropped the rock.

"Now get out of here."

The man threw them a hate-filled glare then took off.

"Shit, Sean. Were you going to shoot him over my window?"

"If I had to, I would. You said this was going to get bad. Don't go acting like I was wrong."

Cole watched the man disappear around the corner of the rental place. "Yeah, you're right. I have some hunting rifles and ammo, but I don't know if it's enough. What about you? Did you pack anything more than that?"

"Oh yeah. I have four handguns, a shotgun, and a hunting rifle."

Sean engaged the safety and shoved the gun into a holster beneath his left arm. He covered it with a loose work shirt.

Cole knew about the shotgun and the hunting rifle now that he thought about it. They used to go hunting now and then. Their dad had been a big hunter and Sean had loved the trips. Cole hadn't been as interested but was glad that they both knew how to handle a weapon. The skill might come in handy.

Jenna pulled into the parking lot and Sean looked over his shoulder, then leveled his gaze at Cole. "Don't tell Jenna or the kids about this. I don't want to scare them."

"Yeah. Sure. Thanks for saving my ass."

Sean nodded. "That's what brothers do."

Chapter Eight

"But I need to get back to Atlanta…that's where all my data is. I need to compare—yes, I know I can look some of it up on the computer, but the Wi-Fi here is unreliable. I've been booted from the system four times in the last five hours."

Elly paused and listened to her boss at the CDC tell her how she was needed in Chicago and there was nothing he could do to help her. She knew everyone was stretched thin at the office and didn't mind the work, but she felt handcuffed.

"Sure. I'll keep doing the best I can." She got another call coming through, so she said goodbye and switched to the next call.

"Elly Jackson." She rolled her eyes. Frank, from FEMA. Perfect. "What do you need, Frank?"

The guy was competent, but he was as frustrated as she was. She'd been sent to Chicago, while others in her office had been dispatched to New York, Los Angeles, Houston and other major metro areas. They were to work with FEMA to coordinate emergency management efforts and to make sure all proper precautions were taken when setting up quarantine centers.

"No, you can't compromise on the N95 masks. The surgical masks aren't adequate for airborne precautions."

She waited as he explained that they'd been sent ten cases of surgical masks and only one of the N95 respirator masks. "I don't care how tightly you tie it, it's not going to stop the virus from getting through. It's not meant to filter airborne contaminants."

"Did you get enough food for the centers?" That was the other thing. The trucks laden with food had been delayed. One truck had been delayed by the death of the driver and the other when it was hijacked by a man earlier in the day. Nobody knew if the first truck was safe for another driver or even the cargo. The driver had helped to load it, so now the contents were considered compromised.

With all the setbacks, they were scrambling to set up the centers. Initially, they were only for people with late signs of the disease, but since those folks perished quickly, the agenda had changed to those who had close contact with someone who had already died. It was meant to contain the disease the best that they could.

So far, only two centers had been set up, but three more were planned. The problem was that several of the workers had already succumbed to the disease, and now she worried about the others contracting it as well. How do you quarantine the people who are responsible for running the quarantine centers?

Elly stared out the window at the lake. Any other day, she'd have been mesmerized by the waves sparkling in the sun, the deep blue of the water and how it contrasted with the lighter blue of the sky. It was gorgeous. Serene. A couple of puffy clouds floated in the sky, and if she focused on them, she could imagine for a moment that all was right with the world. Even a few days ago, when she'd arrived, there had been a dozen sailboats out on the lake, but today, in spite of the unseasonably warm weather, there were no boats of any kind.

She stepped closer to the window and looked down at the chaos in the streets below. Even she hadn't predicted things would deteriorate this quickly. It seemed like days ago that she had spoken to Cole and warned him. Afterward, she almost called him back to say she'd probably exaggerated the situation. The only reason she hadn't was that her phone had been ringing off the virtual hook.

It was either the CDC or news stations calling to set up interviews with her. Everyone wanted her to tell them that this disease would run its course in a few days and then it would be back to life as usual. She gave them the truth; this disease had spread faster than any disease she had ever encountered or even heard of, and that no effective treatments had been found yet. Victims succumbed so quickly that even diagnosing the disease was a post-mortem task—ERs were getting swamped with people who thought they had it, but real victims didn't realize they were even sick until it was too late. Meanwhile, they were spreading the disease far and wide. The media outlets chose to either edit her interviews or not air them at all.

Her phone rang yet again. Her boss. Hoping he'd changed his mind, she quickly hit the 'accept' button. "Yes, Ross?" Her jaw set as she listened to the latest news.

"But…how can they shut down everything? What about people stranded far from home?" Like me, but she didn't voice the thought. Surely she'd get special permission to travel. She had nothing here. Just one suitcase full of clothes. At least at home, she had some food and provisions set up in her cellar. She'd learned to be prepared for an emergency, but none of that preparation did any good when she was stuck so far from home. "So, what about me? How am I supposed to eat? If everything is shut down, things are going to get even crazier."

She pinched the bridge of her nose as he rambled on, then shook her head. "What do you mean, *say a prayer*? That's it? *That's* your advice?"

He hung up. She stared at the phone in disbelief. *Asshole.*

Elly clicked off her cell phone, clenching it in her hand. "I can't believe it!" She fought the urge to fling the phone across the room. She hadn't left the hotel room since yesterday morning, subsisting on what was in the mini fridge and some snacks she'd packed in her suitcase and purse. She'd dealt with most matters by phone since traveling the streets was next to impossible. Besides, she didn't even have a car. She'd taken a cab from the airport to her hotel. Now she wished she'd have rented a car.

Her stomach rumbled, and her throat was raw from so much talking on the phone. Just thirty minutes ago she had hung up after talking to someone at FEMA. They had been slow to deploy, and now she feared their efforts were too little too late. What needed to be done was a full-scale deployment. She flipped through the channels on the television. Two news feeds showed reporters at the scene of a riot in Los Angeles. It looked even worse than what she saw outside her hotel, but the virus had hit there a few days earlier. It was working its way in, although it was already well-established, thanks to air travel.

Even as she watched, someone in the background of the shot, an older man, his head topped thinning gray hair, crossed behind the reporter, and suddenly staggered, collapsed and began convulsing. After thirty seconds or so, he stilled.

The reporter looked over his shoulder for a moment and then returned his focus to the camera. "That's at least the tenth person I've seen who dropped dead in their tracks."

At least the live reporter was wearing a respiratory mask, not some flimsy paper mask. She just hoped he had been wearing it the entire time he was on assignment.

"Carl, how do you know he's dead?" The news anchor looked horrified as she asked Carl the question.

"Diane, just be glad his face is turned away, but I guarantee that if he faced us, we'd see a pool of blood around his head. That's how it's been with all of the others. They drop, begin convulsing and vomit up massive amounts of blood. That's it. It's how they die. One second, they're walking and talking, the next..." He made a spiral motion with his finger along with a whistling sound reminiscent of a falling missile. He shook his head.

Suddenly, all of the televisions flashed a Special Report screen. The scene shot to the familiar podium in the White House press room.

"Ladies and gentlemen, the President of the United States."

ELLY'S HANDS SHOOK. *Martial law?* She had wanted precautions but not this. She thought back to what the President had said. Martial Law wasn't going into effect until midnight two days from now. That meant she had two days to get out of the city. She had no food and no way to get any more up here. Room service had stopped delivering yesterday. A precaution, she'd been told, to keep contact to a minimum. She couldn't blame the hotel, but it left her in a predicament. She was down to a tiny pack of peanuts she'd received on her flight here. She had nothing to drink except water, and she wondered how long the infrastructure would hold up. When too many people died, there would be too few left to work, or those who were left were too afraid to show up for work out of fear of catching the virus. Then, society would break down completely.

She had been warning them for weeks, ever since the first three sailors had died out on Aislado. She'd asked if it was a bioengineered virus that had escaped from the lab, but the Navy had remained tight-lipped. If they created the virus, they should have an antidote or treatment for it, but apparently, they didn't. Or if they did, they weren't sharing it with the public.

Where could she go? She thought about the people she'd worked with while out here and tried their numbers. Some calls never made it through, and the others weren't answered. She went down her list, trying everyone in the area, hoping she could seek shelter with one of the FEMA people or some official in Chicago would tell her where she could ride this out. There had to be some kind of provisions made for those trying to combat the spread of the disease, but she was finding out that wasn't the case.

It seemed as if everyone was already in full survival mode, and if she wanted to survive, she had to make plans. Now.

Chapter Nine

Cole turned onto his street and slammed on the brakes. "*Holy shit!*"

Yellow barricades like police used when trying to hold back mobs of demonstrators blocked off the street. Three men with guns manned the roadblock. Cole tensed as one of the men approached his vehicle.

Sean was right behind him with the truck and Jenna and the kids following Sean. He hoped his brother wouldn't jump out and start waving his handgun around. He was grateful for Sean's forethought to bring the weapon, but it was three against one, and now Jenna and the kids were around.

Cole rolled his window down a crack, squinting at the man who was backlit by the sun and wearing a baseball cap pulled low. "What's going on? I live on this street and need to get home."

"Do you have proof of residence?"

Cole glared. "Since when do I need proof that I live in my house? My key is proof, now get those barricades out of the street and let me through." He had his license, of course, but that wasn't the point. He jabbed his thumb over his shoulder. "The two vehicles behind me are family. Let them in, too."

"Cole, is that you?"

He blinked up at the face. "Who wants to know?"

The man pulled off his cap. "It's me. Jerry Keeling."

"Doctor Keeling? *The dentist?*" He'd taken Hunter to the guy a few times after their regular dentist had retired. He'd also spoken to him at the annual block party, but he'd never had the impression the man would become militant in a situation like this.

"Yeah. We've had outsiders trying to seek shelter in the neighborhood. They think because we're upscale here, that we're safe."

Cole bit back a retort. Their neighborhood, while nice enough, was hardly upscale. "Look, Jerry, I just need to get home. It's only going to be for a few hours, then we're leaving." Crap. He probably shouldn't have said that.

Jerry scratched his cheek, his gaze wandering to the other two men as if seeking permission. "Okay, I guess I can let you pass, but the truck and the other car will have to stay out. Only residents allowed." He smiled as if he was doing Cole a favor.

Cole fixed Jerry with a hard stare. "Listen, Jerry, that's my brother in the truck and his family in the red Ford. Now, unless you're going to *shoot me*, they're coming, too."

Jerry glanced back, his grip shifting on the hunting rifle. He cast a nervous look at the other two men still on the other side of the barricade. "I don't know. We're only supposed to let residents through—"

Cole had had enough of this. He put the car in park and opened his door. He looked at the other two men, their rifles pulled closer to their bodies as if they were ready to aim them. He spread his arms, palms out. "Listen, I live here. Right over there, in fact." He pointed to his house. "We're coming through here, getting my belongings and then leaving. We're not stealing anyone's stuff, and we want to keep all contact to a minimum. I don't even want to be this close to any of you. I'd recommend that you keep back from anyone trying to approach the barricade and get yourselves some good masks."

"Who the hell are you to tell us what to do?" One of the men circled the barricade. He was taller and heavier than the short, slim dentist, and he shouldered Jerry out of the way. "We say who comes and who goes."

Cole narrowed his eyes and straightened his shoulders. "As it happens, I know a thing or two about diseases since I'm an epidemiologist. I worked with the CDC for many years and even went to Africa to help manage the Ebola outbreak. Do you have better credentials?"

The man's mouth dropped open.

"Yes, that's what I thought." He turned sideways, jabbing a finger at the truck and the Ford. "These two vehicles behind me are my family, and they're coming in. Get those barricades out of the way."

The man grunted but waved at the other man to move the barriers. "Yeah, okay, but this is the only time."

Cole rolled his eyes, but let the man keep his dignity and didn't press the issue. He only needed this one time. Retreating to the car, he put it into the drive and drummed his fingers on the wheel while the barricades were moved. He gave a curt nod to Jerry as he passed. He sure as hell hoped neither men had Sympatico Syndrome because they'd been within three feet of him. That was closer than he felt was safe. He wanted to maintain at least a six-foot buffer zone, preferably even bigger.

He kicked himself for not having his mask on already. He hadn't counted on hostile encounters, but he wouldn't be caught unprepared again.

The first thing he was going to do was instruct everyone to wear a mask whenever they might possibly come in contact with someone outside of their group.

COLE HELD his hand up in a stop motion. "That's good, Sean. We need room to get the ramp down."

Jenna crossed the front yard, the kids trailing behind her. "Cole, is everything okay? What was going on with those men?"

Piper darted a look at the men. "Why did they have guns?"

"Were they going to shoot you, Uncle Cole?" Trent's voice held a note of excitement and Cole gave him an incredulous look.

"Were you hoping they would, Trent?" He smiled to soften the accusation. Trent was just at the age where something like this seemed incredibly exciting, and the danger was secondary.

"No, but man, they had rifles and everything! It was crazy!"

"Yes, it was insane, I'll grant you that, but they were just protecting the neighborhood. I guess some outsiders were trying to come in, thinking they would be safer here for some reason. The first guy with the gun, he's a dentist. He'd never shoot anyone. He's only dangerous when he has a drill in his hands."

Trent's face fell, and Jenna shook her head with a wry smile.

The truck door slammed, and Sean approached. "Good job dealing with those guys, Cole. What did you say to them?"

Cole shrugged and faced the keypad for the lock on his garage door. He keyed in the code and stood back as the door lifted. "Nothing. Just told them I lived here. I knew the first guy. He's Hunter's dentist." Cole didn't want to get into too many details with the kids around.

"No kidding? Jeez."

"Yeah, anyway, we have a lot to do." He pointed to the supplies he'd left in the garage. "All of that has to be loaded, and I have more stuff in the house."

The kids groaned but Sean sent them a stern look, and they began carrying the boxes to the truck.

Jenna said, "I'm going into the house and see if I can organize it." She left the garage.

"Sorry, guys. I know you've already worked hard today, but once we get settled in the cabins, it'll be like a great vacation. There's fishing and a beach. Kayaks—"

"Kayaks? Cool! Will you show me how to use one, Uncle Cole?"

"Sure will. And when Hunter gets there, you guys can learn together."

"Hunter's cool."

Cole smiled. Trent had always followed Hunter around like a little puppy, worshipping his older cousin. "Yeah, he thinks you're kind of cool too."

Sean started arranging the boxes, and when Cole went to help load, Sean waved him away. "We got this. You go and help Jenna in the house."

"Okay. If you see anything in here you think we'll need, pack it in. We have plenty of room." He waved a hand towards the tools hanging on the wall.

As he entered the house, he sighed as he smelled something cooking. Something good.

He turned into the kitchen to find Jenna stirring something on the stove. "I hope you don't mind, but I saw some pot pies and frozen chicken breasts in the freezer. And this," she pointed to the pan, "is something that was labeled 'soup'. I think it's split pea'."

"Oh, yeah. I made that about three months ago. I made way too much since Hunter wasn't here and froze it. Just be warned—I'm no gourmet cook."

She smiled. "It smells good. I figured I'd cook as much of it as I can so we can eat it now and save some for later. Otherwise, it'll go to waste."

"Good thinking. Get the kids to drink up the milk and juice and anything else you find in the fridge. I have some ice and a cooler so we can take some of the frozen items, as long as we cook them when we get to the island."

"I've been meaning to ask, how are we getting to the island, exactly?"

Cole rubbed the back of his neck. "Um, well, I'm assuming the boathouse has a boat in it. One is listed in the will as part of the holdings, so I hope it's in working order. Since Uncle John did, apparently, still use the island, I'm assuming he had to get there somehow and would have a boat in the boathouse."

"Will it be ready to go?"

"I guess we'll find out."

"I'm not sure I like the sound of that."

Cole pinched the bridge of his nose, closing his eyes. Fatigue and stress tapped against the inside of his skull. "Look, Jenna—I don't like this any better than you do, but do you have a better idea? You saw what's happening out there." He flung his arm out, pointing to the front door. "Do you think it's going to get better?"

She set the spoon down on the spoon holder, and her shoulders sagged. "I have no idea. I feel like this is all some kind of bad dream that I'll wake up from any minute." Her eyes welled, and Cole shoved his hands in his pockets, uncomfortable with the display of emotion. He willed Sean to appear in the kitchen, but he was still out supervising the loading, so Cole gave Jenna's shoulder an awkward pat then moved past her to the get some bowls out of the cupboard.

"I have some cold cuts in there too, for sandwiches. Those need to be used up. I'm going to go see what else I can find to bring. I might have something useful in the basement."

Cole trudged to the basement and opened the storage closet. He couldn't remember the last time he'd looked inside. It contained mostly boxes of old clothes Hunter had outgrown as a child and Cole had intended to drop off at the Goodwill but never got around to it, and old pieces of furniture that Hunter might need for an apartment of his own. He shoved past all of that but took the card table and folding chairs and set them aside. Those were easy to transport and could always come in handy.

He found a box of old tools—hammers, screwdrivers, loads of different size screws and four boxes of nails. Most of it had been left-over from when he'd finished off the other side of the basement ten years ago. Building supplies might come in handy on the old resort, so he put the box beside the card table and kept digging farther back in the closet.

He found a vacuum sealed package that looked to contain quilts and blankets. He smiled when he remembered Brenda buying some late night infomercial gadget that promised to revolutionize storage closets everywhere. You put the items into the bags, attached the vacuum device and sucked all the air out so the package was easier to store. He had to admit, it had worked well, and they had stored all kinds of things until they ran out of the special bags and never got around to order more.

The back of the closet contained six of the bags. He squinted at one that showed a familiar logo through the plastic. So *that's* where his heavy duty winter coat had gone. He vaguely remembered looking for it the winter after Brenda had died and just assumed she must have dropped it off at some cleaners and had been killed before she had a chance to pick it up. But here it had sat for all these years. He picked up the stiff plastic bundle. To think that the last person to touch this had been Brenda made his breath catch. It had been a long time since he'd felt such a wave of grief. He swiped the back of his hand across his eyes and set all the bundles he found beside the tools and card table.

S<small>EAN BARRELED INTO THE KITCHEN</small>. "We got a problem, Cole."

Cole took the last of the non-perishable items from his pantry as Jenna handed it to him, and tossed it into the large plastic bin and snapped the top on. "What?"

"A couple of those guys who tried to stop us this morning are trying to get in."

"Get in? They tried to enter the *house*?"

Piper and Trent rushed in behind their dad, with Piper heading straight to Jenna, wrapping her arms around her.

"Yeah. I locked up the truck as soon as I saw them heading our way and got the kids in the house. They're acting like maniacs—shouting and laughing as though they're drunk. One pretended to take aim at us."

Cole dashed to the front door, keeping out of sight in front of the living room window, and looked through the peephole.

"Evans! Come on out! We're gonna go hunting! Wanna come?"

Cole recognized him from across the cul-de-sac, his house was several doors down. The guy had three girls. Where were they now? He tried to spot anyone else moving around in the neighborhood, but his vision was too limited by the peephole.

The man had been one of the men guarding the gate earlier. Cole tried to remember his name. Elliot or something like that. He observed their behavior, flinching when Elliot fired off a shot, luckily the barrel was pointed skyward and not aimed at anything in particular, but he crawled over to the window, dropped the blind and drew the curtains.

"Sean, get the curtains in the kitchen and den. Jenna, take the kids to the basement." The windows there were covered by plastic bubbles to deflect rainwater. That should make it harder for anyone to shoot inside.

"Aw, come on, Evans. We know you're leaving, and we wanna give you a going away party!"

He didn't bother answering and from the manic way the men were acting, he didn't think either was drunk.

"Bring your whole family. We don't care. My wife is loading up the grill."

"Yeah, you're all invited. Everyone is gonna be there! Join the party. We'll have a blast!" The second man added his plea, shooting his gun off to punctuate his request.

Cole swallowed hard. It was just as Elly had described. They seemed euphoric, as though they really wanted to have an impromptu block party.

Glad he'd brought his guns in the house, he found the cases in the mess of his living room and dug through the paper bag for the ammo.

Sean entered. "I got them in the basement. Piper is shaking like a leaf." He stalked to the front door, peering through the peephole. "I'm ready to kill those assholes."

"I don't think you'll have to."

Sean shot him a look. "Why not?"

"They're displaying symptoms of the disease. I have a feeling that soon, both will be dead."

Sean took another peek outside and shook his head. "Shit. They sure don't look sick."

"Nope. Apparently, that's how it goes." Cole pointed to the hunting rifle. "I just bought that yesterday. Haven't even taken it out of the case."

"We could have used this when we were picking up the truck." Sean sat on the side chair and dug in the box of ammo, loading the rifle.

"Yeah, well, I didn't think we'd need it so soon. I bought it for hunting deer if we need more meat. Eventually, we might need to protect ourselves, but I didn't believe it would happen so soon."

"Me neither, and if you hadn't come to our house yesterday, we'd have been completely unprepared."

Cole met his brother's serious gaze and nodded. He worried about Hunter. Was he in danger of running into people like this? He pulled out his phone to call, but dove for the floor when a bullet came through the window. Glass shattered, the blinds rattled, and Cole swore, coming up to a crouch. He poked the shotgun through the empty square where a pane of glass had been just moments before. He fired off a round, aiming high. Cole didn't really want to shoot anyone. Not if he didn't have to. "Elliot, get the hell away from my house! The next round won't be a warning!"

"Aw, man. We were just having fun."

Chapter Ten

Cole kept vigil by the front window while Sean watched the back of the house. Elliot had been true to his word about a party brewing as loud music blasted throughout the neighborhood, the beat emphasized periodically by gunfire. It set Cole's nerves on edge and several times, he had to fire warning rounds at people trying to venture close to the house.

He rose and peered over the edge of the window frame, his blinds bent all to hell to allow him a narrow gap to look through while still providing some cover. His last warning round had been just a minute or so before, and he wasn't even sure anyone noticed it. Three women, several children, and nearly a dozen men ran around in the street, playing some kind of game. It looked like tag, except that nobody seemed to be 'it'.

Either they were all drunk off their rockers, or they were very ill. Maybe it was a combination. As he watched, a woman staggered and fell. He waited for her to get up laughing. It wasn't the first time she'd fallen. All of the partiers had hit the ground at least once but always staggered back to their feet. This time, the woman stayed down. She moved briefly, in a spasmodic way, then became still.

Cole stood and pushed the blind out of the way. Was she struck by the last round? He'd been confident he'd aimed high enough to avoid hitting anyone, but maybe he hadn't? What if he'd killed her?

One of the kids stopped beside the prone woman, nudging her with his toe. Then the child pulled his foot back and planted a solid kick to her head. Cole started. There was no reaction from the woman. The kid raced away. His laughter sent a chill down Cole's spine.

Not long after, three more people dropped in their tracks, and nobody seemed to care. Nobody went out of their way to abuse them as the child had, but several were stepped on and tripped over in the course of the 'game' of tag. Cole's stomach churned after a little girl dropped and a woman snatched the child by her long blonde hair, dragging her across the lawn. He was pretty sure it was the girl's mother from the color of her hair.

"Sean!" Cole didn't want to shout and kept his voice low, but he needed to talk to his brother.

"You got something?" Sean entered the living room, sending a nervous glance over his shoulder to the backyard.

"No new threats but four people seem to have died in Elliot's front yard, and nobody gives a shit about them."

"How do you know they're dead?"

"Well, I don't know for certain, but the others have gone up and kicked, stomped, and in one case, dragged around a little girl, and none of the fallen have reacted at all. I'm pretty sure they're all dead."

"They dragged a little girl? What kind of monster would do that?"

"Her mother." Cole turned away and retched into the planter of a ficus tree beside the window.

Reaching over, he grabbed the cover of the armrest from the sofa and wiped his mouth, then dropped it into the planter. "I think we need to plan our escape for early morning. I'm hoping that, even ill, they might be less active at that time." Or maybe they'd all be dead by then. It was a morbid thought, but just knowing the virus was mere yards away made his skin crawl. Every time a breeze blew through the broken pane of glass and rattle the blinds, he instinctively held his breath. Thinking that there was a slight possibility of the virus floating on the breeze, he pulled his mask from his pocket, where he'd crammed it earlier. He put it on.

Sean's eyes widened. "What are you doing?"

"Just a precaution but I think we should all wear them until we're in the car and on our way, and even then, if we run into any other people, we need to have them on. I have extras in the garage."

"We might have packed them already."

"Shit." Cole thought for a minute. "Well, you guys should stay in the basement then. Use the bathroom and what have you, but then try to get some sleep. The sofa pulls out into a bed, and I have the bedding from my bed and Hunter's bed I can bring down for the kids to sleep on."

"Yeah, sounds good. But what about you? How are you going to stay awake all night and still drive tomorrow?"

"I'll manage, don't worry. Maybe when we get away from towns, we can pull into some little side road, and I can take a nap."

Sean looked doubtful.

"Look, how about this? We'll have to take turns guarding the house. I'll take first watch. I may have another mask stashed away somewhere. Look around my laundry room down there." He was pretty sure he didn't have one but wanted Sean in the basement where it was safer.

"Okay, but I'll go get the bedding. You stay here and keep an eye on those guys." Sean jabbed a finger at the window, already turning to go up the stairs to the bedrooms.

"Is something wrong, Cole?"

Cole turned to find Jenna standing in the threshold of the kitchen. She eyed the mask on his face. "It's a precaution, but I only have one mask here. The rest are in the truck already. We'll have to get them in the morning."

"Oh. Okay. Well, I'm too keyed up to sleep right now and can get some packing done while the kids sleep."

"I don't think we can right now. I'm worried about the virus. I'm not convinced that it could travel this far in the open air, but I just don't know for certain. I think the basement, with the door closed, will be the safest place for your family right now."

Her eyes darted to the window. "Okay. Well, I guess we got most of everything boxed up anyway. Where's Sean?" She pressed a hand to her forehead, before smoothing it back over her hair and blowing out a breath.

"He went to get blankets and pillows."

When Sean came down, he tossed a blanket at Cole. "Here."

Cole grabbed it. He didn't intend to sleep, but maybe he could stuff it in the hole in the glass. "Thanks."

Sometime towards morning, the shouting and gunfire tapered off. Cole couldn't tell if everyone had just fallen asleep or if they were dead. The music still played, but he was starting to recognize the songs and realized it was someone's playlist which repeated every hour or so. Nobody was manning the stereo.

As soon as Jenna and Sean had gone downstairs, Cole had turned off all the lights so he could see outside better. Since then, he'd only had two partiers attempt to approach the house. One dropped on the sidewalk in front and hadn't moved since, and the other had headed back, apparently drawn by something. Maybe someone had called his name or maybe the music had drawn him back to the party.

Cole yawned and lifted the mask long enough to rub his nose against his arm and take a sip of the coffee he'd made. He was worried someone outside would smell it, but he had to have something to keep him awake. He settled the mask back over his nose and mouth. The first hint of dawn brightened the eastern sky and birds were starting to chirp. Just a few more minutes until light, then he'd wake up the others.

———

"COLE!"

Someone shook his arm, and he bolted awake. "What?"

"Hey, calm down. It's just me."

Cole blinked up at Sean, who was wearing a mask. The room was bright, and as he looked around, he saw all of the boxes and bags that had littered the room were gone.

"We got everything packed. You might want to take a walk through to see if there's anything else you want to take."

The rifle was leaning against the wall. "Shit. I fell asleep." He groaned at the stiffness in his back, and he rose to his feet.

"Not for too long, your coffee was still warm when we came up." Sean pointed to Cole's mug.

"Oh. Good." He stretched. "What time is it?"

"Just a little after six."

So, he'd had about an hour and a half of sleep. It was better than nothing. "How are the kids?"

Sean rubbed the back of his neck. "Freaked out, but they're holding up. Didn't give me any trouble when I woke them to help pack the truck."

"Any sign of life from...?" Cole nodded towards the window.

"Nope. After I got a mask from the truck, I went to the front with the shotgun and made sure nobody was lurking." His eyes met Cole's. "It looks like a war zone, though. At first, I thought people had passed out in the street—I mean, it sounded like a helluva party, right? But all of them are dead. Most are lying in pools of blood, but I don't see any wounds. Looks like they puked it up or something. I took an old sheet and covered the guy on the sidewalk in front. I didn't want the kids to see him."

"You didn't touch anything, did you?"

"Do I look stupid? Of course not."

Cole nodded. "Sorry. Habit."

"Forget it. Let's eat up whatever you have in the fridge and hit the road. Hanging out here with all of those bodies out there is giving me the heebie-jeebies."

"Yeah, sounds good. I just want to try to reach Hunter." He'd left his phone on the charger all night, and unplugged it. He hoped he'd see a text or missed call from his son, but there was nothing. His stomach clenched. He tried to call, but the call went right to voice mail. He left a message, but not trusting his son to listen to it, Cole dashed off a text asking Hunter to call ASAP.

Where was he and why wasn't he answering calls and texts?

Chapter Eleven

Hunter spent the night parked on an abandoned back road, huddled in his pile of clothes and sleeping fitfully. His stomach rumbled, and he dug through his supplies, but he was down to one cereal bar, a pack of peanuts and a bottle of water. No matter the risk, he'd have to stop somewhere soon to gas up and get some more food. As soon as the sky had lightened in the east, he was awake.

His eyes felt gritty, and he'd kill for a shower. It was chilly, but he stripped off his shirt and let the rain cascade over him. The downpour made goosebumps rise, but it felt so good, especially when he looked in the bag where he kept his shaving gear and pulled out a bottle of body wash. He used it everywhere, looking around to see if anyone was watching, then shucked the shorts for a few minutes to get completely clean. With the threat of the virus, he'd felt dirty and contaminated just from listening to the news. He knew the impromptu shower hadn't lessened his chances of contracting the disease, but at least he felt better.

Pulling the shorts back on for a few minutes, Hunter checked the garbage bag he'd rigged between the car and a guardrail. Duct tape was something he always carried in the car to make repairs, and he'd used it to tape one short end of the trash bag to the car, the other to the guardrail. He angled it so it sloped down towards a small plastic container he'd used to hold snacks in his dorm. The snacks were long gone.

As he noted the several inches of water in the bottom of the container, he grinned, proud of his ingenuity. At first, he'd thought to just set it out and get whatever fell into it, then thought of awnings and how they always dripped water in rivulets. He could make an awning.

His backseat was an even bigger mess when he dumped the trash bag of junk from his dorm onto the floor of the car, but it was worth it now that he knew it worked. The bag would effectively triple the amount of rain that could collect in the container, and he had empty water bottles he could fill with whatever he collected.

He wished he had a funnel. It would make the awning even more effective. Maybe he had something he could turn into one. He rummaged through the mess and came up with another empty bottle. He cut in half and rigged it so it would fit inside the top of the bottle below it. Duct tape would make it perfect makeshift funnel. That would be for next time, though. He had five more bottles of water now. That would last him today at least.

He held off on eating right now. He was hungry, but it was tolerable. Grabbing a towel from his pile of stuff in the backseat, he dried off while sitting in the passenger seat. Hunter reached back and dug through the pile until he came up with a clean t-shirt, another pair of boxers and shorts. Feeling better than he had in a few days, in spite of his hunger, he looked at the maps he'd downloaded and traced a route with his finger that would take him back in the right direction.

Hunter leaned forward to peer at the flashing police lights in the middle of the road a quarter of a mile in front of him. Two squad cars blocked the highway. Steady rain and the reflection of the lights on the wet pavement lent the scene an eerie quality. A few people milled around the wreck, although nobody seemed to be doing anything to either help victims or remove the wreckage. Puzzled, he slowed, coasting to a stop about fifty feet from the first squad car, cringing at the four car pile-up behind the squads. It looked bad, with one car flipped onto its roof, and another had the driver's side caved in nearly to the other side of the car. Could anyone have survived that?

He didn't see any bodies lying on the road, but they could still be in the car.

Something struck him as off about the scene. Where were the tow trucks? What about rescue squads? The accident must have just happened, and none had yet arrived. The lack of urgency shown by the two officers on the scene he explained away by assuming there were no major injuries. A few people stood around and observed the wrecked cars, hands jammed in pockets or tucked under opposite armpits. One guy threw back his head, appeared to laugh, then leaned over and spit a glob of something on the ground. Hunter blinked. Had that been blood? While the sun was up, the sky was dark with thick clouds, and he could have been mistaken, but he could have sworn the guy had spit blood. He supposed the guy could be a driver and injured his mouth. That was the most likely explanation. They all must be the drivers, and since they appeared uninjured, bloody glob notwithstanding, that would account for everyone's casual behavior.

Up until now, Hunter had managed to put the weird vibe he'd had from the group he'd fled from yesterday morning out of his mind. He avoided most news stations on the radio, and when he started to get more static than music when he was between stations, he switched to his own playlist on his phone. He knew he should listen to the news to try to get some information, but the few times he had turned on the radio, the reports had freaked him out. Yeah, he was burying his head in the sand, or figuratively sticking his fingers in his ears, but he didn't want to hear all the depressing news about the thousands who had already died. Listening wouldn't change anything. Thousands were said to have died already. How had it gone from hundreds to thousands in just a few days?

He scouted for a way around the accident, but between the police cars, glass, and car parts scattered across the two lanes, the only way around was through the median. Hunter took one look and knew that wasn't an option. Water was filling the depression between the lanes and he knew it was a good way to get stuck. *Crap.* The right shoulder was narrow and dropped into tall weeds and brush. For all he knew, it was filling with runoff as well.

Sighing, Hunter put the car in park and reached into his center console for his phone. He studied the map for a moment, trying to decide where to go from here. Route 83 seemed to run parallel to I-80, and he could probably swing north into South Dakota, then hop on I-90 and zip straight east into Wisconsin. From there, he could take a smaller highway to Oshkosh, then get on the main road up to Green Bay.

While he was glad he'd downloaded the map to where he needed to go, he was happy to have found an atlas at a gas station when he'd last filled the tank. His cell phone signal had been spotty, which he remembered had happened when he'd driven his car out to school in the fall, but he'd forgotten about it. He looked for any new messages from his dad, but there was nothing. He only had one small bar of signal, but he decided to try it anyway. It rang and rang, and never even went to voicemail. What was going on? Had his dad caught the virus? Why wasn't he trying to contact him?

Hunter drummed his fingers on the steering wheel. Uncle Sean would know what was going on. He searched his contact list, hoping he had the number saved, but didn't. But he had Piper's number. He held the phone to his ear. *Please answer…*

"Hello? Piper? It's Hunter—"

"Where are you?" Piper cut him off. "Your dad has been going crazy."

Relief swept him, and he rested his forehead on the wheel. "So, he's okay?"

"Yeah. We're all okay. You would not believe how crazy it's been, though. We had to hole up in your basement all night while your dad stood guard—with a rifle! Someone shot out one of your living room windows."

"What? Why?" Hunter couldn't imagine what Piper was describing.

"I guess they were sick and kept trying to invite us to a party, but your dad kept them away."

"Let me talk to him." He longed to hear his father's voice. Needed to hear it.

"I can't. He's driving the rental truck. We packed it with a shitload of stuff."

"Where are you?"

"We're in your dad's car, following the rental truck. My dad is behind us in his truck. We're like a caravan."

It hadn't occurred to him that things were moving so fast at home. He'd envisioned his dad sitting in the living room watching television or playing on the computer while waiting for Hunter to get home. Then they'd all go up to the lake together. Sure, he had the map, but thought that was just a precaution. "Oh. Okay. I'm stuck right now somewhere in Nebraska. There's a big accident on the road, and I can't get through. Hold on...the state trooper is waving to me...what the hell?"

"What's happening?"

"It's weird, he's grinning at me and waving to me to come out. Hold on." Hunter rolled his window down, made a move to put on his mask, but hesitated. Hiding behind a mask when faced with a cop didn't sound like a good idea. But as Hunter studied the cop's strange grin, the hairs on the back of his neck rose. It reminded him of the look from the group in the last town he'd been in the other day.

His heart knocking against his ribs, Hunter lifted the mask and slid the window back up. He wasn't taking any chances. He'd expected several tow trucks to come along and maybe a rescue squad or two as he didn't see anyone who fit the bill. The people he'd thought had been victims of the accident started laughing, and one started doing a jig—right in the middle of the highway. Hunter ignored Piper's questions coming through his phone. He didn't know what was going on, but he knew it couldn't be standard procedure for a traffic accident. Scanning the road, he calculated the chances of getting around the crash versus doing a u-turn and driving the wrong way until he got to a place where he could cross the grassy, flooded median.

The cop's grin faltered and turned to a scowl as his eyes settled on the mask Hunter wore. He took another step towards Hunter's car, but when the other police officer called to him, he turned away.

Hunter locked the doors. "Hey, Piper, I have to go. This cop is creeping me out. Tell my dad I'll try to call later, okay? I downloaded the map to the island, so I guess I'll see you guys there in the next day or so."

He didn't wait for her to answer because now both police officers were approaching. Each cop wore the same, crazy, shit-eating grin Hunter had only seen on stoned students at parties—never on a policeman's face. A few cars had pulled up behind him, and he saw another in his rearview mirror. If he didn't do something fast, he would be trapped.

Chapter Twelve

Cole calculated it should only take them about three hours to get to Oconto, where the boathouse was located. That was the closest town to the island, located about a mile offshore in Green Bay. He vaguely recalled riding down a river for a little ways before they reached the bay and then the boat trip had been longer. He supposed that the boathouse might have been on the river. It made sense.

Worried about losing Jenna or Sean, he kept darting glances at the side mirror. They all had the directions written down as well as the map on their phones, but after the ghoulish night, he was paranoid about anyone coming into contact with someone carrying the virus. It only took one of them to catch the virus for them all to be at huge risk. He just prayed they hadn't already been exposed, either when getting the truck or shopping the day before. He'd worn a mask and Jenna said she had as well. Thank god she was a nurse and had the foresight to take the precaution before he had mentioned it to her. The kids hadn't been around anyone since Cole had delivered the bad news a few days ago. Chances were, they were safe as long as they stayed away from anyone until they got on the island.

Traffic this morning was heavy, but he peered into other cars and noticed most contained families, and belongings were piled high. SUVs had bikes, canoes, and luggage carriers attached to the top, many pulled pop-campers or were RVs. It seemed like other people had the same idea—to get away from people. Was Wisconsin big enough to put enough room between all the people? The number of Illinois license plates made him aware that many out-of-staters who owned cabins up north were probably heading up there. If they could afford a cottage, they could afford to prepare for something like this. What about those left back in the towns? Those who didn't have cabins or islands to retreat to? Guilt crept into his heart, and he tried to push it aside. He had to take care of his family. He couldn't do anything for others until they were safe.

Cole took a moment to check his phone. No messages from Hunter. Damn that kid! He dialed the number, but it never rang, just went straight to voicemail, but the voice told him the mailbox was full. Probably full from all the messages Cole had left. He tossed the phone on the passenger seat.

To keep calm, he reminded himself of the bad cell phone service he and Hunter had experienced when he'd followed him out to Colorado last August. They were constantly in and out of dead spots. That was probably what was happening now.

His phone rang, and he answered, unable to take his eyes from the busy highway to see who had called, but hoping desperately to hear Hunter's voice on the other end of the line.

"Hey, Uncle Cole, Hunter just called me." Piper, not Hunter, but her words had almost the same effect as if it had been his son. Cole sagged in relief, his foot slipping off the gas for a moment, causing the truck to lurch. He winced when he heard Jenna swear in the background of Piper's call and knew he was the reason. He pressed the gas again, watching Jenna in the mirror. She gripped the wheel of his SUV and shook her head as though she knew he was watching her. Cole grinned. "Tell your mom sorry about that. My foot slipped. What did Hunter say? Why did he call you? Where is he?"

"Whoa, hold on. He's okay. Stuck on a highway somewhere in Nebraska, and he tried calling you but couldn't get through."

"Just now?"

"I guess so."

"Damn, he was probably calling me at the same time I was calling him. Okay, so what's this about him being stuck on the highway?"

"Oh, there was an accident, and the police had it blocked off. But, he didn't say anything more because the cops there were freaking him out."

"What were they doing?"

"I'm not sure, he didn't really say, but said he had to go and to tell you that he'd meet us at the island."

"Okay." Cole blew out a large breath, breathing easy for the first time in days. His son was safe for now, although the cop thing niggled at the back of his mind. He hoped Hunter was being cautious. "So, how are you all holding up? Think you can make it another…" he glanced at the dashboard clock, "hour and a half without a bathroom break?" He really hoped so because he didn't want to take the chance of running into anyone if they didn't have to.

"Yeah, we're all good here." There was a muffled voice in the background and then Piper's squeal. "Gross!"

"What's going on?"

"Trent said he has to go, but he'll just take a whizz in an empty water bottle. *So gross*, Trent!"

Cole smiled. "Well, if he has to go, that would be the safest alternative."

"Whatever." She didn't quite use the tone he'd heard her use with her own parents, but it was close. He chuckled, glad for the only bit of normalcy they'd had in the last few days.

The rest of the ride was uneventful, and when he spotted the exit to the town, he signaled well in advance and made sure Jenna and Sean exited behind him. Now, to find the boathouse.

THE CAR in front of Cole suddenly swerved left, hit another vehicle, and both crashed into the cement median. Braking hard, he managed to avoid hitting either of the cars, but the wheel crunched over something. He coasted and glanced in the side mirror to make sure Jenna and Sean had come through the mess okay. Both of their vehicles looked like they came through unscathed. His instinct was to see if the victims needed help, but he fought it. The way the car swerved in front of him made him leery of the reason for the accident and even with a mask, he didn't want to risk exposure to the virus. He gunned the engine, hoping the other two would take the cue and follow as well.

They both did, but Cole's cell phone rang, and he saw Jenna's name flash on the screen. He answered it.

"Cole! We can't just drive off and leave them!"

"We have to. We can't risk it. Just opening the door near another person could allow the virus into your car. Granted, it's a small risk, but it's there. I drove behind the car that caused the accident, and the guy driving looked like he was having a grand old time. He was dancing in his seat, his arms flailing. Frankly, I'm surprised he managed to keep from crashing five miles ago."

"Do you think…"

"…he had the virus?" Cole finished for her. "Yes, I do. I feel sorry for the occupants of the other car, but it's too risky."

Jenna didn't say anything; she just clicked off and followed the truck.

It wasn't the last accident they saw. In fact, the longer they drove, the worse it became. Cole had never seen anything like it in his life— not even when the roads were covered in snow and ice in the middle of a blizzard.

By the time they got to the middle of the state, the good news was that most of the traffic had disappeared, but the bad news was that they had to pick their way around accidents and Cole worried about glass causing a flat tire. If one of them had a flat, they'd have to abandon the car. He just prayed the truck would make it through.

Chapter Thirteen

Cole matched the address to what he had and what Google Street View had shown him. This was the place. It was an empty lot along the river—empty except for a gravel road leading up to a boat ramp beside a decent sized boathouse. He exited the truck and waited for Jenna and Sean to park beside him.

"This is the moment of truth, I guess." His whole plan hinged on there being at least one boat in the boathouse. There had to be. How else would Uncle John have returned from the island the last time he was there? He studied the keyring he'd received with the paperwork. Some were labeled with bits of paper taped to the metal, but the tape was wearing off, and the paper was dirty and yellow. He held the key at arms-length. He was just starting to need reading glasses and reached into his shirt pocket to get his, settling them on his nose. "Main house, one, two, three, four..." he sorted through the keys, assuming the numbers were for the guest cabins his uncle had on the property. With any luck, a few were still standing. "Ah, here we go." He found several labeled boat, and one boat H. He strode up to the door of the boathouse and tried the key. It didn't fit. Shit! He jiggled it. "It's not fitting. Is there another door somewhere?"

Sean jogged to the left to look, and Trent took the right side and shook his head. Sean said, "Just on the river."

"Here, let me look." Piper took the keyring, and flipped keys, before settling on an unmarked one. "This looks about the right size." She put it in the lock and it turned easily.

She pushed open the door and gasped.

Cole's heart sank at the sound until he followed her in and discovered a pontoon boat. It was perfect! It was raised on a lift, and he'd have to figure that out, but taking all of their gear out to the island would be much easier on a pontoon. The flat deck would make loading and unloading simple.

Sean came in and gave a low whistle. "Sweet!" Then he turned to Cole. "Does it have gas?"

Piper and Trent entered, with Trent walking along the pier beside the boat. "I know how to work this." He pointed to a small box on the ground between the two boat slips. One slip was empty, but the other held the pontoon up out of the water. "It'll lower the boat into the water if you turn this lever," he kneeled and pointed a yellow-handled lever, "and turn it on here." He pointed to something else on the box.

"Good, Trent, because I've never done that before. If you have any other tips, feel free to share."

Jenna approached, crossing her arms as she watched her son eye the pontoon boat. "I'm sure he will, Cole. He spent a month at his friend's cabin up north the last two summers. They have two or three boats, I think."

"Does he know about gas? I'm at a loss here. I don't know if there's gas, and if there isn't, what kind and where to get it. I'm assuming there isn't any gas in it now."

"All of you, come out of there now with your hands where I can see them!"

Cole shot a look at Sean. It hadn't occurred to him to have someone keep watch outside. Damn it. "I'll go out. You guys stay here."

Sean shook his head. "No way. I'm going with you." Cole hadn't even been aware he was carrying, but after their experience getting the truck and last night, he should have expected it. Sean had given a second handgun to Jenna, and from the way she was bending to get something from her ankle area, he guessed she had one too. And his gun was in the truck. Perfect place for it. He should have carried it with him. Cole vowed to never make that mistake again. Things were different now.

"I'm not asking you again! Get out now before I come in shooting!"

"I'm coming out. Calm down!" With no time to argue, Cole stepped through the doorway, squinting into the bright sunlight after the darkness of the boathouse. An older man, probably sixty or so, balding and wearing a dirty t-shirt, stood twenty feet away, a shotgun aimed right at Cole.

"What do you think you're doing? Here to steal something?" The man snarled the question, his finger on the trigger.

Cole shook his head. "No. I own this boathouse. That's my boat in there." He jabbed a thumb back towards the boathouse.

"Bullshit. I know the owner and you ain't him."

"You knew my Uncle John? John Evans?"

The man hesitated, the end of the shotgun sliding to the right, away from Cole. "I know John. You say you're his nephew? What's your name? And if I don't recognize it, you and whoever you got back in that boathouse better pack up your stuff and get the hell outta here."

"I'm Cole Evans, and my brother, Sean, is in there...with his wife and kids." Cole didn't know if he should give that information away, but he sensed this guy wasn't generally hostile.

His eyes narrowed, and he raised the end of the shotgun, aiming at Cole's chest. "Why didn't John call me and tell me you were coming up? I got a feeling you're trying to steal his boat to get away from the sickness. Already had a couple of people show up trying to break in, but I chased them away." He spit on the ground. "Damn thieves. I can't wait to be rid of them. Just waiting for John to show up—then we're heading out there."

Cole had trouble forming a coherent thought while staring down the barrel of a shotgun but he managed, "I'm sorry to tell you that he's not coming. My uncle passed away."

The news startled the man. His eyes widened as pain and disbelief flashed across his face. The end of the shotgun tilted towards the ground. "John's dead?"

Cole nodded. "I'm sorry."

"The sickness got him?"

"No. He passed just before Christmas. Heart attack." Cole slowly lowered his hand, palm spread. "I have the papers from his lawyer right here in my pocket. They prove what I'm saying is true."

The barrel inched up, but not as it had before. The man hesitated. "Nobody told me he died. I'd have gone to pay my respects." The man blinked hard. Cole felt sorry for him.

"I'm sorry, sir. His wishes were cremation and no fuss. We had a small memorial in January. If I'd have known, I would have called you."

"Wait a second, if you're his nephew, you'd know his birthday."

Cole's mind went blank. "I can show you my driver's license. That proves he has the same last name as me, and the papers will prove that I own this boathouse."

"Maybe you are who you say you are, but a nephew should know his own uncle's birthday."

Then it came to Cole. His uncle had died just before his sixty-seventh birthday. The memorial had been the day before his birthday. "January fifth. He would have been sixty-seven this year."

The man appeared to deflate, his bravado escaping in a large sigh. "Yeah. I missed him this year. He always came up unless there was a snowstorm or something. I just figured he decided to go someplace warm this year. He used to joke about that all the time. Why the hell he was spending his birthday freezing his ass off in an ice fishing hut instead of lying on a beach in the Caribbean."

Feeling as if the danger was diminished, Cole held his hands wide, then raised the mask he'd taken to leave around his neck when he was alone. "Just a precaution—to protect both of us." He pulled the documents from his pocket and extended them. "Here's a copy of the paperwork."

The man barely glanced at it. "Nah, that's okay. I believe you." He stood, as if in a trance, his gaze on the boathouse, but it looked like his mind was a million miles away.

Cole had an idea. "Listen, sir…what's your name?"

"Joe. I'm Joe Miller. John never mentioned me?"

"I'm sorry. If he did, I don't recall. I'm afraid I wasn't an attentive nephew and didn't see my uncle often over the last few years."

"John sometimes talked about you and your brother. Said you two and your kids were his only family. He told me all about you having some fancy degree and your brother having his own business. Electrician, right?"

Cole nodded. "That's right. I think we have some distant cousins, but nobody close."

Joe's eyes swept the boathouse and out to the river. "We used to spend almost every weekend in the summer on the island. I'm gonna miss that." He gave a sad shake of his head. "Anyway, I stocked the island up some. Got the generator all ready, and the boats are gassed up. Even got some extra fuel stored in the shed there. I know that's not a good idea, but circumstances." He shrugged. "You're welcome to it. Might as well not let it go to waste."

"Wow. Thank you, Joe." Cole reached into his pocket and pulled out his cash, peeling off a couple of hundreds. "Here, take this for your expenses and time."

Joe waved the offered money away. "Keep it. Won't be worth nothing anyway in a few days."

"That's probably true." Cole tucked the money back in his pocket. "Hey, Joe? How about I go tell my brother that everything is okay? Knowing him, he's getting a bit antsy in there."

Joe nodded and started to turn away.

"Wait, don't go. I want to ask you something. Just hold on a second, okay?"

COLE HURRIED BACK into the boathouse, slamming to a halt when his entrance caused Jenna to jump, her gun centering on his chest. Her eyes wide, she blinked in recognition and lowered the pistol. She blew out a deep breath. "Next time, tell us it's you, Cole." Piper huddled behind her, and Sean had an arm out, keeping Trent behind him. The teen's sulky expression showed what he thought about that.

"Take it easy. Everything's fine. That guy was a friend of Uncle John's. He was protecting this place for him."

"Yeah, that's what I gathered, from what I could hear." Sean holstered his gun.

"He said he was hoping to go to the island with Uncle John when he got here. Said he expected him any day."

"Expected him? How could he be expecting him?" Sean shot a look out the door.

Shrugging, Cole said, "He didn't know Uncle John died. He seemed genuinely shocked, so I believe him. I have an idea, but I want to discuss it with you all before I said anything to him. The thing is, we don't know that island at all, but it sounds like he does. So...I have a proposal, but you all have to agree."

"Proposal? What kind of proposal?" Jenna took a step closer to Cole but motioned for the kids to stay where they were.

"What if we ask him to come to the island with us?"

Sean's mouth went to the side, his expression doubtful. Jenna just gave a hard shake of her head. "No way."

"Why not?"

"*Why not*? Are you crazy?"

Cole sighed. "Look, I know it sounds insane to invite a stranger and under normal circumstances, I never would, but this guy has been to the island a lot. He knows the boats too. And we're going to need all the help we can get to make it through the winter."

"But I have a daughter. I don't want a strange man living with us." Jenna's eyes sparked with anger.

Cole hadn't considered that. "I see your point. I'm also leery that he could have the disease, so that's a consideration too."

"I don't want a strange man near the kids either, but didn't Uncle John have a bunch of cabins out there?"

"The deed lists several buildings, but I don't know how good a shape they're in."

"Okay, well, what if we tell him he can join us, but he has to at least be quarantined in one of those? The weather is nice now so he can fix it up to make it as comfortable as possible." Sean jabbed a finger at Cole. "But, if he so much as looks at either of the kids cross-eyed at any time, he can swim his ass right back here." Sean looked at Jenna then Cole. "Well?"

Cole met Jenna's gaze. It was really her call. Jenna looked at Piper, who shrugged.

"If he can help us this winter, maybe we need to ask him, Mom.

It's not like I'm a little child, and look how tall Trent is already. I don't think he's in any danger, and soon Hunter will be here too. Besides, I would have gone off to school in a year anyway."

Piper's logic made Cole smile briefly.

Jenna reached out and drew her hand down Piper's hair, letting the strands sift through her fingers before turning to Cole, the anger was gone, but concern lingered. "But what about food for another person?"

"Here's the other thing. This guy, his name is Joe Miller, stocked the island in preparation, thinking Uncle John was going to arrive. The boats have gas, there's some food, so I guess he's taken care of his own needs already. I offered to pay him for the goods, but he refused my money. Said it would be useless and he didn't want it to go to waste. If we leave him here, with no food, what will happen to him?"

"Why don't we go out and meet this guy?"

"Okay, but everyone put your masks up." Cole replaced his as well.

"I left mine in the car." Trent shuffled his feet and gave his mom a guilty look.

Sean gave his son a hard look. "You stay here. Someone will bring your mask in. And keep it on until I tell you otherwise, got it?"

Cole led the way out, wondering if perhaps Joe would have left already. They had taken several minutes to discuss Cole's idea. Was he making the decision? Should they just leave Joe here?

Joe was leaning against a tree looking out at the river. He didn't move towards them but nodded at Cole. "What did you want to ask me?"

"Joe, would you like to come out to the island with us? I know it seems like an odd offer, but you know the island. I'm sure we'd manage fine after a while, but you already have your supplies out there."

Joe's gray bushy eyebrows went up in surprise at the offer. "You want me out there with you?" He looked at Sean and over to Jenna. "You both agree? You don't have to, you know. I'll be fine here. I got a little bit of stuff here that I hadn't moved out to the island, and I can just hole up in the house."

Sean took one step forward. "Listen, mister. I think you can help us, and we can help you, but there are some conditions. There's more than one cabin there, right?"

Joe nodded. "Yeah. Three that aren't too bad, and one that's got a hole in the roof."

"Good. You can have the one that's farthest from us—"

Cole cut in and met Joe's eyes. He spoke in a tone he hadn't used since he left the Navy. "And stay quarantined for at least three weeks. That's for all of our safety. At the first sign of illness, you'll be put in one of the canoes listed in my documents, and off you'll go. As far as the kids go, stay away from them unless one of us is around, and that's after the quarantine, of course."

Joe nodded. "I wouldn't have it any other way. I had a daughter."

Cole waited for him to explain what happened to her, but Joe cleared his throat and only said, "I'd be happy to stay there and share whatever I got with you folks. Times like this, decent folks have to stick together."

Chapter Fourteen

Elly looked down on the street. More bodies than she could count littered the sidewalks and cars blocked the streets, either crashed into other cars or just stopped for no apparent reason. Emergency services had tried to keep up. At first, it had seemed like a giant street party. Music had blared and even up in her room, she'd heard laughter and singing down on the street. But now, it looked like the aftermath of a riot. Windows at street level were broken, and she hadn't left her hotel room in three days. Water hadn't been an issue; it still came from the tap and electricity functioned.

The last two days, she had watched them collect bodies and put them into large trucks, having given up on trying to revive anyone after the first day. The workers, what few who were left, now wore biohazard suits, but some of them must have caught the disease before they took proper precautions because she saw several bodies wearing the suits as well.

Among the dead had been police and rescue workers, and when they fell, the others, in the throes of their illness induced euphoria, desecrated the bodies. Elly had stopped watching then. She'd tried calling her office at the CDC for the last twenty-four hours, but nobody answered anymore, and she didn't know what that meant. Were they all dead? Or were they just so busy they were unable to answer the phone?

She barricaded her door with the bed and had stuffed a blanket beneath her door. She'd closed the air ducts, and covered them with pillowcases as well. She wished she could create a negative pressure in the room to make the flow head out of the room instead of in, but she couldn't think of a way to do it. She contemplated breaking a window but thought the pressure from the air conditioning in the building would probably have the opposite effect.

Elly sat on the bed and tried not to think about the gnawing hunger in her stomach. She hadn't eaten anything for two days, having cleaned out the mini-fridge.

The first two days, she'd heard doors slamming and loud voices in the hallway and adjacent rooms. The last twenty-four hours, her floor had been silent. Did she dare leave her room and try to scrounge up some food?

Standing, she dug through her suitcase. At least she had some protective gear with her. She had a small box of gloves and one of the masks. She had learned from her past missions to not take anything for granted. The one thing she hadn't packed due to space constraints was a biohazard suit.

She sorted through her clothing trying to find anything she could use, but all of it would have to go on over her head, and she didn't want to take that risk. She wanted something she could wear over her clothing, like a long coat. Her eye fell on the bathroom door, and she had an idea. She'd ignored the hotel robes, preferring sweats to lounge in, but now a robe could be exactly what she needed. She held one up and decided it would work. It was long on her and over-lapped in front. She could easily wear it backward, to protect her better and keep her regular clothes from getting contaminated.

Tossing it on the bed, she dug into the pocket of her suitcase, pulling out her sneakers. She always packed a pair for comfort but hadn't worn them out of the hotel. They would be her 'clean' shoes. The loafers she wore and left just inside the door when she'd last entered her room would be her 'dirty' shoes. After this, they would be left outside the room.

Suddenly, the television that she'd left on to provide news and sadly, the sound of another voice, turned off as the bathroom light flickered. Elly gasped. Was this it? Had so many people died that nobody was left to work the power plants? Worried about a blackout, she filled the tub, sink, the ice bucket and every empty bottle she had in the room. She also plugged her cell phone in. She wanted power for the flashlight if she needed it. She had an extra power bank already charged. At least she wouldn't be completely in the dark if she had to leave the hotel down the fire stairs.

Slipping the robe on backward and her mask in place, she pilfered a shower cap from the bathroom amenities, Gloves on, she found the plastic grocery bag in her suitcase. She'd intended to transport dirty socks and underwear back home in it, but she wouldn't be going home anytime soon.

Her next dilemma was how to get into the other rooms? She didn't have any tools. She'd seen doors opened with credit cards in movies, but had only attempted the feat once, and that was on her mom's door when she'd been a teen and had been locked out accidentally. Only she'd used her school identification instead of a credit card. Flipping her wallet open, Elly pulled out her license and a credit card so she'd have a couple of options. Those she stuck in the pocket of the robe. With the robe on backward, the pocket wasn't quite as handy, but she had no trouble reaching it.

As she opened the door, she debated locking it. If the power went out, would she be stuck out in the hallway with no way to get back in? Or would the locks all release? Unsure, she decided to try to prevent the door from latching, without it being obvious that it was open. A sock laid across the latch prevented it from engaging, but still allowed the door to close almost all the way. She tried it a few times from inside to make sure she would be able to push the door open, and then left the relative safety of her room.

Elly's room was near the elevator, but she wasn't about to venture very far from her room yet. Not until she had a feel for what was going on. She looked at the lights and noted that both elevators were on the lower level. Was that just a coincidence or was it because nobody had used them for a while?

Her hope was to find a few unoccupied rooms that still had food in the mini-fridge. She had heard a lot of noise coming from the room adjacent to hers, so she avoided it, knocking on the door across the hallway, instead.

With her ear almost against the door, Elly listened, hoping on one hand to hear a friendly voice, but on the other, if the room was unoccupied, she had a chance of finding food.

Nobody answered her second knock either. She tried the door handle, but it was locked. It was worth a try. She tried the credit card. No matter how much she wiggled it, she couldn't wedge it between the door and the frame so she could slide it down. Maybe it was too thick. Sighing, she tried her license. The edge was a bit thinner than the card. On her third attempt, she managed to squeeze it and then slid it down. The door popped open. Startled at how easy it was, she vowed to always use the chain lock also.

With one hand on the door, and the other clutching the neck of a vase, she peeked behind the door first. Even through her thick mask, she smelled the unforgettable stench of a dead body. Elly wasn't squeamish but worried about contamination. There was too much she didn't know about this disease. Ebola victims were extremely contagious after death. Did victims of Sympatico Syndrome also become reservoirs for the virus after death? Uncertain, she almost backed out but changed her mind. There could still be food in here that was safe to eat if it was packaged and unopened. She had disinfectant wipes to clean any packaging.

The room was trashed. The beds not just unmade, but the sheets and blankets stripped off. She found one body in the bathroom, and another on the floor between the two double beds. Giving them a wide berth, she opened the fridge. All the miniature bottles of alcohol were gone, but she found a package of jumbo roasted almonds intact. She snatched it and tucked it into the bag. There was an orange, and she debated. Was it safe? The skin was unblemished, and unless the victims had injected it with a syringe, there should be no way they could have contaminated the edible portion. Her stomach growled. Into the bag it went.

The can of Pringles was opened with only two broken chip in the bottom. She sighed. The salty crispiness of a chip would have been heaven right about now.

That was all that was in the fridge, but she took a look around the room and saw a suitcase shoved into a corner. Guilt nudged her conscience as she rummaged through the luggage, but she tamped it down. The owner wasn't going to claim this luggage ever again. All guilt was forgotten when she scored an unopened box of chocolate mint truffles. The shrink wrap was still in place! Her mouth watered.

That was all she found in the room so she headed down the hall to the next room. This time, it only took her a couple of tries to pop the lock and the room, other than a faint stale scent, didn't assault her with the smell of death. "Hello?"

Nothing. She entered and found the room unoccupied. Wanting to shriek for joy, she darted to the fridge and laughed aloud. Everything was there. She cleaned it out. Every bottle of alcohol, every candy bar and a package of M&Ms found their way into her bag.

Buoyed by the find, she ran into the hallway hoping to find another empty room, but she couldn't get the door open. Her license opened the latch, but the occupants had used the heavy chain. From the lack of response inside, she guessed they were dead.

Elly only had one more room to try on her side of the floor. She wedged the license in the door, and it popped open like the others had. This entrance wasn't secured with the chain, so she crept in as she had the previous two rooms, only to come face to face with a woman. When she spotted Elly, instead of being alarmed, she grinned.

"Come on in! I was just about to have a drink! Want one?"

Elly hesitated. "Um, sorry. I guess I have the wrong room." She tried to pass off breaking into the room as a mistake. The woman waved off the apology.

"No worries. Things have been crazy, am I right? I just feel so good to have survived the apocalypse that I was going to celebrate with a drink or two. Screw the hotel and their minibar rates. Just let them try to make me pay." She laughed and waved for Elly to come in, not even commenting on Elly's unusual attire.

"I should be getting back to my room. Enjoy your drink."

"Hey, don't leave me here to drink alone." The woman's smile faded, and an angry gleam came to her eye. "Get in here."

Elly turned and bolted for her room. Dashing inside and slamming the door an instant before the woman pounded on it. Sliding the chain into place, Elly leaned her forehead against the wood, she gasped in relief. It took a moment, but with a groan, she realized she still wore all of her now contaminated gear. "Shit!"

At least she hadn't gone beyond leaning on the door. She'd left her wipes by the door and so used them to wipe all the surfaces she had touched, then wiped off her shoes, taking them off and setting them in the corner behind the door. She still considered them contaminated, but she didn't think she'd be able to sleep with them in the room and not wiped down.

Next, she wiped down the bag and all the contents, tossing them onto the bed to keep them from coming into contact with anything near the door. An orange rolled off the bed, but that wasn't a big deal. The bottles, she had to set as far away as possible, not risking the glass breaking on her bed and losing the contents. Even beer had precious calories.

When the food was decontaminated, she removed her robe, hanging it on the hook on the back of the door, the contaminated side facing the hallway. She would be able to just slide her arms into it without touching it next time she wore it.

Pounding on the door made her jump away from the door.

"Hey, bitch! Are you too good to have a drink with me? What's your problem?"

Elly called out, "I'm sorry. I'm just tired. I think I might be coming down with something."

"You're sick? You got that disease? Ew! Stay away from me! You better not have contaminated me, you dirty slut!"

Elly's eyes widened. Where had that insult come from? She would have smiled if the circumstances hadn't been so dangerous. She couldn't remember the last time she'd had a date. The accusation would have been hilarious on any other day.

A door slammed down the hall, and Elly sagged in relief. She was almost certain the woman was showing symptoms of the syndrome.

The power flickered again, but didn't go off, and so she took the orange into the bathroom and washed it to be on the safe side. Then she peeled it and ate it with a handful of almonds and a few peanut M&Ms. She wanted to consume everything she'd acquired but decided to save it.

At least her stomach wasn't knotted in hunger, and she could think of something besides food. She couldn't stay in the hotel much longer. She needed to leave and get out of the city without getting sick. She turned on the television, but the once slick TV news was reduced to a couple of channels showing reporters in full biohazard suits and bodies piling up in cities across the country. There was mention of other countries starting to feel the effects of the disease as well. Chicago had been in the first wave, and the local news channel showed only a test pattern. She hadn't seen one of those in years. She switched back to the station still on the air.

The only thing good about the news was that maybe so many people had died that she'd stand a chance of getting out without meeting anyone else.

Elly took one more almond and chewed it while she devised a plan, such as it was. If she were home, she would have been safely ensconced in her bugout cabin. Her friends had all thought she was nuts, but working in war-torn areas, she'd come across too much suffering and starvation. She had the means to stock provisions, so why wouldn't she?

She wondered how Cole was doing. Was he still alive? Had he made it to a safe place?

Elly scanned the pile of bodies the camera panned over. Out of habit, she noted the measures taken by officials—what was left of the officials, anyway. She imagined they were being decimated at a rate similar to the general population.

She had no doubt that the higher brass would have bugged out some top secret location, their close family all safe and provided for. Elly shook her head. Had the scientists been protected too? They should have been because they were the key to finding a cure or treatment but would the bureaucrats care as long as they were safe?

One thing puzzled her. Why hadn't the scientists at Aislado Island created some kind of vaccine, or at least a treatment before making the disease so deadly? Of course, officially, the disease had an unknown origin, but she knew in her gut that it was manufactured. It was too deadly to have never been seen before. Diseases didn't work like that. You could always go back and dig around and discover a few scattered cases of a mysterious disease that had only affected a handful of people at first. It had been that way with both AIDS and

Ebola. Sympatico had come from nowhere. She'd been spending most of her time while holed up researching everything she could find. As long as the internet still functioned, she was going to use it to investigate what might have happened. She'd been able to connect with some other researchers in other countries, and none had ever seen anything like this, nor had come across it in research.

Elly was certain that this was the same disease that she had investigated for the CDC and when she had first met Cole. He had been stationed at that base. He had shown her around and been the official Naval contact to the CDC—until he became ill. She remembered that vividly because she had been quarantined for three weeks on the island. It had been the three longest weeks of her life. Her supervisor had not been happy. He had worried it had all been a ploy to keep the CDC in the dark about some new biological weapon.

When she was released from quarantine she'd learned that Cole had been ill, and that his illness had been the reason *she'd* been quarantined. But that never made sense to her. Three weeks? His commanding officer had informed Elly that Cole had meningitis but had recovered. Meningitis, while certainly serious, was treated with antibiotics. She should have received a dose immediately, but they never gave her anything. They just quarantined her and she learned later that several other people who had close contact with Cole had also been quarantined. Whatever he'd had, it hadn't seemed to be too contagious.

She had run into him when she went to retrieve some paperwork in the lab and contrary to the report she'd received on his health, he didn't look fine at all. He'd been pale and gaunt, hardly resembling the handsome officer she had met upon her arrival on the island. However, nothing more was said about his illness. When she saw him again in Africa, he'd looked to be fully recovered, and they hadn't discussed it.

Had his illness had anything to do with what was happening now? It had been several years ago, so it seemed as if there should be no connection. In fact, she had forgotten about it until now. It didn't seem related except for the location.

She glanced at the television, shaking her head at the sheer number of bodies, and she knew it was just the tip of the iceberg.

Those were just the bodies that had been collected so far. From looking down on the streets below her hotel window, she knew thousands more were lying in streets. Too many to collect given the reduced number of people healthy or brave enough to collect them.

At least most of the dead were ensconced in body bags, but the top layer of the pile held some that were exposed. The sight should have horrified her even more, but she was becoming numb to it, except for the children. Her eyes welled at the sight of so many small bags. This disease seemed to attack everyone equally, but the death of a child always hit her hard and to see so many in one place, made her catch her breath, unable to hold back a sob.

If she extrapolated what was happening in Chicago to all of the other cities in the U.S. she put the death total up in the millions already, and she was sure it hadn't even peaked yet. It wouldn't taper off until the majority of the hosts were dead— or until it was cured.

The only thing good about the news was with so many dead now, she stood a better chance of escaping the hotel and evading other people. But where could she go?

Chapter Fifteen

Hunter stared at his gas gauge, willing it to move off the red. He'd tried to find an open gas station, but luck hadn't been with him. The main highways had all been closed to traffic, and he'd been forced to take side roads. His GPS still worked, but he'd turned it off when he had to keep making detours. It just wanted to send him back to the highway. So, now he was using a paper map, but tracing a route through the rural roads was hard to do, and he had to keep stopping to make sure he was still on the correct road. He kept the car pointing east whenever he could so he knew eventually he'd reach either Wisconsin or worst case scenario, Illinois.

All of the detours had contributed to him making much less progress than he'd anticipated. Instead of already being in Wisconsin, he was somewhere in Minnesota unless he'd crossed into northern Iowa without realizing it. If he hadn't screwed up a turn anywhere, he should be in Minnesota.

On his left, there was nothing in sight but flat fields, but on his right, he saw a farmhouse about a mile away. He was wary of approaching any people, but he was down to two bottles of water, a few sticks of beef jerky and two apples. When he'd bought supplies, the boxes of granola bars and snacks had seemed plenty, but he'd also counted on being able to go through some fast food restaurants along the way.

With no gas, he couldn't sit in the middle of the road forever. He had a hunting knife and the bow and arrows so he wasn't completely vulnerable, but they were no match for someone with a gun. He glanced west. The sun wouldn't set for a few hours yet, and he didn't want to be left out in the open with no place to seek cover. He hated leaving all of his supplies where anyone could come by and take them. He'd already passed several cars stripped of everything or worse, burned beyond recognition.

Hunter stepped out of the car and scouted a location he could hole up for a few hours before approaching the farm yard. He knew that while the ground looked flat, it was deceptive, and so he walked into the field, heading for a small rise just beyond the front of the car. Crossing the newly sprouted rows of corn, he wondered if anyone would be around to harvest it come late summer? He took a small sip from his water bottle as the field rose even higher. From the rise, he spotted a line of brush and trees winding towards the farm. With luck, it was a creek, and he could pitch his tent there. The brush would hide him, and he could cart all of his supplies there, safeguarding them from anyone who might come along.

His biggest fear was someone at the farm spotting him as he moved his gear to the creek. He found a spot with thick brush, hacking some of it out of the way to create a space for his tent. He filled in gaps in the coverage with what he hacked from inside the camp site. It took him three trips to bring everything from the car to his site, and another hour to pitch the small tent. His stomach growled, and he ate a beef jerky stick, saving the other two for the morning. He selected the smaller of the two apples, leaving the last one for tomorrow, and set it on the ground beside his pack. At least he had water, and he dug out his filter and purification tablets, sending a mental thank you to his dad for telling him to get them. At the time, he'd thought it was over-kill, but now he wished he would have bought even more.

He knelt by the stream to wash the apple and started when a fish jumped just a few feet away. Jumping up from the stream, he grabbed his pole from where he had set it beside the tent. He took the pole, a small tackle box he'd bought as well, along with a net, and put them on the stream bank, then, using his knife, dug a few worms from the ground. With his line baited, he scouted for a likely place. The creek was only about eight feet across but looked pretty deep. He caught a few more flashes of fish in the current. He hoped they were hungry. Good thing it wasn't late summer because he had a feeling the stream would be a lot lower then. He dropped the line in a likely looking pool.

It took a while, but as evening approached, he got a few nibbles. Then a fish stole his bait. At least they're biting. He dropped to his knees and found another worm in the soft dirt next to the stream. It took only a few moments, and he dropped the line again.

Something hit his line hard, and he grinned and set the hook. "*Yes!*" Hunter stilled, looking and listening for anyone who might have overheard him. *Stupid mistake.* What if someone had heard him? His mouth went dry as he strained to listen. When nothing happened after a minute, he relaxed. From now on, he'd celebrate silently. His smile returned as he reeled in a nice-sized trout. He strung it and tried for another one. The next hit was a small bluegill. As he brought it out of the water and onto the bank, he sighed. For such a little guy, it had put up quite a fight. Ordinarily, he'd never consider keeping a fish as small as this one, but he was hungry and didn't know if he'd get another fish. In the end, he kept it and was glad he had because he had to stop when it started getting dark.

He cleaned the two fish and set up the stove. The scent as his dinner cooked made his mouth water and he just hoped the aroma didn't carry too far. He ate the apple while the fish cooked and peeked through his brush fence. No signs of life anywhere—not human life anyway. Plenty of birds darted through the air. High above, two hawks circled lazily in the clear sky. It had turned into a perfect spring day. Letting the brush fall back into place, he checked his fish and took a last bite of the apple, tossing the core into the stream. Instead of filling him, the apple only whet his appetite, and it was all he could do to wait for the fish to cook.

Hunter ate the fish and swiped his plate with his first finger, licking it to get the last trace. He was no longer hungry, but he was far from full. With a sigh, he took his plate to the creek and scrubbed it with a handful of coarse grass and water. It might not be sanitary, but at least it looked clean. He shrugged and tucked it back in with the other gear.

Before settling in to sleep, he left the protection of the creek and walked to the highest point in the field. It was nearly dark, and if anyone was around, they'd have a hard time spotting him. He just wanted to see if there were any lights visible. A highway would be great because there was bound to be a gas station near a highway entrance. Hunter turned slowly in all directions, looking for signs of people. A few lights burned in the farm-yard, but the house was dark. The hoped for glow from businesses near a highway or even a small town, were nowhere within sight. His shoulders slumped. What if everyone else was dead? He couldn't possibly be the only survivor, could he?

There was a barn on the far side of the house, and he wondered if any animals were in it. At the moment, the building was just a dark shadow, except for a light, probably above the main door. It illuminated a small circle of the yard, but other than packed earth, there was nothing for him to see.

As he stood there, the only sounds were natural—frogs, crickets, the wind rustling the leaves of the trees, and far off, a dog barking. He tilted his back, taking in the Milky Way. He'd never seen it so clearly. Granted, he'd been around too many city lights his whole life to ever see anything but the brightest stars and planets let alone the Milky

Way, but was it because he was out in the middle of the country, or was it because fewer lights were polluting the night sky?

There was no rumble of traffic, no airplanes overhead and no sirens. The airplanes he understood because one of the last news reports he'd heard had said all planes were grounded. It was a last ditch effort to stop the spread of the virus, but Hunter suspected that window of opportunity was long gone. He'd picked up enough from his dad to know a little bit about the spread of disease. He'd wondered why they were so slow to stop flights and guessed it was probably the airlines worried about backlash from customers, but now there wouldn't be any customers.

The silence unnerved him. It seemed like half of his drive so far had been accompanied by the shrill wail from emergency vehicles. Most of them he never actually saw, but the tones sent his heart hammering. Sirens had never bothered him before unless it was a cop car coming up behind him—then he had the normal panic thinking he was getting a ticket—but earlier in the day, the sirens' constant droning sounded of doom and death. Now, there were no sirens, and he was missing them. At least he'd known someone was still out there trying to save lives.

He looked over the land, managing to pick out dark shapes in the distance that might be neighboring farms. Far, far away, he spotted headlights on some distant road. They were heading parallel to him, so he wasn't worried, and the sight brought him comfort. It was proof that he wasn't the last person left on Earth. Not yet, anyway.

"TRY IT NOW!" Sean hollered from the back bedroom, having found the breaker box and tripping the switches.

Cole flicked a switch, heartened to see the light come on. "It's working!"

For how long, he didn't know, but they would take what they could get. Right now, it was almost dark, and they had spent the whole afternoon ferrying over their belongings and supplies. Joe had manned the boat while Sean, Trent, and Cole had loaded and unloaded. Jenna and Piper had made up beds for everyone except

Joe, who was staying in another cabin. The main house had three bedrooms, a den, and a living room. The furniture was old and musty, but solid. The den had a sofa-bed—which Trent had promptly called dibs on, and best of all, the kitchen and living room shared a fireplace. An old woodstove was in the den, and Cole hoped it worked. It looked to be vented to the outside, so he felt confident it would.

For the first time, he started feeling like maybe everything would be okay. They could hide out here at the cabin, fish, grow some food, and manage just fine. If only Hunter were here.

He pulled out his phone and tried calling him. To his shock, Hunter answered on the third ring.

"Hunter? God, it's good to hear your voice. I'm sorry I missed your call earlier today."

"It's okay. I think we were calling each other at the same time."

"Are you almost here? We're on the island now, and it looks great. We still have electricity. The only bad part is you'll have to bunk with me initially. There are some other cabins here, but for now, we're staying in the main house. Joe's going to take one of the cabins."

"Who's Joe?"

Cole chuckled. "It's a long story, but he's an old friend of Uncle John's, and he's going to be staying with us. He had the island pretty well stocked before we even got here. Now, we just need you here, and we'll be set."

"Here's the thing. I'm out of gas."

"*Out of gas*? How could you let that happen?" He didn't intend for it to sound like he was blaming Hunter, but he was upset and blurted out the question before he had time to think.

"It's not like I did it on purpose, Dad. All the highways have been closed, and I've been trying to find my way through a maze of back-roads. Every gas station I've come to has been closed."

"I apologize. I should have anticipated something like that. We encountered a whole slew of accidents on the way up here—in fact, I was going to tell you to avoid the main highways if you can. Do you have a map that shows smaller roads?"

"I bought an atlas at a gas station the other day because it was hard to look at my phone and see it when I zoomed out. I know where the island is and everything, but not sure how that's going to help me until I can get some gas for the car."

Cole pinched the bridge of his nose. He wished he could just go pick up his son. That's what he *should* do. "Hey, do you have coordinates from your GPS? I can plug them into my phone and figure out exactly where you are. Then I can just come and get you."

"I guess I could, but I don't want you leaving there. I'm not that far away. I think I can get some gas from this farm I'm on and if not from here, then the way things are going, I can siphon a few gallons from a car crashed on the side of the road. From what I saw, I think most of the drivers are dead. I would have done it today, but this stretch of road is really out in the boonies. I didn't see any other cars —but I'm sure I can walk a mile or so and find one eventually."

"Okay. Keep me posted. Send me texts. How's the charge on your phone?"

"It's okay. I'm at about sixty percent. I've only been using it to check to see if you've called. And now."

"Good. Why don't we set a time to check in? That way you don't have to keep your phone on. How about ten a.m. tomorrow? Are you sleeping in the car? Are you wearing a mask all the time?"

"I left the car on the road because I was worried about someone coming along. It just didn't feel safe."

Cole didn't like the sound of that. The car offered the best protection, but then again, if it couldn't move, whoever was in it was trapped if someone was determined to get in. "Where are you going to sleep then?"

"I grabbed the camping gear you told me to get and found a little stream cutting through a farm, and there are a bunch of trees and stuff along it. I caught a couple of fish and cooked them for dinner."

There was a note of pride in Hunter's voice, and Cole smiled. "Good job. Okay, just lay low, and call me in the morning. Love you, son."

There was a pause. "Yeah. Me too. Bye, Dad."

Chapter Sixteen

As planned, Cole called Hunter at the designated time, but it rang only twice, then stopped. He didn't know if there was something wrong with the service or if Hunter's phone was out of battery. If he'd had turned it off last night, it should still be close to fifty percent. Cole stared at the screen, his mind spinning through scenarios. What if someone found him by the stream? He should have insisted that Hunter send him the coordinates. He had no idea where his son was. What kind of father was he? Why hadn't he jumped in the car and driven to Colorado to get his son when he'd first heard about the disease? He could have been there and halfway back by now, and he'd know exactly where his son was, not wondering if his only child was dead or alive. What kind of father was he? What had he been thinking? The knot in his gut, present since he'd seen the first news reports, twisted. Hard.

Jenna used tongs to set a strip of bacon on a platter. "What's wrong?"

"Hunter. He's not answering."

"He probably just hasn't turned the phone on yet. You know how teens are." Sean turned from mixing the pancake batter. It was the first real meal they were cooking at the cabin. They had several boxes of pancake batter Jenna already had in her pantry, but soon, they'd eat the home-made variety. The bacon would probably be the last they would have in a long time. The mouth-watering aroma inspired warm memories of lazy weekend mornings, camping trips and pancake breakfasts with Hunter's Boy Scout troop. The memories clashed with the reality of a world descending into chaos.

Cole nodded, his throat too tight to speak. He left the kitchen and wandered into the living room. It was really more of a great room with its high ceiling. The cabin had a fantastic view of the bay, and as he gazed at the sparkle and flash of the sunlight as it danced in the waves, he fought to quell his worry for Hunter.

Joe walked past the window, a toolbox in hand. While he was welcome on the island, they had agreed that he would take the far cabin and stay there in a modified quarantine. Cole had given him a mask and was glad to see he wore it now, even outside. It seemed a waste that Joe had to cook for just himself, but for now, it would have to be that way. Everyone had been exhausted from unloading the truck and their vehicles last night and then carrying them into the cabins. Cole had awakened only an hour ago, but it was so strange to him to realize that he didn't have any place to be at a certain time, but while they didn't have a schedule to keep, there was plenty to do on the island.

After breakfast, they were going to discuss what everyone would do.

With the addition of Joe, they had another set of hands to get things done, but Cole worried how they'd survive once their food ran out. They needed a short term plan for the summer. Plant a big garden, fish as much as they could, learn how to preserve the food, and hopefully, in the fall, they could hunt some deer. At least there should be plenty of those around.

As long as the stoves were working, they had an advantage, but once fuel ran out, they would need wood for the stove and fireplace to get through the winter. That was a lot of wood. Joe had already created a nice pile and said there was a chainsaw in one of the sheds, and he'd had a few extra gallons of gas stored in a shed far from the other buildings. Already, Joe had proven to be a valuable asset to their survival and Cole was glad they had invited him to join them on the island.

As Joe passed again, carrying what looked like a small boat

engine, Cole became curious. Were there more boats on the premises? A small fishing boat or two would be nice to have. The pontoon, while great for getting supplies to the island, used a lot of gas.

His stomach growled. Food, shelter, water, and cutting wood for the winter. Those were the priorities for the summer. And soon Hunter would be here to help with all of that. He had to believe that.

Even as he convinced himself of Hunter's survival, he worried that maybe none of them would escape the virus. He'd been watching everyone carefully for any signs of it, and so far, everyone seemed okay. He didn't know Joe, but the man was quiet and from what Cole knew that was the complete opposite from the symptoms. When some time had passed, and they were reasonably certain none of them were infected, they could lift the quarantine and Joe could join them at meals. It didn't make sense for them to waste any food or fuel by cooking separate meals.

As much as Cole hated to do it when Hunter arrived, they'd have to quarantine him. He decided that when Joe was cleared, he could move to the cabin beside the main house. If Hunter arrived in the next few days, he'd have to take the middle cabin. It was set back a little from the rest. Of course, they would provide food for him, they'd just have to leave it on the picnic table beside his cabin. It wasn't an ideal set-up, but Cole hoped it would be adequate.

Then another problem occurred to him. How would they even know when Hunter had reached the dock? If his phone worked, they'd be okay, but if his phone wasn't working, he'd have no way to contact them.

They would have to make some runs back to the mainland every day to see if he'd made it. He wished he could just leave a note, but that would alert anyone who happened upon it, that people were on the island. He had a feeling things were going to get a lot worse before they got better, and the fewer people who knew anyone was living here, the better.

Cole wished he knew the incubation period of the virus. It seemed as though it wasn't prolonged, the way it was spreading, but what if most of the people succumbing to the disease now were actually infected days or weeks ago? For all he knew, they were all incubating it, but it was too late to do anything about it now. If one of them got sick, likely they all would. His only comfort was that victims didn't seem to suffer. Death came suddenly and after a period of euphoria. It was creepy to see, but he supposed the victims didn't realize they were even sick. He'd seen victims of Ebola and death for them had been slow and torturous.

The electricity was on—for now—but it flickered at times, and Sean wasn't sure if it was a problem with the island's feed or if there was an interruption in the power supply from the mainland. There hadn't been any storms to explain a power outage, but his fear was at some point, if the mortality rate continued unabated, there wouldn't be enough people left alive to run the power plant. The whole supply chain was in jeopardy. Despite the heavy automation, people were still required to get the coal from the ground, onto the trains, and to the power plants. The same with all the fossil fuels. He remembered his idea for a windmill to power the well. That would be first on the list if the power went out—but he hoped it wouldn't come to that.

Cole couldn't wipe out the images of all the car accidents they had passed yesterday. The kids had told him every detail as if forgetting that he had passed the same scenes, but he let them talk and tried to allay their fears by reminding them they hadn't had any close contact with anyone now for at least three days. To them, that sounded like a long time, but he knew it wasn't nearly long enough. He wouldn't breathe a sigh of relief until they had reached three weeks on the island with no signs of illness. The danger time might be less, and it might be more, but he couldn't be sure—not without thorough research and access to patient records.

"Breakfast is ready, Cole." Jenna had approached without him being aware. She reached out and rubbed her hand across his shoulder. "He'll be okay. Hunter's smart. He'll get here as soon as he can." She headed back to the kitchen.

He felt both a rush of parental pride that she had said Hunter was smart but also a measure of guilt that he'd had doubts. Sure, Hunter had always seemed intelligent to him, but after years of watching his son struggle through school, as a father, he'd wondered if his bias had blinded him to his son's faults. It was hard to be both mother and father, and the death of Brenda had hit Hunter just as he'd started first grade. No wonder he never liked the beginning of a new school year.

What if Hunter didn't make it? Cole drew in a deep breath. His son was out there— alone—probably scared—and he had to find gasoline, water and probably food too, and yet avoid contact with anyone.

He tried to take comfort in Jenna's words. She was right. Hunter *was* a smart kid. This wasn't school. Some things he learned quickly and easily and the more Cole thought about those skills Hunter had picked up with ease, the better he felt. He recalled their hunting and fishing trips and how his son had learned to clean his kill and fillet fish. He wasn't the least bit squeamish either. They had joked about how apt his name was.

Feeling a little better, Cole joined his brother's family and ate breakfast.

HUNTER AWOKE to the sound of birds chirping and somewhere not far away, cows mooing like they were going insane. He'd never heard anything like it. Scrambling from his sleeping bag, he peered outside. The trees shaded his campsite, but he guessed it was later than he'd thought. He'd spent the night tossing and turning, every sound, fear that someone had found him. At some point, he'd heard snuffling outside of his tent and had lain, eyes wide, until whatever it was left. He knew enough about camping to keep food out of reach of animals. Four years of Boy Scouts had taught him that, but he didn't have much food to begin with. There was just the jerky and the apple.

"Shit!" Whatever it was he'd heard had found his pack and shredded the jerky package. Bits and pieces lay scattered on the ground. The apple had one bite but several claw marks and he kicked it against a tree. "Thanks a lot. At least you could have eaten it all, instead of just ruining it for me!" He whisper-yelled into the trees, knowing a raccoon or opossum, one of which was the likely culprit, would never feel guilty, but it made him feel better to vent his anger.

Then he looked at his pack and groaned. He'd changed into sweat-pants for the night instead of jeans because the jeans had picked up a fishy smell. Maybe the critter had smelled the fish on the denim, but for whatever reason, it had dragged them across the campsite, abandoning them half in the stream. Only one pant leg draped over a root from a nearby tree kept the jeans from being swept away— all the pockets were submerged.

"Shit! *My phone!*" Hunter dashed to the stream, praying for a miracle as he pulled the sodden jeans out of the water. His phone was there, but it was soaked.

Hunter sank to his knees.

COLE SHOVED his phone in his pocket and swore. His instinct was to set out in search of Hunter, but he had no idea where he even was the last time they had spoken. Why hadn't he asked for at least the name of the road where Hunter's car had run out of gas? He grabbed the shovel standing upright in the ground and slammed his foot against the top edge of the blade, slicing the weeds and grass. Dirt fell to the ground as he gave the shovel a shake, trying to get most of the weeds separated from the dirt. When most had fallen off, he grabbed the tuft of weeds and tossed it into the growing pile.

He surveyed the large area they had already dug up and wondered if it would be big enough. There was still a bit of clearing left, but not a whole lot. He'd leave the decision to Jenna. She was the expert here. He was just the hired help. She'd had to go to a location a hundred yards away from the cabins to find a clearing because all of the land around the cabins was heavily shaded. A small creek trickled through the east side of the clearing and Cole was glad to have a water source so close. Maybe they could divert a few channels towards the garden if they needed to.

His arms ached, and he felt a twinge of guilt that he was glad that Trent was on garden duty tomorrow. Cole was pretty sure his arms were going to hurt like hell when he woke up in the morning. He never knew digging in the dirt was such hard work.

Sean and Trent were spending the day inspecting the cabins and repairing anything that needed fixing. After that, Sean was going to see about creating some kind of windmill to run the water pump if the power went out. Water was a priority. Sure, they had a lake all around them, but Cole worried about contamination in the coming months if sewage plants stopped running. A lot of untreated waste could make its way into the lake. The water might be okay out in the middle of Lake Michigan, but where they were, it could be unsafe to drink.

"I hope the deer and rabbits don't get to it all." Jenna raked the clumps that Cole turned over. Piper did the same, picking out as many weeds as possible.

He paused, swiping his arm across his forehead. Even with the gloves on, blisters dotted his palms. He'd thought the last few years of regular physical work that he'd put into remodeling houses before he re-sold them would have conditioned him to this kind of physical labor. He'd thought wrong. "We have some tin foil. Isn't that supposed to help scare them away?" It wasn't the reason he'd bought a giant roll of aluminum foil, but when he'd seen the industrial sized roll, he knew it would come in handy at some point.

"Yeah, we can try it." Jenna leaned on her rake, dragging her arm across her brow. "I'm wiped. This is, by far, the biggest garden I've ever worked on."

Cole dug one more shovelful of earth and flipped it over, jabbing the tip of the shovel in to break up a big ball of dirt. "Yeah, Brenda used to like to garden, but I haven't worked in one since she died."

"I remember. She was a great gardener. She taught me a lot. I remember Hunter and Piper racing around the yard while we worked, digging for worms and once, Hunter got Piper to kiss one."

Cole smiled. That sounded like something Hunter would do. His smile faded as the worry pushed the amusement aside. He'd already lost Brenda—he thought that was going to destroy him, but he had to keep it together for Hunter's sake. If something happened to Hunter, he didn't think he'd even try to keep it together. Not now.

OKAY, so he had no phone. It wasn't as if his dad could do anything for him anyway and he knew where he had to go. Hunter tucked the phone in his pack. Maybe it would dry out and work later. He wrung as much water out of his jeans as he could and hung them to dry on a branch.

He packed up his tent and stashed it under a bush then brushed his feet across the ground trying to erase any sign that he'd been there. He wasn't sure why he should hide it, but it seemed like a good idea. They did it in movies all the time. With his pack on his back, he decided to follow the stream until it reached the farm yard to keep out of sight for as long as possible.

It wasn't a long hike, but he followed the creek as it curved around to the front of the farm so it took a few minutes to get close to the buildings. He stopped to search for signs of life every few yards. He heard plenty of farm animals with the cows still making a lot of noise, he thought he heard a horse somewhere.

A dog barked too, but there wasn't one in sight. Was it locked in the house? The fact that it was still here meant the dog's owner was probably here too. Unless they had run out intending to come back. He hadn't heard any car doors or engines this morning, and there was no reason to believe the people would have tried to be quiet. He watched the windows, looking for movement, but didn't see anything. A beat-up car was parked in the yard. Did it have gas in it? Then he noted the flat front tire.

Hunter tried to memorize the layout of the yard. The house was closest to him now with the barn on the other side of the yard, slightly behind the house. A couple of smaller buildings were next to the barn and behind the house. The smallest building looked like a chicken coop, and he saw movement within it, but it was just flapping of wings, not a person. The next building had wide double doors, and he decided they would be wide enough to fit a tractor. A fenced pasture came off the barn and circled around behind it. It was empty right now, but the cows were in there. Their lowing continued sporadically.

He waited for what he guessed was about thirty minutes, and nothing changed. The dog still barked occasionally, and the cows lowed. A couple of times, he heard the chickens squawk. While he had been on a few farms over the years, a friend at school had one, he was no expert on what constituted a normal farm day, but on a beautiful late spring day like this, he thought the cows should have been let out to the pasture. The cows on his friend's farm were always out when he went to their house.

Hunter took one last look around and decided he'd have to go closer. He couldn't stay in the woods all day. He decided that making his presence known was probably the safest course of action. If they were okay, they might help him, or at least let him take a few eggs or something. If they weren't, then, he supposed he could take what he wanted. His worry was that they were sick. If they were, he wasn't sure he'd recognize it. Just before he stepped from his cover, he remembered his mask and dug it from his pack, along with a pair of gloves. He'd felt stupid buying them, as though he was pretending to be a doctor or something, but now he was glad he had them.

"Hello?" Hunter strode into the farm yard like he had nothing to hide. "Anybody home?"

With no answer, he decided to go right up to the door. "Hey, anyone here?" He trotted up the steps and knocked on the door. The dog went nuts inside, and he heard toenails clicking against the floor. He waited then tried the doorbell. He heard it ring so he waited again. "Hello?"

It went against everything ingrained in him his whole life to enter a strange home uninvited, but he reached for the doorknob anyway to test it with a quick turn, not expecting anything so when it turned in his hand, he jumped away from the door in surprise. His heart raced.

Taking a deep breath, and one hand turning the knob, the other knocking on the door again, he entered the house. The stench of death assaulted him along with the dog he'd heard. Only the dog assaulted him with happy yips and licks, not at all fazed that he was a stranger. He gagged on the stench. Where was it coming from? He eyed the dog, a black lab, looking for signs of blood around his mouth, praying the pet hadn't feasted on its dead master.

"Hey there, buddy. It's okay." The dog was so happy to see him, it circled Hunter's legs like he was a long lost friend. Hunter scratched behind the dog's ears, looking around to see if the source of the stench was lying nearby. He or she wasn't.

"Come on, buddy. Let's find your master." Hunter glanced into the living room, taking in the scattering of dirty glasses and empty beer cans. It looked like a party had taken place. A dining room opened off the side of the living room, and that was empty and neatly kept. The party had not made it into that room, apparently. Hunter moved through it to the kitchen. Two bare feet, dead white on the bottom as they faced the ceiling, were attached to an older woman. He guessed her age at around sixty. She lay face down, a puddle of dried blood near her mouth. The stench penetrated the mask, making him gag as he back-pedaled. The dog whimpered and wouldn't go near her.

"Smart dog." He stroked the dog's head, finding the action as comforting for him as it was for the animal.

Hunter had never been this close to a dead body except for at his mother's wake, and he'd been so young then, he hadn't really understood what death meant. He'd just wanted his mom to open her eyes and smile at him. That was his clearest memory of seeing his mom in the casket. This woman hadn't been washed and made to look like she was merely taking a nap. With her wide, unseeing eyes, and contorted, blood-stained mouth, she looked anything but asleep.

On one level, he felt sorrow that she had died, but he hadn't known her so there was no grief. On another level, he was repulsed by the sight and the smell. He turned away, bending over and gagging until he was afraid he'd puke. He couldn't do that because that would mean removing his mask. Closing his eyes, he concentrated on willing his stomach to settle.

After a moment, he opened his eyes and glanced at the dog who whined at a door to Hunter's left. Afraid of what he might find, but having to know, he reached for the doorknob.

Cringing as he pulled the door open, he blinked in surprise. Instead of another dead body, he'd found the pantry. On the floor was a large bag of dry dog food. So that's why the dog was whining. Poor guy probably hadn't eaten in a few days.

Canned goods lined a shelf. Beans, peas, soups and several other items. He cast a glance over his shoulder. It wasn't as if the woman was going to need this food, but what if someone else who lived here needed it? Only, where were they and why hadn't they at least removed the body in the kitchen? Hunter shook off his hesitation. The food was fair game and better to take it than let it waste here. He snatched a few of the paper bags with handles that were hanging on a hook inside the door. Not picky, he took as much as he could carry and hauled it outside, setting the bags on the grass.

Hunter grinned. He'd feast tonight. But first, he had to find a way to clean the cans. He wasn't worried about the contents, but what if the woman had touched some of them before she'd died?

Returning to the pantry, he found a bag of rice and another of lentils and a few pouches of tuna fish. It wasn't his favorite food, but he'd eat it if he was hungry enough. Right now, it sounded delicious. The sugar and flour were opened, so he left them alone. It was the same with a package of crackers and boxes of cereal. He even wondered if the dog food was safe, but he hadn't heard anything about dogs being susceptible. Rolling the top of the bag down so it wouldn't spill, he lifted it in one arm, and took the bag with the rice, tuna, and lentils in the other hand.

He dumped the bags on the grass beside his first pile and lifted the mask, drawing in deep breaths through his nose to erase the putrid odor that seemed permanently lodged in his nasal passages.

The dog had slipped out behind him, and Hunter chuckled when the poor pup raced over to the nearest tree and lifted his leg. Had he been holding it for days? Hunter called the dog over when the animal was done with the tree and squatted down, looking into the trusting eyes. Hunter smiled but backed away when the dog tried to lick him. "Easy, fella."

He wasn't normally opposed to a dog licking him but worried the black lab might have been nosing the dead woman. Dogs might not get sick from this virus, but what if they could carry it? Why hadn't he paid more attention to his dad's comments around his work? Maybe then he'd know what the chances were that the dog could contaminate him.

Hunter straightened and surveyed his haul of supplies. Food wasn't going to be an issue for a while. With any luck, this would take him all the way to the island.

He looked at the house, his relief at finding the food tempered by the reality of how he'd acquired the items. What he felt wasn't guilt, exactly, but close to it. It was crazy to think that only a few weeks ago, the lady lying dead in there was going about her life, buying these groceries, probably chatting with the cashier as she completed her purchase, and then putting the items in her pantry. She probably never thought she'd be dead before she had a chance to eat the food. It was a lot to wrap his mind around.

Had the epidemic already begun when she bought them or were these just staples? It seemed like an awful lot of food for one person, and he had a feeling she wasn't the only body he'd find on the property.

HUNTER SHOVED MORE gloves into his front pockets and an extra mask into his back pocket. It was time to check the car and the other buildings. He'd had to toss the other mask, not sure if it was contaminated or not. He already worried he'd somehow contracted the illness just from being in the same home. After gathering the food, he'd made another run through the house for any other useful items and found a bottle of bleach and rolls of paper towels. With them, he'd made some wipes and cleaned everything he'd taken.

In his sweep of the house, he hadn't found a set of car keys. It was possible whoever else lived here had them or maybe he had missed them. The car was unlocked, which was a relief, and before he did anything else, he wiped every surface he could reach with the wipes. It wasn't a late model car but wasn't a junker either. He sat behind the wheel, checked the visor and the glove box for a set of keys. Nothing. He got out and ducked under the wheel to check beneath the seats. Shit. Empty except for a few crumpled receipts and a scattering of loose change. Well, he didn't need a car anyway. He just needed gas. And a container for it.

"Come on, Buddy," Hunter called to the dog and smiled when the dog responded to his new name. It seemed he'd decided that since Hunter had fed him, they were best buddies now. It made the name a natural fit for the dog.

When he approached a small shed, Buddy stopped and whined. His tail tucked between his legs and he refused to go any closer to it.

"What's the matter?" Hunter eyed the shed. Nothing about it looked scary, but before approaching any closer, he circled around the back, found a window and peeked into the building. Flies dotted the inside of the window, and Hunter tapped it, scattering them long enough to see inside.

He'd found the farmer.

"Ugh..." He pulled away from the window, gagging. The body looked to be in advanced stages of decomposition compared to the woman in the house. The man must have died a day or so before, and the heat in the small shed had sped along the rate of decay.

Despite the glimpse of tools hanging on the walls of the shed, he decided any he needed would have to come from some other place. Hunter pulled out one of his homemade wipes and used them on his hands where he'd touched the window although he knew logically the chance of the outside of the pane being contaminated was low.

Shuddering, he imagined he could feel the virus crawling up his arms. Scrubbing the wipe across his skin then using it to wipe the bottom of his shoes. Throwing the dirty wipe aside, he gave the tool-shed a wide berth as he crossed to the barn.

The cows were still making a lot of noise and Hunter wasn't sure what to do for them. They weren't in the big red barn he'd been watching, but another building next to it, hidden from his view when he'd been at the creek. He was sure they needed milking but other than a few times he'd milked a couple of squirts from one at a county fair demonstration, he wasn't going to be able to help them. Even if he knew how to run whatever milking equipment the farm had, he couldn't stay here and milk them indefinitely.

About all he could think to do was to make sure they could get out of the barn. There was lots of grass and a creek nearby. A few might live. He slid open the barn door, wrinkling his nose at the smell, but here, it was just barn smells. Not pleasant, but expected. The cows set up an even louder racket when the door opened. There were no conventional stalls, but a center section covered in straw and where some cows were standing and others lying. More cows wandered freely in the aisle that was almost like a track around the center.

Hunter thought about trying to milk one, but what would he do with the milk? He didn't have a way to keep it cool and no way could he milk this many animals. He took a quick look around for anything useful and spotted a bucket hanging on a hook beside the door. He grabbed it.

He went to the chicken coop and left that door open too, knowing most of the chickens would end up as a meal for some coyote, but he couldn't leave them to die slowly of thirst or starvation. Digging in the straw, he found nine eggs and wrapped them in a rag he found in the coop. He set the bundle carefully into the bucket and found a bag of sawdust, using it to protect and insulate the eggs. He had two more buildings to check.

One was locked, and he couldn't get in. The other was a small pole barn. The pasture he'd seen ended on one side of the barn. He opened the door and was greeted with a loud whinny and stamping of feet from the two horses in stalls. The barn reeked of manure and urine, but he ignored the odor as a glimmer of an idea took root.

Horses could take him home. It might be safer too since he could cross remote land and stay away from people and highways. The horse in the stall closes to him pressed against the door, his head bobbing and his nostrils flaring. Hunter held out his hand. "Hey there. Whoa, shhh…it's okay." He stroked the silky muzzle. Peering in, he noted the bone dry bucket. "Thirsty, aren't ya? I'll get you a drink. Just give me a sec to find the hose."

Chapter Seventeen

Elly shook out the last M&M and looked at it. *Green.* In high school, green M&Ms had some meaning, but she couldn't recall what it was. Maybe they were lucky. She popped it in her mouth and sucked, making it last as long as possible. She had only a few chocolate mint pieces and a bag of potato chips left from what she'd scavenged. She wasn't too hungry yet, but water was going to be an issue in the next day or so. She had enough left in the tub to fill the eight bottles she had about three times. That was about two more days' worth of water after today. By then, she'd be completely out of food and getting really hungry. Did she dare wait until she was desperate? Or would it be better to venture out now while she still had plenty of energy? What if she didn't find food right away?

When the world had realized what was happening four days ago, the news had reported on the run on grocery stores and showed footage of bare shelves and people fighting over a box of crackers. But surely there had to be plenty of food in a city this big. She might have to risk getting close to contaminated bodies to get it, though.

Last night, the power had gone out and had never come back on. The taps had run dry when the power had cut off. As she looked out at the city in the early dawn hours, there were only a few patches of light— even the roads were mostly dark. Normal power outages would have light from vehicles illuminating the roads, but she saw only a few cars picking their way through the crashed and stalled cars in the streets below.

She still had a charge on her cellphone and had dial-tone when she turned it on. There was only one person she knew. She found Cole's number and took a deep breath. Was he still alive? She pressed the call icon on the screen and said a prayer.

He answered on the second ring, and she closed her eyes, blinking back tears of relief.

"Elly?"

"Cole...you're still alive."

"Yeah. So far." There was a pause, and Elly swiped at the tears pouring down her face. She hadn't realized how worried she was that everyone she knew was dead until she heard his voice over the line. At least one friend was still alive.

Elly drew in a shaky breath. "Where are you?"

"We made it to an island my uncle left me in his will. We're out about a mile or so in Green Bay, just east of Oconto. Where are you?"

She hated the tremor in her voice, but couldn't stifle it. "I'm still in my hotel room. The power went out last night, and I don't think there are many people still alive here. They stopped removing bodies from the street two days ago, and I haven't seen a car moving all morning."

"Shit. I knew it was bad, but I've been so busy we haven't had much time to listen to the news. Last time I tried, all I got was static, but I didn't know if it was because we're too far away from a station or what. We don't have television or internet out here."

"There was nothing on TV yesterday. The stations were off the air. I've never seen that before, Cole. And now, I couldn't watch it even if there was anything on, without electricity." She fanned her face with the hotel's room service menu. It was getting hot.

"Do you have food and water?" The concern in his voice was almost her undoing.

She shook her head, forgetting he couldn't see her. "Not really. I have a couple of pieces of chocolate, a few chips, and half a tub of water. I found food in some other rooms on my floor, but there was a crazy lady in one room. I'm pretty sure she was infected. I was too scared to go out again. I have my door bolted and a chair wedged under the handle."

"Elly, you have to get here. I could come and get you. I have a car."

"No, you're safe. You need to stay there with your family. Hunter needs you."

There came an odd sound over the phone, almost like a grunt or sob. "He's not here yet. I...I don't know where he is. His car ran out of gas, and now he's not answering his phone."

"Oh, Cole..."

"But he was healthy. I think he's alive still—in fact, I'm sure of it. I'd feel it if he was dead. He's just unable to get here. He was camped out and said he caught some fish in a stream, so at least he had some gear."

Taking her cue from the forced positivity she heard, she agreed. "He's smart. He'll make it to you."

"You will too. Do you have a car?"

"No, and even if I did, the streets that I can see are full of stalled or abandoned vehicles. I don't think I could get through. The sidewalks are full of bodies. It's a nightmare out there. Literally."

"What about a bike? There has to be a bike lying around. It would be quite a ride, but you could do it. I guess it'd be a few hundred miles, though, but maybe the roads won't be so bad once you get out of the city."

"That's an idea. I could try and find one." A sliver of hope crept into her voice. "How do I get to the island? And are you sure you want me there?"

"Elly, you know you're always welcome. *Especially now.*" He gave her directions, and she jotted them on the back of the menu. "If power is going out, I expect the phones are going to die soon. I haven't been able to pull up the Internet in over a couple of days now, but I barely have a signal at all. Just get here as fast as you can. We have food, there are several cabins, and we're isolated."

"I'll need to find some supplies somewhere along the way."

"Do you still have a way to protect yourself from the virus?"

She looked at her box of gloves and the other one of masks. "Yeah. At least I have that going for me." It was going to be hell riding a bike with one of the masks on but with luck, out in the country she could take it off. She turned to the window, pressing her cheek against it to look north towards safety. Towards Cole.

There was a lot of city to get through first.

"Also, Elly, try to find a gun. We've already had some problems, and that was three days ago. It could be a lot worse now."

Elly gave a short laugh. "Well, I *am* in Chicago. Finding a gun shouldn't be an issue."

"GET OUT OF MY WAY, Sean. I'm going to find my son." Cole stood on the pier, toe-to-toe with his brother. His goal was the small fishing boat Joe had found in the shed. He glared, his fists balled at his sides. He hadn't hit Sean since he was thirteen and they fought over something stupid when they were teens, but now, he had a good reason. The best reason. "Let me get to the damn boat!"

Sean pressed a hand against Cole's chest, balling up his shirt and not letting him pass. "You can't leave, Cole. You don't even know where Hunter is. Seriously, what are the chances you'll find him just wandering around? Elly told you the power was out there, too. Even if you could find him, what about the disease? What good are you going to do Hunter if you catch it and die? Your friend Elly said there were bodies all over Chicago. Don't you think that the situation is like that everywhere by now?"

"Are you implying my son is dead?" Cole shoved Sean. "You bastard! Hunter's *alive*—"

"No! I didn't say he was dead. Listen to me. I meant there's too much risk now, Cole, with too little chance of finding him. What if you two pass within a mile of each other? How would you know? The phones are out now. The only thing we know for sure is that he's on his way here. You need to be here when he arrives."

Cole's gut twisted at the truth of Sean's words but every instinct he had pushed him to find his son.

"What are we going to tell him when he gets here, Cole, and you're not here?" Sean flung an arm towards the mainland. "What if you die out there?"

"Listen to him, Cole. He's right."

Cole narrowed his eyes at Jenna then turned the heat of his glare back on Sean. "What if it was Piper or Trent out there? You'd go find them."

"I *get it*, Cole. I'd be in your shoes right now, and you'd be holding me back and telling me how I need to be here for the kids when they arrive." Sean bit his lip, his throat working as he blinked hard. Sean's tone softened. "We love him too, you know." His voice broke on the last part.

The anger drained out of Cole, but it was all that had been keeping the true fear at bay—that he might never see his son again. "But he's all alone..."

HUNTER PULLED the saddle off the bay mare, setting it out of the way, and brushed her. Horses were something he knew a little bit about from when he had gone to summer camp three years in a row. It wasn't a riding camp, but they got to ride almost every day, and he always volunteered to work in the stable, preferring that over washing dishes in the kitchen.

The mare was well trained and easy to ride. The other horse, a chestnut, was also good but seemed younger and more excitable. That made him fun to ride, but Hunter hadn't ridden since last summer. He was rusty and didn't trust his skills to keep the horse in check if the animal spooked. If he had a few days to feel comfortable, it would be an easy decision, but he didn't want to hang around any longer than he had to. The knowledge of the bodies lurking within the building not only creeped him out but made him uneasy in regards to the virus. Everything he came into contact with on the farm had the potential to harbor germs and he had used the wipes so much that his hands were red and sore. He just wanted off the property.

As he curried the mare, he glanced out to the pasture at the chestnut. What a beautiful horse. He hated to leave him. For sure he'd leave the gate to the pasture open and let the horse run free so he wouldn't die a slow death in the barn, but wished he could take him as well.

Then he thought about it. Why couldn't he? It wasn't as if anyone was around to stop him. He could take some feed, and there was plenty of grass along the way. He was pretty sure water wouldn't be a problem either. Creeks, ponds, and lakes were plentiful. He didn't know how he'd get the animals to the island, but he'd worry about that later. After tending to the horses, he let them out in the pasture, making sure they had access back into the barn and to fresh water. They could come back to their stalls in the night if they wanted to. He was going back to his campsite for the rest of the day. Hunter called out for Buddy before he headed back to camp. The dog came running from under the shade of the large tree in the farm yard. "Come on, Bud, let's get back to camp."

He used the camp stove late in the afternoon to cook up a bunch of eggs he'd gathered from the chickens. After tonight, he'd probably have to make wood fires as the propane was pretty much gone. He'd pack the stove in case he came across more fuel, but wondered at the likelihood of finding a tank that would fit his model of stove.

He'd found a good cast iron skillet in the farmer's kitchen. It was heavy but well worth the extra weight. The only thing that would have made the meal better would have been a few slices of buttered toast, but he didn't trust the stale bread he'd found in the house. The bag had been opened too, and that was the biggest worry. What if the woman had touched it before dying?

Eating directly out of the skillet, he dug into the eggs. It was the best meal he'd had in several days, and he didn't know if it was because he'd cooked them just right or because he was just glad he hadn't had to dip into his stores of packaged food.

In addition to the skillet, he'd taken several knives, a few forks and spoons, and a can opener. He'd almost forgotten that. It would have sucked to have been hungry and unable to open the cans. He'd seen some video on social media a few years ago about how to open a can by scraping it on a sidewalk, but he looked around. Not many sidewalks around here and he his plan was to stay out of towns and cities. The fewer people he encountered, the better.

When he finished eating, he took the skillet to the creek along with a few handfuls of coarse grass and scrubbed the pan, getting all the bits of cooked egg from the sides. The pan was so well –seasoned that the eggs peeled right off better than any non-stick pan he'd ever used.

Not that he'd used many. Scrambled eggs, tacos, and spaghetti with sauce from a jar were about the limits of his culinary skills.

The rest of the afternoon, he practiced with the bow. He'd dragged a couple of bales of straw back to his camp working up a good sweat in the process. The effort was worth it when he dug an old red t-shirt out of his clothes, and using mud, drew a crude target then duct taped the shirt to the stacked bales. He paced off about thirty feet or so. His first few shots went low, and he adjusted the sight down a little to bring his aim higher. Even though his circumstances were dire with the fear of the virus ever-present, he couldn't help enjoying the practice. His muscle memory kicked in, and soon, he was back to form. He inspected his arrows, making sure they were all in good condition before he returned them to the quiver he'd bought as well.

The next morning, Hunter awoke early and packed up his campsite. With it all packed, he pulled his phone out and turned it on, hoping it had dried out enough to work, but it was dead. He shoved it back in his pocket wondering why he even bothered keeping it.

Today he was moving on, and dread filled him. The farm had felt like a safe haven, of sorts, as long as he was careful about wearing his mask and gloves. Now, he had to venture out into whatever the world had come to, and he wasn't looking forward to it. He made sure he had a couple of masks ready, shoving one in his pocket and put one to hang loosely around his neck. It wasn't the most comfortable way to wear it, because it wasn't a flimsy paper mask, but one that was thick and stiff, with a metal nose band. It scratched his neck from time to time, but no way was he going to risk coming into contact with someone who could be sick without a mask handy.

He whistled for Buddy and smiled when the dog responded, bursting out of the brush. He had packed a leash he'd found, but it wouldn't be practical to use it while traveling. He hoped the dog would keep up on his own, and from the way he followed the horses when Hunter led them to the road hinted that Buddy had gone on more than one trail ride with his masters before.

Leaving the car was one of the hardest things he had ever done. Gas wasn't his worry—he could siphon it from other cars if he had to, but after what his dad had said about how he too had run into lots of problems with car accidents. Hunter's own experience several nights ago with the accident and the cop approaching his car made him wary. What if he was trapped in a traffic jam full of diseased people? What if they swarmed his car like something out of a zombie movie? Just imagining it made him shiver, and he wanted no part of it.

True, the sick people weren't zombies but what he'd heard on the radio before the stations had cut out, was that the sick sought out the healthy. They probably didn't mean to infect others, but the disease seemed to force them to become overtly friendly and helpful. Was that why his cellphone had blown up with texts from friends the day his dad had told him to head home? A lot the invites to parties had come from students he barely knew and only shared a class or two with. He'd thought it odd he was suddenly popular and realized that spilling soda on his computer might have been the luckiest thing he'd ever done. It had forced him to actually crack open the books and read them instead of just going over his notes. That meant no time for partying.

His dad would have a theory about why the disease caused people to act weirdly outgoing he was sure, but whatever the reason, he didn't want to encounter it firsthand ever again. The mob in the street on the first morning, then the cop at the accident, had been enough for him.

He hitched the horses to a speed limit sign a few feet behind the car and popped open the trunk. Rummaging around, he dug out the tire iron, a basic tool kit, some flares, and a first aid kit. The kits went into one of the large saddlebags he'd found in the tack room, and he slid the tire iron into the saddle bag on the right side of the mare. It would be within easy reach if he needed it.

Hunter had lashed the tent behind his saddle with extra straps he'd found in the tack room. In addition to the straps, he'd found two long lead lines for the horses' halters and hoped he'd be able to stake the animals out at night. He tied his sleeping bag and an extra tarp he'd found lying in the hayloft behind the saddle he'd put on Red, his name for the chestnut horse. The second horse and saddle would be nice to have on the island if he could transport the animals out to it somehow. Maybe he could teach Trent and Piper how to ride. With some careful planning, he was able to fit everything onto the two horses.

With the bow tied on top of the tent, the quiver tied onto the side of his saddle, and a baseball cap shading his face, he was ready to leave. Hunter shoved the keys in his pocket, not really sure why he even bothered because he doubted he'd ever see his car again, but on the outside hope that things weren't really as bad as he thought they were, maybe he and his dad could return to pick up his car.

Taking Red's lead rope, and wrapping it around his hand, he mounted the mare, took a last look at his car, and then urged his mount forward.

Chapter Eighteen

"Dad, can't I just take it out a little ways?" Trent stood on the pier holding a fishing rod and tackle box. *"Please...?* I helped plant the garden all day yesterday, and today, I," he motioned to the fish cleaning shed that Cole had just left, "even scrubbed out the fish shed. It was beyond disgusting." He made a face.

"Kid's got a point. He's been working hard." Cole nodded. "You've done a great job, Trent."

Trent beamed.

Sean sighed and looked at Cole. "Do you mind?"

Cole held his brother's gaze. "First of all, from here on out, everything here belongs to all of us. You don't need to ask permission for you or your family to use anything here so if you're okay with him out in the boat, it's fine with me." He turned his attention to his nephew. "However, unfortunately, you need to stay close to the island, Trent. Gas is precious now."

"I know, Uncle Cole. I will. I just want to fish a little. Relax. "

It sounded tempting to Cole as well, but there was still so much work to do. One of their biggest chores over the next several months would be to chop enough wood to last the winter. Cole thought about taking the pontoon and seeing if he could find any abandoned houses along the coast that had wood stacked in their yards but he wasn't sure if it would be worth the gas without concrete knowledge of where the wood piles were located. But Trent was just a fourteen-year old kid. He'd worked as hard as the rest of them without complaint. He deserved some time to have fun.

"Let me show you how to work the engine." Cole started down the pier, but Trent scrambled into the boat and said, "I already know how. My friend, Scott, has a boat just like this and his parents let us take it out on the lake all the time."

Cole looked back at Sean, who confirmed, "They do." Then Sean pointed at Trent. "You got a life jacket in there?"

Trent glanced around and spotted the jacket Cole had left in it earlier. He held it up. "Right here, Dad."

———————

HUNGER FINALLY FORCED ELLY to leave the hotel. For the last few days, she had rationed her food in the hope that things would get better. Despite her education and experience, she had thought that somehow the government would come through. At the very least, the National Guard would have shown up to help clear the streets and enforce the curfew, but nobody ever came.

Before the power went out, the internet and television had shown the virus active across the world. Some places weren't as hard hit, but those places were remote. As she had broken out the window to ventilate the room the day before, she had stared at the hundreds of buildings in sight. Her location was anything but remote.

Since she was on the eighteenth floor, there was a good breeze, and she was high enough that the stench of decaying bodies on the street was diluted by lake breezes, but at night, the sounds from street level terrified her. The yowling of cats, snarling of dogs, and incessant squeaking of what she guessed were rats, filled the night as they feasted on the bodies below. During the day, the constant sound of birds reminded her of the old Hitchcock movie. Worried they would fly into her room, she had tacked the shower curtain over the window. It was loose enough to let in air but would deter most birds. Fortunately, most were only interested in the banquet lying on the pavement.

She stripped the bed, rolling the bedding up and securing it with belts from the guest robes in the room. She considered leaving her computer, but if she made it to Cole's and he had electricity, all of her notes and data about the disease was on the hard drive. If nothing else, she wanted to transcribe it onto paper for future historians. It sounded like a silly reason to lug the computer, but when she thought of all the prior scientists who had created notes of deadly diseases like the plague and cholera, she knew she had to try. Maybe in a thousand years, they would help someone figure out what had happened here.

She ditched her makeup, kept her sunscreen, and left the paperbacks she'd brought along to read on the plane. Her expensive heels were tossed aside. She kept her 'clean' shoes but packed them in her bag. On her way out, when she was in her gear, she'd slip on the dirty shoes in the hallway.

Elly surveyed the items of clothing lying on the bed. She hadn't expected to be in Chicago for more than three days, so had packed lightly. Thankfully, she had tossed in a pair of jeans to wear on the flight for comfort. It was a compromise between the sweatpants she wanted to wear and the dress slacks she should wear. She changed into them. It would be easier to wear the jeans instead of toting their weight around in a bag, and tucked the sweats she'd been wearing the last few days into her suitcase.

The case had a retractable handle and rolled, but she didn't know how long the wheels would last on the pavement. They were meant for smooth tile inside of airports, not miles of rough streets and sidewalks.

With her jeans and a t-shirt on, she made her way down to the first floor, the bedroll strapped to the handle of the case and a pillowcase, fashioned into a bag. She had taken the cords from the drapes and cut slits around the open end of two pillow cases and threaded the belt through them. The double thickness added strength to the bag. She added a few towels from the room and her plastic bottles of water to the bag. She only had two full bottles left.

Settling her mask over her face, she opened the door. The halls were dark and abandoned. She located the stairs and headed for them. She paused before pushing the bar to open the heavy door. What if there were dead bodies on the stairs? She looked back at her hotel room door, tempted to return, but she had no choice, she had to leave or die of thirst.

Bracing herself for whatever she would find, she entered the stairwell. The steps were clear and she lifted the case down, worried that thumping it against every stair would break the wheels off, but by the tenth floor, her arms were burning. She stopped to rest. Breathing through the heavy mask was difficult when she was exerting herself. She leaned against the wall and fought the urge to raise the mask. The moment she thought of lifting it, she was hit with the urge to take a drink of water, but not only did she have to conserve it, but she also didn't want to risk lifting the mask even for that brief moment it would take for her to take a drink.

Her goal was to reach some area of the city that wasn't littered with dead bodies. All the streets could be as bad as this one. Pushing away from the wall, she continued her journey, finding only one body in the stairwell, slumped into the corner of a landing, and she was able to avoid it easily.

Finally, after only one more rest on the fifth floor landing, she made it to the first floor. There was a door right there to the outside, and she started to open it, but something blocked her from pushing it open more than a few inches. She tried to peek around the edge but recoiled when she saw a part of a bare foot lying on the ground. It looked like some animal had gotten to the body. Gagging, Elly stumbled back and found the door to the first floor hallway. She opened it, thankful that whatever automatic locks would normally prevent the door from opening, must have been deactivated when the power went out.

The stench in the hallway slammed into her and made her remember an old trick she should have done before she'd left her room. A little smear of toothpaste inside of the mask would have cut most of the odor, and she'd have just smelled spearmint. More bodies in varying states of decomposition were strewn down the dark hallway, and she grimaced at the dark stains on the carpet beneath the bodies. Some of it was no doubt blood but some also much of it was various other body fluids. Trying not to look directly at the victims, she picked her way to the front lobby with the same care she'd use if she were crossing a minefield.

The poor lady at the reception desk lay dead at her desk. Elly hurried to the front door, but the gift shop by the entrance caught her eye. She wondered if any food had survived. There might be something else in there that she could use as well. The glass display had been broken, all the jewelry missing, and most of the snack food was gone or destroyed. She spotted a door behind a toppled rack of designer cocktail dresses. Moving the rack out of the way, she tried the doorknob and found it unlocked. After opening it a crack, she listened for any sounds from within, but it was silent. The silence in the building was unnerving. She almost welcomed the cawing of the crows outside over the dead quiet within the building.

The first thing she did was carefully remove her gloves, making sure her bare hands never touched the outside of them, and set them on an empty spot on a shelf. Normally, she would just toss contaminated gloves, but she had a finite supply now. She fished a new pair from her back pocket, having stuck them there before leaving her room. She slipped them on.

This room looked like it hadn't been touched by anyone sick, so while she didn't consider it safe, she felt that whatever was in the boxes would be and didn't want to contaminate any of it with 'dirty' gloves.

The room wasn't big, but shelves stacked with boxes lined the walls, forming a narrow corridor for her to walk through. She propped the door open so she could see what was in the boxes. A box cutter sat on a shelf, and she grabbed it and looked for another one. It wasn't much as far as weapons went, but it was better than nothing.

The first few boxes she cut open contained t-shirts, sandals, and scented candles. She didn't want the weight of the heavy jar candles but stuffed all the votive candles in her suitcase. Hopefully, she'd find matches too. She held up a t-shirt, emblazoned with the hotel logo, and cocked her head. It should fit, and it was a good, heavy cotton mix. Most of what she had in the way of clothing was business attire. Dumping a skirt, she replaced it with three t-shirts. When she found a hoodie that fit her, she took that too, tossing aside the dress slacks in her suitcase to make room. Tying the arms of a second hoodie around her waist, she moved on to another box.

As soon as the cardboard parted and she saw the familiar dark blue bags with the yellow lettering, she let out a squeal of delight. Peanuts! The packages claimed they were perfect for snacking. She stuffed a few packs in her pockets and fit the rest into every crevice of her case. Her mouth watered at the thought of eating them even though she had never been overly fond of peanuts before.

Another box, already opened, held a few bags of dried mixed slices of dried fruit. So, she had protein and fruits covered. Grinning, she shoved them in to her case as well, sacrificing a silk blouse in the process. It had cost her over a hundred dollars a month ago. She shook her head. What a waste of money.

The rest of the boxes held nothing of value to her, just postcards, souvenirs, and stuffed animals.

She put the box cutter in her back pocket and removed her gloves, sticking those in the pocket as well. Replacing the gloves with the dirty pair, she returned to the gift shop to get a better look around. The small shop had three victims on the floor, so everything around them was off limits. Elly frowned when she saw three bags of potato chips sitting in a dark stain beside one body. *Damn.*

Spotting a bottle of soda beneath a rack of swim suits, she bent to retrieve it then pulled back at the smear of brown on the label. It looked like dried blood. She backed away, checking to make sure she wasn't standing in any blood. Navigating the small shop was like crossing a minefield. If it was this hard here, how would it be outside? She drew a deep breath to steady her nerves.

A revolving rack of sunglasses caught her eye. It appeared intact and untouched. They weren't the expensive brands that had probably been in the jewelry case, but she took several pairs, knowing they would come in handy.

A cloth bag emblazoned with a trendy fashion logo and sporting shoulder straps made of thick string, hung by one strap from a hook. She grabbed it. While it wasn't quite a backpack, she could wear it as one. She dropped the sunglasses inside and scoured the shop for anything more. A sealed travel sized box of toothpaste joined the sunglasses, along with a couple of toothbrushes.

She found five packs of pain relievers, a sealed lip balm and a tube of hand lotion. She almost left that, deeming it too frivolous but changed her mind. Dry and cracked skin was a bad thing when a deadly virus lurked about. She needed her skin intact.

Tucked back on a shelf at the rear of the store, apparently untouched by looters or whatever the victims became with infected with the virus, she found a baseball cap—a white cap with a Chicago Cubs logo. She supposed it was the boutique version of the cap. She plopped it on.

A rack beside the caps held silk scarves. Deciding a scarf could double as a rope or belt, she took several, stuffing them in her bag. Besides, they were light and easy to carry. Elly took one more and tossed it around her neck, catching a glimpse of her reflection in the mirror beside the display. With her hands on her hips, she twisted like a model on a catwalk, chuckling at her behavior. In light of all the death around her, she welcomed the brief interlude when she had forgotten her circumstances. As if it really mattered what she looked like? Then she shrugged at her image. If she had to survive the end of the world, at least she could apocalypse in style.

COLE DRAGGED THE WHEELBARROW, loaded with cut wood, to the small but growing stack near the house. He'd discarded his t-shirt earlier and gazed out at the bay, enjoying the refreshing breeze. The water looked inviting. It wasn't a hot day, but the exertion had him certain that he wouldn't miss his gym membership in the least. Maybe a quick splash or two would cool him off enough to get one more load of wood in before he had to go see how Sean was doing working on an old windmill set behind the houses. Joe said it had probably pumped the water before the island was connected to the mainland via buried cables. It was a priority.

He thought of all the things they needed to make it through the winter. Hell, everything was a priority. But in the winter, water above ground would freeze. The well went down far enough to where the earth was a stable temperature year round, but the water had to move, or it would become ice.

The beach was on the other side of the house in an open stretch. Cole rounded the corner of the house, intending to follow through on his idea of cooling off in the lake. He gazed at the water lapping at the sand, pausing to watch a bald eagle swoop down and snatched a fish right out of the water not twenty feet into the bay. What beauty and grace. As he tracked the raptor's flight west, fish clutched in its talons, he caught sight of Trent in the fishing boat. He was a little farther out than Cole was comfortable with, and he lifted a hand to wave to him in an attempt to get the kid to bring the boat in closer.

The drone of an engine made him freeze mid-motion. Trent's boat wasn't moving, and Cole swept the bay, searching for the source of the noise. A speedboat skimmed close to Trent, making his boat rock precariously in the water. They shouted something Cole couldn't make out, and Trent shouted back and spun on his seat, watching the boat. The hairs on the back of Cole's neck prickled. The passengers whooped and hollered as they sped over the waves, only to make a sharp U-turn.

"What the hell?" Cole cupped his hands around his mouth. *"Trent! Get back to the pier!"*

Trent scrambled in the fishing boat, tossing his pole down and yanking the cord on the motor.

The speedboat made a return pass, zipping near enough for one of the passengers to lean over and drop something in Trent's boat. Trent bent and scooped whatever it was up, tossing it over the side. The wake from the speedboat threatened to capsize the smaller vessel.

"What's going on?" Sean raced down the path from the work shed.

Cole pointed.

"Who are they?"

"I don't know. They just showed up."

The boat closed in a third time, this time, throttling back and idling within a few feet of Trent, who was furiously yanking on the cord. The engine sputtered. In his haste, he probably hadn't primed it. Finally, it caught. Cole breathed a sigh of relief, but it was short-lived as Trent reached for the anchor over the side of the boat. He started hauling it up, but the other boat closed in. Cole darted ten yards out into the lake, and yelled, "Cut the rope! Cut the anchor!" The advice was too little, too late and he knew it.

The boat circled Trent, causing his boat to spin. His fingers must have pinched between the metal side of the boat and the rope, because he suddenly let go, shaking his hand as the rope slithered over the side, the anchor dropping to the bottom again. He reached down, and Cole saw a glint of steel as Trent sawed on the rope, having either heard Cole before or thinking of it on his own.

The speedboat stopped alongside Trent and one guy leaped into Trent's boat.

Sean lifted a hand, shading his eyes. "Oh, shit. *Trent*!" He cupped his hands around his mouth. *"Leave him alone!"*

Cole raced for the pontoon boat. It was slow and cumbersome, but it was all they had. Sean pounded on the deck behind him, yanking on the tether, then ran to the rear tether, pulling it off the post.

"Hurry, Cole!"

"I'm trying!" The boat started immediately, but it seemed to take forever to back clear of the dock.

"They're holding him down and..." Sean stopped, his voice puzzled. "Forcing him to drink something."

Cole looked to his left, trying to make out what was happening. Trent's boat rocked wildly as now two guys wrestled with him, laughing as one held him down, guzzled a can of something, then put the can to Trent's lips. The boy flailed, his legs kicking as he turned his head, but the one holding the can followed his actions, laughing like a hyena as he forced Trent to drink.

Suddenly, the guy holding Trent yelped and shoved Trent against the side of the boat. "You stabbed me!"

Trent crouched the knife in front of him.

Whatever anger the man had felt dissolved in a fit of laughter. His buddy joined in as both men almost collapsed in amusement as blood welled over the injured man's hand where he held it against his thigh. It looked as if Trent had stabbed him in the thigh. Both men, still laughing, returned to their own boat, high fiving those waiting for them.

The speedboat took off, the front of the boat at a forty-five degree angle as it headed out into the bay.

"Do you think those people were sick?" Fear coated every word Sean uttered.

Cole stared at the receding speedboat, replaying the brief scene.

He couldn't be certain—not from here—but the way they moved, and their over-loud laughter, was not reassuring. He shook his head. "I don't know. I wish I could give you an answer."

"Trent! Are you okay?" They were close enough to see the fear on the boy's face. He nodded, and moving mechanically, returned to work on the anchor, tossing the knife aside as he pulled the rope and brought the anchor over the side of his boat.

As they got closer, Trent waved them away. "I'll follow you in!"

Cole waved that he understood and made a wide turn.

"Go back! I want to make sure he's okay." Sean stood beside Cole and reached for the steering wheel.

Cole pushed his hand aside. "He said he was okay."

"What if they come back?"

"I'll stay close enough to get to him if they do, but I can't even hear their boat anymore." His worry about the boat returning was secondary now. His first worry was about Trent, and whether he was exposed. His training taught him that they had to assume he was and respond accordingly, which meant full quarantine. How was he going to convince Sean that was the proper course of action to keep everyone safe?

Sean sank onto the seat beside Cole's, running his hands through his hair, elbows propped on his thighs. He let out a soft groan, almost like he was going to be sick. "Shit! What are we going to do?" Sean bent at the waist and groaned. "What happens if they were sick?" He jumped to his feet, pacing in the short length of the boat.

He had never seen his brother so agitated, not even when he had first discussed the virus with him. "Sean, just take it easy. We have the cabin ready, and Trent can just stay there. That's why we made plans."

Sean dragged in a shuddering breath. "What if he gets sick?"

Cole closed his eyes briefly. How many times had he asked himself that exact same question about Hunter? The answer wasn't pretty. There was no cure. No treatment. Even diagnosis was based on behavior until the stricken died. The terror in Sean's eyes ripped through him. As a father, he knew that fear. Had felt it first hand and was feeling it now. He didn't wish that same feeling on anyone.

How could he tell Sean that there was nothing they could do?

Helpless to offer advice, Cole simply reached over as Sean's circuit brought him close, and pulled him in for a brief hug. Giving his shoulder a quick squeeze as he returned to steering the boat, he said, "I'm sorry, Sean. We have to do what we talked about."

Sean slowly dropped onto the seat again, staring behind them to Trent's boat.

Cole followed his gaze, watching Trent steer the boat just to the left of their wake. It sounded cold and barbaric now that he was facing the reality of putting his nephew in isolation, but he took a deep breath. He had to put aside his feelings. His job was to keep all of them safe.

He faced forward, spotting the small cinderblock building. It had probably been a changing room for beachgoers, but Cole's background made it look like a perfect isolation ward. They would have to get Trent to go in there for a few weeks until they were sure he was going to be okay.

Joe was staying in one cabin, and while it had worked well for isolating purposes, Cole remembered with a shudder how his neighbors had acted. A truly sick individual wouldn't pay any attention to quarantine rules.

The cinderblock was a better choice than a cabin. The building had a heavy door, a bathroom, and protection from the elements. It would work well as an isolation unit if they put a mattress in it. There was only one door, and it already had a place for a padlock on the outside. He supposed that was added so anyone who docked when nobody was in residence didn't trash the building or to keep the door from blowing open from the narrow gap between the roof and the top of the walls. He was certain it had never been used to keep anyone inside.

He docked the boat but caught Sean's arm as he started to disembark. He couldn't let Sean get too close to Trent.

"Wait. We have to implement our isolation protocol." He nodded towards the changing room building.

Sean followed his look and stepped back. "No way...Cole, you can't be serious?"

"I'm sorry, Sean. We all agreed."

"But I didn't think we'd need to actually use it. I thought we were safe here!"

The boat engine slowed as Trent approached the pier, and Sean spun and sprinted to meet the boat as Trent moved closer to the slip.

Cole raced after him. "Sean, get back! Don't touch him! Don't touch the boat or anything in it." *Shit!* "And for God's sake, put your mask on!" He pointed to Trent, shouting, "Where's your mask?"

Trent shook his head and held his hand by his ear. "What?"

Yanking his own mask from around his neck where he wore it when he wasn't speaking to Joe, he put it in place, forced to slow down as he did so. He pointed to it with both hands, hoping Trent would get the hint.

Trent looked around in the boat, then reached down and held up his mask. It was torn and the straps no longer attached. The boat bumped against the dock, and he bent to secure the ropes.

Cole darted between Sean and the edge of the boat, teetering on the narrow pier but he'd prevented Sean from catching Trent's outstretched hand holding the second rope.

"Uncle Cole, what are you doing?"

Sean took a step back but glared at Cole. "Get the hell out of my way!"

"You can't, Sean. You know that. Where's your mask?" Trusting his brother not to toss him off the other side of the dock, he twisted and met Trent's eyes. "You can't touch anyone or anything. You have to go straight to the building on the beach." He ignored Sean's grip on the back of his shirt. Maybe he was trying to keep Cole from falling in.

"Why?" Trent looked confused. He clung to the torn mask, his hands shaking along with his voice when he said, "I didn't know they were going to jump into the boat. You saw me trying to get away. Didn't you?" The last word cracked as he pleaded with Cole and Sean. "They *made* me drink the beer. I didn't want to. I didn't want them anywhere near me...they weren't acting right." His adam's apple bobbed. "I...I stabbed one and made them go away."

"We're not mad at you, Trent. You fought hard. We saw you." Cole wanted to give his nephew a hug and knew it was even harder for Sean not to be able to hold his son and make everything okay.

"Even though it's not your fault—not at all—you understand, Trent?" The boy nodded. "You still have to be isolated."

"Am I going to get the virus?" He sounded like a small child.

"No, son. You'll be fine." Sean gave the assurance as he glared at Cole.

It was the hardest thing he'd ever done in his life, but Cole couldn't give in—as much as he wanted to. He turned, arms outstretched to prevent his brother from coming into contact with Trent. Sean's hand bunched Cole's shirt as he tried to move him out of the way. Trent climbed onto the pier, but stood, uncertainly. "We know it's not your fault, Trent. But remember what our plan if anyone was exposed?"

Trent nodded, his eyes wide. "We have to go into quarantine."

Sean's shoulders sagged. "No...no."

"Sean, we have to think of Jenna and Piper." He pulled out of Sean's grip, his brother's hand slipping off without a fight. Cole's mouth was stiff, his voice flat as he said, "Please put on your mask."

Sean nodded, pulling his mask from his pocket, his eyes never leaving Trent's face.

Trent's gaze darted between his dad and Cole, his shoulders straightening. "It's okay, Dad. We all agreed."

Chapter Nineteen

Hunter shifted in the saddle as the horse crested the small hill, his thighs protesting a second long day in the saddle. He drew back on the reins and Red slowed and stopped. Stroking the mare's neck, he promised her that he'd find a new stream for her to drink from very soon. He was tired, and he was sure the horses were tired too. None of them were used to riding all day long. Even Buddy lagged behind. While Hunter couldn't imagine leaving the dog to fend for himself, he also worried how he'd feed the animal once his supply of food ran out. At least the horses could graze, but last night, he'd dismissed all of his second thoughts about Buddy's presence.

As he'd tossed and turned, every noise had pulled him from the brink of sleep. What if someone sneaked up on him in the middle of the night? What if the horses were stolen? He'd staked them as close to the tent as he dared without worrying about the animals treading on the tent, but someone could creep up and lead them away without him ever knowing, but then he'd observed Buddy. The dog had curled up with his head at the entrance to the tent, his head on his paws and not long after Hunter had settled in, the dog had stood, his ears pricked. It had turned out to be just an opossum passing through the camp, but it made Hunter realize that he had a watchdog. Buddy would let him know if anyone came near his camp. With that knowledge, he'd slept better than he had since his last night in his dorm.

One problem solved, but another surfaced. He was lost. Was he in Iowa or Minnesota? He was sure he wasn't in Wisconsin because he hadn't had to cross the Mississippi yet, but that was the only thing he was certain of.

He had never really found out where he was when he'd abandoned his car. Why hadn't he at least checked the mail at the farmhouse? He could have narrowed where he was from the address on an envelope, but it hadn't occurred to him to look. He'd been focused on supplies.

He had ridden east yesterday, but today was overcast, and he wasn't sure of his direction anymore. If only his phone worked. He had an application that showed direction, stars, and everything. Of course, if his phone worked, he could just call his dad.

His riding experience had been on a few trails near his friend's small farm and in their paddock. They had never paid attention to how many miles they'd covered so he had no frame of reference to calculate the distance he'd traveled since he'd started his trek the morning before. Hunter twisted and dug a bottle of water out of his saddlebag. He eyed it and grimaced. Half-full. It was the last bottle he'd filled at the farm. As he sipped it, he surveyed his surroundings. From the rise, checkerboard fields stretched in every direction, a white farmhouse or red barn dotting a few of the squares.

He'd skirted around all other homes he'd come across so far, but he might have to stop at one to find water. The last stream had been muddy and slow moving, and he hadn't trusted drinking from it. He'd had enough water at the time to hold off, but now if he didn't find a house with a working water source, he'd have to take his chances with the purification tablets and straining the water through an old t-shirt.

In the distance, he spotted a winding ribbon of highway and debated whether he should try for it. A highway meant signs and mile markers. He could figure out where he was, but a highway also meant people. He squinted, trying to determine if there was movement on the road, but he couldn't make a determination from this distance. Would it be worse to find it devoid of life or to find it full of people who might infect him? He rubbed the back of his neck, feeling the grime and sweat. What he wouldn't give for a real shower with hot water.

Hunter didn't just feel lonely, he felt *alone*. Two weeks ago, he wouldn't have known there was a difference, but now he knew. Loneliness sprung from being among other people but not feeling connected. Alone meant zero human contact and no opportunity to make a connection. He drew a deep breath. He was tired of being alone—completely and utterly exhausted. It was as if the face of the Earth had been swept clean of human beings except for him.

Up until a few hours ago, he'd followed a stream that twisted and turned, but he'd managed to keep the sun in front of him in the morning or behind in the afternoon. The stream had petered out, so he was forced to abandon it.

It freaked him out that he had seen absolutely no signs of human life since spotting the single set of headlights his first night on the farm. What if *everyone* was dead? Then he confronted his worst fear. What if his dad was dead? His gut knotted. No, his dad was safe, and he'd keep everyone else safe too. That's what he did. Convinced he was right Hunter banished the thought to the deepest, darkest crevice in his mind.

Instead of dwelling on the doom and gloom, Hunter had conjured up a fantasy that everything was fine. It was based on silly hope, but what if the disease had been contained and everyone was going about life as usual? He grinned as he imagined his dad's reaction to his solitary journey through the countryside. His cousins would laugh at him, and he'd chuckle right alongside them. Then he remembered the farmer and his wife and the grin faded along with his hopes.

Nobody had noticed their deaths. If they had been dead only a day, he could understand, but he was pretty sure they had been dead at least two before he'd arrived and he'd been there a couple of days. So, four days they had been gone and nobody noticed? None of the farms he'd passed had shown any activity either. Hunter hadn't seen a single tractor crawling across a field, not even in the distance. Periodically, he checked the sky for contrails or the flash of a plane high above, but the sky had been a blank, blue, expanse broken only by occasional clouds until today. It looked like rain was heading his way.

Hunter took one more sip, screwed the cap on and tucked the

water back in his bag. He could try to rig another water catcher if he couldn't find water. His dad was too smart to be dead. He knew about diseases and how to take precautions. Growing up, Hunter had been teased by friends for his washing his hands so much. Some had even suggested he suffered from obsessive-compulsive disorder, but Hunter had laughed it all off and reminded them that his bedtime stories had consisted of tales of scary diseases run amok.

Of course, his dad never told him those kinds of bedtime stories, but he had pressed home the point of thorough hand-washing to the point it was ingrained into Hunter. Especially after his dad had become so sick just before he got out of the Navy. He had said he forgot to wash one time and almost died. Hunter thought there was something more to it than that, and when his dad finally came home, he had looked terrible—pale and thin. It had taken him a year to get back to normal.

Hunter glanced around. The horses had taken the opportunity to grab a few tufts of grass, and Buddy had flopped onto the ground, his tongue lolling as he waited for Hunter to decide what to do. "Come on, Buddy."

He gave the mare a light kick and pointed her in the direction of the highway.

ELLY RACED DOWN THE STREET, vaulting bodies on the ground. Dragging her case over the corpse, she made a mental note to wipe down the whole case with a homemade wipe made from paper towels, bleach, and water. She'd been careful so far, but now, there wasn't time to be careful. Something was coming. She ducked behind a stalled car. As she caught her breath and her heart slowed, she strained to hear. Since leaving the hotel, she had seen no one alive— just bodies. Everywhere, bodies. The stench penetrated the mask and filled her sinuses. She didn't think she'd ever get the stink out of her head. But, she'd grown used to it and had picked her way through the streets, heading for the lake.

She'd downloaded a map to her phone before ever coming to Chicago and had just enough juice left in the phone to consult it.

Sheridan Road would take her as far north as Racine in Wisconsin. It was the most direct route north. If she had a car, the highway just west of Chicago would be her best bet in normal times, but now, it was the worst solution. Every street was clogged with bodies and cars. There was no way she'd be able to navigate to the highway, and even if she risked taking one of the multitudes of cars abandoned everywhere, and made it to the highway, she figured it was probably as choked with cars and bodies as the city streets.

The clacking sounded louder now. What the hell was it? She made sure her mask was firmly in place and inspected her gloves for any holes. The rhythmic clacking grew closer, then it stopped. She held her breath. It had sounded mere feet away.

After what felt like several minutes, but was probably only thirty seconds or so, Elly couldn't stand it. She *had* to look. Rising up on her toes while still crouching behind the car, she peered over the trunk.

She hadn't known what she was expecting. Maybe some gruesome cadaver come to life or a pack of wild dogs, but what she found was a teenaged boy on a dirt bike—the kind of bike kids used with ramps to perform various tricks. It might be good for stunts, but it wasn't the best for long distance biking, but perhaps the teen wasn't planning on going far.

His back was to her as he scoped out the intersection. When he looked left, Elly noted the bandana tight across his nose and mouth. He'd taken precautions, even if the measures weren't the most effective. That gave her hope he wasn't infected because she hadn't encountered a single dead body wearing a mask or gloves. That led her to believe the infected hadn't been worried about catching anything. Maybe they had before symptoms started, but since the symptoms were so different from any other illness, most never even realized they were sick. The last thing the virus would want was for its host to take precautions.

He wore studded leather bands on his wrists, black leather driving gloves and a knit cap on his head. She'd seen the caps before but never understood why anyone would wear a cap in the middle of summer, but what did she know of fashion? Blond scraggly hair escaped the back of the cap.

Other than the bandana, he sported a tattered black t-shirt and ripped jeans. The tough guy image was spoiled by the Sponge Bob backpack. It hung low on his back, bulging with whatever he had in it. The backpack might have made her smile, but when he stretched up on his tip toes to see farther down the road, she spotted a gun tucked into the waistband of his jeans. It gave her pause.

The boy lounged on the seat as he used one hand to steer the bike into a circle. It was then she realized the clacking had come from a playing card stuck between the spokes. Why would he have that in there? She ducked back down before he had completed his turn.

Should she wait him out and hope he went away? Or should she try to make contact with him? He had a gun and could take her supplies without a fight, and she needed everything she had. Silence was the best option. Now, if only he would go back the way he'd come.

The clacking, slow and intermittent now, crept closer. He was at the end of the car. *Damn it.* Of all the cars she had to dive behind why had she chosen this one? She should have gone farther down the street and hidden behind one of the others.

And then suddenly, he was right there. Even though she knew he had been close, his appearance at the end of the car caused her to start. But if she was surprised, he was so shocked he almost fell off his bike.

"*What the fuck?*" He staggered sideways as the bike tilted, then he regained his balance. He straddled the bike, facing her, but he didn't reach for his gun. Instead, he eyed her with a mixture of curiosity and apprehension.

She rose, holding her hands out to show she meant no harm. "Hi."

He rolled back a few feet and nodded, his eyes flashing to her suitcase. She pulled it close, stepping in front of the case as she leveled a hard look at him. "Don't even think about it."

His eyes widened, but then he must have grinned behind the bandana because a dimple dented his cheek. "Don't worry, lady. I don't want your shit." He swept a gloved hand out. "The city is full of stuff. Everything you could need or want. You just have to be careful to avoid the stiffs."

"Okay. Good to know. Well, I'll be on my way." She backed away, but he followed her, pedaling just enough to keep the bike from falling over.

"Where are you going?" His tone wasn't threatening, but not only was she wary of telling him her plans, she wondered if it was just a casual question or if he was becoming friendly due to the virus. She edged away from him.

She increased her pace. "Why do you want to know?"

He kept abreast but remained several feet away. "Look, lady. You're the first person I've seen in days who wasn't either dead or partying like it's 1999." He shrugged and gave a whistle like a plane spiraling out of the sky, his thumb pointing towards the ground "And then they'd die. I'm curious is all."

She glanced at him as she marched down the road, skirting right of a body while he went left. "I'm meeting some friends."

He skidded to a stop. "You mean other people survived too?" There was a note of wistfulness in his voice that brought her up short.

Had Cole survived? She was counting on it, but she didn't know for sure. "I don't know. Possibly."

"Where?"

She resumed walking, more slowly now. "Why do you want to know?" Two could play the question game.

"I just thought maybe there was a town or something, where everything was normal still." There was a catch in his voice, and she did a double take. The kid looked tough on the outside with his studded wristbands, and she noticed a bar through his right eyebrow, but he'd sounded like a little boy for a moment.

She was too wary to let down her guard completely, but she gave him a sideways look. "What's your name?"

"Jake."

"Hi, Jake. I'm Elly." Last names weren't necessary.

"Nice to meet you, Elly."

"Yeah, same to you. Sorry to be rude, but I really need to get a move on." She doubled her speed. She was almost to Michigan Avenue and from there, could hook up with Sheridan Road.

"Why are you walking?"

"Because I don't think I could drive a car through all of this." She gestured to the cars and bodies littering the street.

"Grab a bike. They're all over the place."

The idea had occurred to her but thought dodging the bodies might be more trouble than it was worth. "Too many obstacles in the road. Besides, I have all of my supplies in this." She rattled the handle of her case.

"Yeah, but if you take the alleys, most of them are clear. And I bet you could find a wagon to hitch to your bike. Or maybe one of those baby trailers. Check the Lincoln Park area. Those people are always pulling their kids in those contraptions. I used to love scaring the shit out of the parents, racing up as close as I could before skidding sideways. It was hilarious."

She rolled her eyes. "I'll bet. Sorry, I missed it."

He must have caught her sarcasm because he shrugged. "It was fun to mess with them, but I never actually hit any of the trailers." His voice hardened. "I don't hurt little kids."

"I'm sure you don't." She thought about what he'd said about a bike, but decided that dragging a trailer behind one wasn't much better than a car. It would be hard to navigate around all the obstacles. As they avoided two more bodies, both in advanced states of decay, she averted her eyes from what was left of the corpses. "How come you don't have a trailer?"

"I do, but I didn't bring it. I'm just out scouting for more stuff."

"How do you navigate around all of the—" she swallowed hard and gestured to another pile of bodies, "dead?"

"Like I said, I stick to the alleys. People were dancing in the streets, not the alleys." He chuckled. "Sorry, just my sick humor."

"Yes, I figured that out." She didn't hold his twisted sense of humor against him. It was a coping mechanism.

She hadn't looked in an alley, assuming they were as bad as the rest of the streets. "Really? The alleys?"

"Yeah. The rats are even gone. They're all out here now." He nodded to a couple gnawing on the leg of what had probably been a young woman. She grimaced and looked away.

"Maybe I'll do that. Thanks."

"No problem."

He continued to tag along. She didn't feel threatened, but it made her nervous all the same. Finally, she halted. "Are you planning on continuing to follow me?"

He straddled the bike, his feet planted on the asphalt. "I could help you get wherever you're going."

"How do you know you could help? I haven't even told you where I'm headed."

"Because I've been riding around the city for the last three days. I know where the sick are still running around and could help you avoid them."

She had assumed almost everyone was dead. There had been no signs of life except in the streets for the last couple of days. At least, none that she had seen. "Why would you do that?"

"You mean, what's in it for me?"

She met his eyes and nodded.

He tipped his chin at her mask and gloves. "I don't want to be the last person in Chicago, and you look like you might survive, too."

JENNA TRIED to push past Cole. "Let me by, Cole. He's my son!"

Cole took her by the shoulders. "I know. I'm sorry, but he has to stay in isolation." He'd taken charge and already put Trent in the building and locked the door. Trent had been in shock and hadn't protested, but Cole had told him he'd be back with some blankets and a blowup mattress. It was all ready to go and had just been sitting on the porch of the house waiting for Hunter to arrive. Nobody thought they'd need it before then. As Jenna glared at him, Cole tilted his head. "It's for all of our protection. We all agreed, remember?"

"Yes, for Hunter! Not for my son!"

At the mention of Hunter's name, Cole felt a stab of pain in his chest. He only hoped the day would come when he had to deal with putting Hunter in isolation. She tried to shove him out of her way, but he held on tight, searching over his shoulder for Sean, but his brother was standing at the end of the pier staring out towards the lake.

"We can put some chairs outside of the quarantine, and you can sit and talk to him through the doors—as long as you're wearing your mask."

Tears coursed down her cheeks, and Cole felt like an asshole enforcing the rules, but he had to stand firm. "It's only three weeks, okay? I know that sounds like a long time, but it's really not so long. And we'll deliver food, and he has a bathroom. We'll stock him with some books and magazines. It'll be almost like a vacation for him." He tried to smile, "He'll be thrilled not to have to work in the garden for a while."

"He hates the garden." She sagged against him. "But he'll be all alone, and you're locking him in." With a sniff, she pushed away. "And what if there's a fire and he's trapped in there?"

"There's not going to be a fire. The walls are cinderblock."

Jenna swiped at her eyes and glared at Cole. "Fine, but just wait until your son is in there. Then you'll know what it feels like."

Cole knew she didn't mean to be cruel. She was just scared and lashing out at him. He didn't point out that he already knew her pain because he was living it every day that they didn't hear from Hunter. First thing every morning, Cole took the boat to the mainland. He'd dock and check around the area, praying that he'd find Hunter waiting to go to the island. If his son made it this far, he'd see Cole's vehicle and know he was in the right place. He was smart—he'd know they'd come for him.

Chapter Twenty

Hunter approached the highway, but the horses balked, Red tossed his head and Hunter had to take the lead in his hand instead of just having it secured to the back of his saddle. "Come on, Red. It's okay."

The mare, while reluctant, was easier to handle. He coaxed them forward, his voice low and encouraging as they neared the highway. He needed to see what the road was like. Maybe driving a car the rest of the way was an option after all although he didn't want to give up the horses. With most places abandoned, he could probably find a horse trailer without too much effort. The back roads, while dotted with occasional wrecks, made him re-think his strategy. Finding a car to drive wouldn't be an issue. What he wanted was one that wasn't potentially contaminated.

The on ramp was devoid of vehicles and had apparently been closed at some point, the gate still lowered, blocking vehicles from entering, but he and the horses simply went around it. Halfway up the ramp, the horses' ears flattened, and they became skittish, even the mare. Hunter had all he could do to get them under control.

The smell of death permeated the air and Hunter secured his mask around his face. He didn't know if dead bodies could still spread the disease, but he wasn't taking any chances. Flies swarmed, and their buzz was like something out of a horror movie. Buddy trotted ahead, the scent didn't seem to bother him, but Hunter didn't want him too close. He whistled, and the dog halted and looked over his shoulder at him.

"Come, Buddy. We don't need to take the highway." Maybe the horses' reluctance had rubbed off on him, but Hunter decided he didn't need to go all the way up to the highway after all. The signs leading up the ramp had given him enough information, along with a sign on the highway, visible once he was partially up the ramp, that told him the distance to the next towns.

He backtracked to the base of the ramp, turning onto a frontage road, following it. He'd discovered that the highway was I-90, and the signage over the road said that Austin was nine miles east so he was definitely in Minnesota. Dismounting, he let the horses graze in the median while he plotted where he was on the map. A slew of fast food restaurants and gas stations lined the road near the entrance and exit ramps.

Deciding to check out a few of them in case they contain something he could use, he headed towards the nearest one—a gas station. It had a good-sized mini-mart and housed a burger chain as well. He stopped in the parking lot, ignoring the cars at the fuel pumps and the dead bodies inside and outside the cars. He was leading the horses, which was a good thing as the mare snorted and threw her head when an empty potato chip bag skittered between her legs. "Easy, girl."

Red shied again, so Hunter tied them to a light pole on the edge of the station, letting them graze in the grassy strip between the station and the road. He untied the bow and the quiver, draping the quiver across his body. He thought about leaving his backpack, but he'd decided early on that he would never let it out of his sight. He kept the lighter, matches, jeans, some food, a water bottle, and his water purification tablets inside it. It contained the basics he needed to survive, and while the station looked deserted, he wasn't going to assume that it was. He looped the bag over his other shoulder and carried the bow in his left hand. It would only take seconds to drop the backpack and grab an arrow if he had to.

He grimaced at the trashed appearance as paper towels blew across his path. A trail of crushed cheese curls led to one of the cars at the pumps where the bag had spilled into a pile of what was now an ant-infested pile of orange crumbs. A body hid half the spill, the bag trapped beneath what was left of an arm.

Hunter averted his eyes and swallowed hard. He was already getting used to seeing corpses, but that didn't mean he liked it.

One look inside the gas station and he almost backed out. The attendant must have died in his plexiglass cubicle, and if he'd thought the smell had been bad on the highway, it was ten times worse in the building. He wasn't the only body, but the windows and plexiglass must have acted like a greenhouse, and the inside of the secure cubicle dripped with condensation. Hunter turned away. It was all he could do not to gag. He kicked through some of the items on the floor. Most were just crushed bags of snacks, but his toe hit a disposable lighter, and he grabbed it but looked for somewhere to stow it, unwilling to put a possibly contaminated item in his pocket. -

He grabbed a package of baby wipes off the shelf. The items on this shelf had been undisturbed. Apparently, nobody had worried about the babies. One of the items was a box of little bags to refill some kind of diaper disposal contraption. Hunter wasn't sure what it was, but he opened the box and thought they looked a bit like mini-trash bags. They were perfect for what he needed. He tore one off and popped the lighter inside.

He searched the shelves for anything more, brightening at two bags of dog food and some doggie treats. Hunter snatched them, tucking the bags inside his backpack. He could barely close it. He carried it by the straps. Looping the quiver over one shoulder with his bow, he stuffed some flea collars in his pocket, along with some pouches of doggy treats. He held one pouch up for Buddy, who'd trailed him inside. "Look what I got you!" Buddy sat down and scratched behind his ear, showing no signs of excitement. Hunter shook his head with a smile. "Ingrate."

In the health area, he found a jar of petroleum jelly. He wasn't sure what he'd need it for, but it seemed like a good item to have. If nothing else, it would help a fire burn. A roll of medical tape and a package of adhesive bandages joined the other small items in his bag.

It wasn't just dead bodies, but rotting food and rancid lunchmeat at the small deli counter.

The shelves had been ransacked, and Hunter wondered when that had occurred. All the snack items were gone or destroyed. Not a single bag of chips or pretzels remained. All the candy was gone too. He supposed the infected people had looked for party food. That's what they seemed to want to do, so it was no wonder all the snack items were gone.

Suddenly, Buddy growled and gave a soft bark, his ears cocking. Hunter froze, watching the dog's reaction, then crept towards the door.

One of the horses neighed. Then he heard voices.

"IT LOOKS SO PEACEFUL." Elly sat on the dock, her feet dangling as she listened to the cry of the seagulls and the soft slap of waves against the hulls of several dozen boats. With the city and all the dead behind her, for just a moment, she could pretend that everything was fine. A soft breeze blew in from the lake, and she lifted her mask, allowing it to perch on top of her head. She'd risk it for a few breaths of clean air.

Jake dumped his bike on the pier and plopped down a few feet away. Boats bobbed in the water, masts moving side to side like aquatic metronomes. Elly had been drawn to the lakefront because of the beauty and serenity. She desperately needed this—a dose of normalcy even if it was false.

While there were still dead here and there, for the most part, people had fled to the streets, not the lakefront. It was crazy to think that just a few weeks ago the owners of these boats had probably just taken them from dry docks or garages, and put them in the water, anticipating a lively and fun boating season.

Jake braced his hands on the edge of the wood and hunched forward, studying the water inches below his sneakers, before his gaze swept the marina. "Do you know how to sail a boat?"

She shrugged. "Sort of. I sailed a bit in my teens and twenties. Never by myself, though. Why?"

"I just thought it might be a good way to get away from all of that." He motioned behind them. "Get out on the water for a while. No more germs."

"Yes, that's a good idea, but I don't know if I could manage it."

She thought of Cole. "That's what my friend is doing. Well, except he's not sailing a boat, but living on an island. I'm going to try to get there, but…" She thought of all the miles between Chicago and Green Bay. Streets were impassable for all practical purposes. There were stretches of open road, but then there would be a pile-up, and there had been nobody left to clean up the mess.

She wondered how many people had survived the virus. Did anyone catch it and live? Or were the only survivors those who never caught it? She itched to get blood samples from herself and Jake, and anyone else still alive to see if there were antibodies to the virus. The CDC hadn't come up with a definitive test yet—there hadn't been time, but there had to be some markers. Given just a little more time, they would have nailed it.

Elly sighed and glanced over her shoulder at the high-rises behind her. Chances were survivors were hiding out, waiting for the danger to pass. It was unlikely that she and Jake were the only survivors in the city—because what were the chances they'd run into each other? No, there were pockets of survivors. There had to be.

"Where's the island?" Jake pulled his bandana down around his neck. She considered pulling her mask up again if he was going without the bandana but didn't bother. He didn't seem overly social, just lonely. He was a good looking kid and not nearly as tough looking now that she could see the lower half of his face. In fact, she thought he probably belonged in this upscale area of Chicago.

"Up around Green Bay."

He did a double-take. "You were planning on walking all the way to Green Bay?"

"I hoped I'd find a car to use along the way. That was before I realized how bad the streets were."

"Ah." He nodded, then waved at the selection of moored boats. "Why don't you take one of those?"

"A sailboat?"

"Sure. Or maybe a power boat. Shit… take one of those yachts." He laughed and pointed to the biggest boat in the marina. "I doubt the owner will miss it."

She gave a wry chuckle. "No. Probably not, but I have no idea how to steer a yacht." She nodded to a small sailboat. "That's more my speed."

He eyed it, his expression doubtful. "That's too small. It would be hard to sail all the way to Green Bay on that thing." He pointed to a good-sized Sea Ray. "There you go. Now we're talking." He grinned at her.

She took in the cabin cruiser, tilting her head as she wondered if she was up to the task. It was bigger than any boat she'd ever attempted to skipper. "You're out of your mind." She shook her head but smiled. "Even if I could manage a boat that big, we don't have the keys and how would we get gas? The electricity is gone, so no pumps."

Elly noted several boats that would be up to the task of sailing up the lake. She had only been out on the ocean, close to shore, not on one of the Great Lakes, but she knew there were differences. Could she do it? Most of her experience was with small sailboats, but her grandfather had a motorboat, and she used to take it out a lot before she became more interested in sailing.

"I bet I could siphon some gas. Same as what you would have had to do with a car." Jake bit his lip as he studied the cruiser.

"That still leaves us trying to hot wire it, and I don't know about you, but I've never hot-wired anything before."

Jake gave her a sly smile but didn't admit to anything. "I doubt we'd have to hot wire one. People are stupid."

"Excuse me?"

"You take that side, and I'll take this one. I bet you a hundred bucks that at least one of these boats has the keys right in the ignition."

She shook her head. "No way."

Jake jumped to his feet. "If I find keys, I get to go with you." He grinned like it was just a game, but she heard a note of desperation.

They had only met a few hours ago, and it was crazy to trust someone so quickly. In normal times, there was no way she'd travel alone with some teenage boy she'd just met, but these weren't normal times.

"You're on." She hoped they found a set of keys.

Jake took off down his side of the dock, jumping on and off boats like he knew a thing or two about them. Elly cocked her head, watching him for a minute. He knew right where to look and didn't waste time. As he leaped onto the dock and on to another boat, she gave a wry chuckle, envying his youth.

She had to climb a few steps to get to the first boat she came to checked the ignition. *Nothing.* She glanced around, hoping it was stashed somewhere, but if it was, she didn't see it. She tried a small glove box but found only a map. She started to put it back, but changed her mind, tucking it in the string bag. She returned to the dock and checked the next three boats with no luck. She skipped the sailboats, not confident enough of her sailing skills to try a long distance trip. She was about to try a small cabin cruiser when Jake shouted to her.

She turned and spotted him on the deck of a medium-sized boat. It was a beauty, and she looked over her shoulder, as a wave of guilt washed over her. This boat cost someone dearly, and here she was thinking of stealing it without a moment's hesitation. There were cameras mounted high on light poles and ordinarily, they would be a deterrent to theft.

Striding around to Jake's side of the pier, she hopped in the boat. "You found one?" She really hadn't expected they'd find a key. Who would leave a key in a fifty-thousand dollar boat?

Jake grinned, dangling a set of keys with a red foam float attached. "You owe me a hundred bucks!"

She chuckled. "Sure, I'll just pop into the next bank we come across and withdraw some money."

His grin flattened, but only for a moment. "Hopefully, the battery has been charged up already."

"You sure sound like you know what you're doing."

He shrugged. "My dad has a boat sort of like this one." He frowned, his eyes distant. "I mean, he did have one." He fiddled with the keys, his voice quiet as he added, "I don't think he's alive anymore."

Elly bit her lip. "I'm sorry." She wondered where his father's boat was and why didn't they use it instead of stealing one, but asking would be cruel.

"He lived in Miami, and I only saw him on school holidays. My mom and I lived here. She was a doctor—one of the first to catch the disease."

She wondered how he'd survived, but didn't ask.

He threw off his quiet mood and found the engine. "It works!" He rushed to the ignition and tried another key, the engine coughed the first time, then started up. "Sweet!" He peered at the dials on the dashboard. "Almost a full-tank!"

"Will that get us to Green Bay?"

"No way, but there are a lot of harbors between here and Green Bay. We can siphon gas when it starts getting low."

She rubbed her forehead with thumb and first two fingers as she processed the change in plans. "So, you're coming with me?"

Jake turned from examining the dials. "I've got nothing here. Everyone I knew is dead—all my friends and their families—everybody. I even went to check on some of my teachers, but..."

Could she trust being on a boat with this kid for a few days? She barely knew him, but he could have stolen her supplies at any time in the last few hours, or tried to attack her, but he hadn't. He reminded her of a lost puppy and her heart went out to him. Sure, he could be lying, but what was the motivation? Like he said, everything he needed to live was easy to find in the city—at least for the foreseeable future. Fresh food was already gone, but things like dried rice, beans were likely plentiful, although they'd have to be found soon or they'd be consumed by rodents. Canned foods would be good for several more years.

But what would Chicago be like in a few days or weeks as people came out of hiding? Fights over limited supplies were a real possibility. Cole had the right idea to isolate his family on an island. She wanted to bring Jake along, not only for his sake but for her own. She wasn't sure she could get this watercraft all the way to Green Bay on her own and having another hand on deck was always a good thing. Plus, he was smart and resourceful—he'd already shown that. Would Cole welcome him, though? She drew in a deep breath. They'd deal with that when they made it that far.

"It's your boat, Jake. You found it and got it working. I should be the one asking if I can come along."

He shrugged. "Yeah, but they're your friends."

"Just so you remember, I don't even know if they're still alive. It's been several days since I spoke to Cole. They could all be gone by now."

"Do you want to stay here?" He swept a hand in the direction of the city, his lip curled.

The last thirty minutes of fresh air had already convinced her that she would do just about anything to not return to the death and decay in the streets and buildings.

Elly shook her head. "*God, no.* And Jake, I would be happy to have you as first mate."

He grinned. "Awesome."

She looked at her watch. It was almost three p.m. She wanted to check a few things first, see what was onboard, get more fuel to have on hand, and check out some of the other boats for anything that might come in handy. "I think we should spend the rest of today getting ready and head out first thing in the morning. See if we can get some more fuel. I don't like the idea of carrying it onboard, but it's not like we can call the Coast Guard if we run out of gas in the middle of the lake."

"Right. I'll get our bags, then I'll check some of the cars around here and look for gas cans in the trunk. If I can't find any, there's a gas station about a half-mile up the road. Normally they'd have some."

"Yes, well, I wouldn't be surprised if they were snatched up by those looking to flee the city, but maybe you'll find one." Now that she had decided he could come with her, she worried about him and didn't want him going too far away. "Just don't go too far. If we need to, we can switch boats at another marina, right? Maybe try a sailboat."

"Good thinking." He started to leave, but turned to her, his expression conflicted. "It feels so wrong to just take a boat."

"Yeah. I know."

He nodded at her then took off.

She yelled after him, "Use your bandana!" He waved over his shoulder. She shook her head at her tone. She'd sounded like the kid's mother.

For the rest of the day, Elly scoured the marina, hopping on and off boats, finding more than she'd expected. She looked at her haul and tried to find a place to stash it all. Her biggest finds were fishing poles, nets, and a tackle box, but she was also glad to find thick gloves, cans of mosquito spray and sunscreen, three boxes of crackers, a jar of peanut butter, and one bottle of fine, expensive scotch. She'd save that for when they reached Cole's island.

Jake was gone longer than she'd expected and she started to get worried when he showed up. He had traded bikes and had a child trailer attached. The dock wasn't wide enough where the boat was to bring the trailer.

"You won't believe all the stuff I got, Elly. I found three gas cans, and two were already full!" He unsnapped the trailer and carried the gas over. "And I found a metal garbage can to store it in. What took me so long was cleaning the can." At her alarm, he waved his hands. "Don't worry, it was just full of grass clippings, but it stunk, and I had to do something. I took it to the pool outside one of those fancy condos and cleaned it in there."

"Good thinking."

He dropped his backpack. "And I got some cans of food. They were in the trunk with the gas cans. And don't worry. I washed the cans too, just in case they were contaminated." He pulled the cans out of his pack and frowned. "Shit. All the labels came off." He reached farther into the bag and pulled out a handful of soggy paper labels.

"It's okay. We'll be surprised every time. It'll be kind of fun."

He nodded but looked worried.

"What?"

"I didn't know if I should say anything because I could be wrong, but..." He faced west, blocking the sun with his hand. "I thought I heard someone yelling. I didn't see anyone, what if they saw me? I took a couple of turns, taking a roundabout way here to make sure nobody saw where I was headed, but to be on the safe side I think we should load up as quick as we can."

Elly scanned the shore, but all was still. Of course, that didn't mean there wasn't someone out there. "You're right."

It took them five minutes to get everything to the boat and stored. Just as they got the gas cans in the trash can, a loud shout, more like the whoop of a fan cheering on their favorite team, echoed through the marina. Elly ducked. Jake froze, his eyes locking on hers.

He whispered, "I have to get rid of the bike and trailer."

Elly rose and scouted the area. "I don't see anyone. Sound carries over the water, and there's no background noise to drown it out. I don't think whoever made the noise is as close as they sounded."

"Yeah, but they could be coming closer." Like a cat, he leaped onto the dock, barely making a sound, and he crept to the bike and trailer on the end.

The shout came again, a little closer, maybe. Jake unhitched the bike and lowered it into the water without a sound. Then he looked around for a place to dump the trailer. She thought he'd dump that in the lake and worried about a splash, but he lifted it and set it in the back of a large yacht. He threw a tarp over it.

Just as he stepped back onto the cruiser, the shout came again.

Elly motioned for him to get into the cabin, and as soon as he did, she shut and locked the door. Her heart raced. She whispered, "Don't move too much. We don't want to set the boat in motion."

Jake gave her a thumbs-up and peered through one of the tiny windows. "Someone's coming."

Chapter Twenty-One

"Mom! I wanna go home!"

Trent's voice carried to the house, wrapping around each of them as they picked at the tuna casserole for dinner.

Jenna, ramrod stiff, stared at her plate. She hadn't even lifted her fork. The noodles clumped into a congealed mass of pasta.

Sean shoved back in his chair and turned towards the changing house two hundred feet away on the beach. It wasn't visible from the table in the kitchen, but Cole knew Sean saw it anyway as if the walls of the house didn't exist. His brother's hands balled into fists on his thighs. He looked coiled—ready to fight for his son. If only he could.

Piper's fork clinked against her plate as she poked listlessly at her dinner. She had her elbow on the table, her head resting in her hand.

All day, they had listened to Trent calling out. Sometimes he wanted to go home. Other times, he begged to see his friends. For a while, he sang at the top of his lungs and seemed happy when Sean stood outside the changing room and played the guitar a little, but Sean could only do it for an hour before he broke down and retreated to a work shed. He said he had to work on the water pump.

Trent hadn't seemed to mind when his dad left. He continued his singing until his voice became hoarse. Occasionally, the singing had been punctuated by moments of manic laughter. He'd called out to Piper and his parents to join him. Once, he even asked for Hunter to come out and play with him and Cole was reminded of all the times Trent had made the same request at family gatherings.

Cole slid his plate away, his appetite gone. He propped his forehead against his palms, elbows splayed on the tabletop. A pea from the casserole had escaped from his plate, and he stared at the green and cream colored glob.

When Hunter had been twelve and Trent eight, his son had complained about it—how he was too old to play with little kids, and Trent had overheard. Dejected, he'd trudged to the backyard. Cole had been about to scold Hunter but held back when his son had followed Trent, apologizing. Not fifteen minutes later they were engaged in a water gun fight, laughing and whooping with glee. If —*when*—Hunter arrived, the news of what happened to Trent was going to devastate him.

"Mommy…*please*?"

Jenna drew in a sharp breath, a hitch in her voice. "He hasn't called me 'Mommy' since he was five." She closed her eyes, tears tracking down her face, dripping onto the table. "I'm a nurse. I should be able to do something for him." Then she stared at Cole. "If we hadn't come here, he never would have come into contact with those guys in the boat."

Cole flinched. She was right. The fact that he probably would be dead already, along with the rest of them, didn't matter. Unfortunately, they couldn't undo the past and take a different course of action.

Sean put a hand on her shoulder, but she shrugged it off. Cole had heard them arguing the night before over the isolation imposed on Trent. Sean glared at Cole, then stood, stalking to the window and braced a hand on either side of it.

"Uncle Cole, are you sure that Trent has it? That he has the virus?"

Cole felt the weight of his family's gaze, but he couldn't meet their eyes. They wanted him to deny it and how he wished he could. He pinched the bridge of his nose and sighed. They knew the truth but needed him to confirm it. He looked at Piper, feeling her pain like it was his own. "I'm afraid so." There was no gavel to bang, but he still felt as if he'd issued a death sentence.

Silence. Even Trent had paused in his singing.

He stared at the table. All the plates were untouched, the food wasted. Not that he cared. He lifted his gaze, but they were no longer watching him. Jenna's lip quivered, Piper stared at her mother, her eyes red and watery. Sean leaned against the wall, his shoulders slumped, eyes vacant.

"*Mommy…I'll be good.*"

Piper jumped up from the table. "You guys have to do something! *Mom! Dad!* You can't just let him die!"

Jenna crumpled, her shoulders heaving as sobs poured out. Sean pushed away from the wall, moving to Jenna, his arms wrapping around her. This time, she leaned into him.

"*That's it?*" Piper looked from her parents to Cole.

His mouth dry, his throat tight, Cole wanted to offer comfort, but had none to give.

With a cry of anguish, she bolted to the counter where Cole had left the key to the changing house after delivering Trent's dinner. She grabbed it and dashed out the door.

Cole, numb from despair, didn't process her sudden departure, but as he pieced it together, he jumped to his feet, his chair toppling as he raced after his niece.

"*Piper! No!*" He flung open the door and took the three steps in one bound, moving faster than he knew he could as he raced after her. He caught her as she fumbled with the lock on the door. He closed his hand over hers.

She turned on him, pounding her fists against his chest, one fist cracking along his jaw, the key in her hand gouging along his cheek.

"I have to let him out! I can't let him die in there alone!"

Trent's voice, just on the other side of the door, encouraged his sister. "Piper? Is that you? Why am I locked in here? Let me out!" He sounded almost normal, and Cole felt a moment of hesitation. Maybe he was wrong? What if Trent was fine?

Then Trent whooped. "Come on, sis. We'll show them we can't be treated like this. Stupid ass parents treating us like shit! I got friends we can go party with. They'll like *you*."

His tone and insinuation made the hair on the back of Cole's neck stand up. Trent never spoke like that. Not the real boy.

Piper froze, staring at the door. She covered her mouth, her eyes wide in horror as she backed away, her body trembling. "*Oh, Trent...*"

Cole reached for the key, and she relinquished it without a fight, her body trembling. Piper looked at him, searching his face...seeking hope? But he couldn't give it to her, and she bent, burying her face in hands as she sagged to her knees.

He blinked hard, swiping his face on his shoulder as he stood beside her, unsure of what to do. She was his niece, but almost like a daughter to him. He couldn't love her any more if she were his own. And Trent—being the youngest of the group— always held a special place in everyone's heart. His chest ached as he watched her, even as Trent hummed on the other side of the door. Cole took a knee beside Piper, draping his arm across her shoulders and giving her a gentle squeeze.

HUNTER PEEKED around a poster in the window of the gas station. Three guys and a teenaged girl were approaching the horses. He swore softly, wondering what they wanted. If they wanted the horses, it didn't make a lot of sense. There had to be plenty of other horses out there that they could find.

The horses snorted, and Red stamped the ground as the men approached. One guy stayed back, his hand gripping the girl's upper arm. Hunter didn't know if he was trying to protect her from the horses or if he was keeping her from bolting. Her body language said she wanted nothing to do with him.

Buddy growled low in his throat, and Hunter tried to quiet him. The dog gave Hunter an anxious glance, obviously wanting to please him, but the animal obviously sensed something with the group that he didn't like. Hunter wished the dog could talk.

He scanned the mini-mart for a weapon, hoping the store owner had a gun. His skin crawled as he pushed open the door to the cashier's area, hoping to find a weapon stashed under the counter, but he didn't see one. His stomach churned from the stench and sight. He backed out as fast as possible.

There wasn't much left in the store, and what was left was scattered on the floor, not neatly arranged. None of it was worth losing the horses. Most of his supplies were on the horses, including his ax. To protect it, he'd rolled it into his sleeping bag. He cursed his stupidity for not carrying the ax on his belt. He hadn't thought of it as a weapon but as a tool. He had his hunting knife, but the ax would have been better if he had to get close. And of course, there was the bow, but while he'd practiced, he'd never shot anything living before, let alone a human. And if they had guns, the bow would be paltry protection against bullets. His only advantage would be surprise and silence.

He looked around for a place to stash the pack, not wanting to be burdened with it, but not wanting to lose it to these guys either. A large stack of large Styrofoam coolers lay on the floor, he righted the stack, stuffing the pack in the cooler in the middle, and leaned the stack against the shelves. He wanted the coolers to look undesirable, so he grabbed a bottle of mustard on the floor, and squirted it over the coolers. Ketchup would have been better, but he didn't see any.

He adjusted the tension on the bow, and drew an arrow, notching it but holding it loosely. Looking around, he noted a backdoor, and moved towards it, remembering the carwash on that end of the lot. He could circle it, bringing him closer to the guys. Besides worrying if they were armed, what if they had the virus? The possibility gave him pause. Should he just abandon the horses, get his pack, and take off across the field behind the gas station? He was pretty sure he could find more horses although he hated to give them up. They were more than just transportation to him.

Hunter made sure his mask was in place and decided he'd get a closer look before deciding anything. For all he knew, the strangers were friendly. Maybe they could help each other.

Then the girl cried out in what sounded like pain. Hunter stiffened. One of the men yelled at her to shut-up, or she was dead. That answered his question about the men's intent, and his decision was made. He had to face these guys and get the horses back.

The guys probably suspected someone was nearby because it was obvious the horses hadn't been tied up for long, but that was assuming the men noticed the absence of manure and the health of the animals, but these guys didn't look too bright. They'd made a lot of noise, for one thing. Hunter crept to the corner of the gas station. There was a twenty foot gap between the station and the car wash he'd have to cross. Only part of the gap would be visible to the strangers, but if one of them happened to be looking, they'd see him. But, if he crossed it, he could come up behind them to within fifty feet before they'd see him.

Hunter took a deep breath, darted across the gap. Buddy came with him, thankfully, not making any noise. When he reached the cover of the car wash, he stroked Buddy's head, then crept around the back of the car wash, taking care not to kick anything on the gravel-strewn blacktop. Weeds grew out of cracks as the asphalt gave way to the grass that surrounded the lot.

When he reached the corner, he whispered and motioned for Buddy to lie down and stay. The dog obeyed, his ears perked as he watched Hunter.

Crouching behind the air pump, he watched the men circle the horses. The mare shied away as far as the rope would let her go while Red snorted and took a few quick steps towards the strangers. The men backed off, throwing suggestions to each other.

Hunter looked to see if they had any weapons, but if they did, he couldn't see them. It was then he noticed that the girl's wrists were tied together in front of her. He was close enough to see a bruise on her cheek. Anger rose in him. Just because there was nobody around to enforce the laws didn't give the men the right to do anything they wanted to another person.

He watched for several more seconds not seeing any weapons, but he had a feeling they were armed. Guys like that probably had a whole arsenal. They just didn't see a need for it now.

Out-numbered, and his only weapon a bow and arrow, he wasn't sure what his next move should be.

The girl yelped, raising one foot and that's when Hunter noticed she was barefoot. The guy holding her arm, shoved her forward, laughing when she fell to her knees. Her shoulders shook, and although Hunter didn't hear her, he imagined she was crying.

The one who had shoved her pulled a gun from behind his back and aimed it at the girl.

"I've had about enough of your crying. I think it's time I put you out of your misery." He turned to the other men, who watched Red, their hands out as though to calm him, but apparently neither had any experience with horses because their sudden lunges for his halter only made the horse more skittish. "You guys care if I get rid of her? I've had all I can take of her crying."

The tallest guy shrugged. "Whatever. We're kinda busy now. Do what you gotta do." Red snorted, and both men backed off, cursing the horse.

The one with the gun grinned and leveled it at the sobbing girl's head.

Hunter didn't think; he just reacted, letting the arrow fly and notching another before the first had even reached its target. His hours of studying speed shooting videos on Youtube and practicing the techniques paid off. At the time, he'd pretend he was in a video game, shooting at imaginary foes, but these guys weren't imaginary, and this was no game.

The gun went off, but Hunter's shot had hit the man in the chest, and he'd pulled his arm back reflexively, his aim at the sky when he'd fired.

Red reared at the gunshot, catching one of the men in the head with his hoof. Hunter winced at the impact. The other man stumbled back, shouting for help. He reached behind himself and withdrew a gun, leveling it at Red, but when the shooter didn't reply, he turned, his gaze locking on the shooter, now down on the ground. The other man's jaw dropped at the sight of Hunter's arrow sticking out of the man's chest.

Then he crouched, his gun leveled as he sought out the source of the attack. "Who's out there?"

Hunter drew back behind the air pump, but peeked between the coiled vacuum hose, still able to see the gunman. Buddy huddled at his side, alert, but not alarmed and Hunter suspected the dog had been hunting a time or two. His heart hammered in his ears, and he fought to control his ragged breathing. Fear and adrenaline made him feel as if he'd just sprinted a mile. His mind raced even faster than his heart. Should he let another arrow fly? Or wait to see what would happen? If he shot and missed, he'd be a sitting duck. But he couldn't crouch here forever. Already his thighs burned.

The girl had curled into a fetal position, and even from his distance, Hunter saw her shaking in fear. Any second, the remaining guy standing could decide to finish her off. Hunter took a deep breath and waited for a good shot. He had to take it. Not only did his life depend on it, but he had a feeling that her life did as well.

The man stepped over to the shooter, nudging him with his toe. Hunter's jaw tensed, willing the man to face him and give him a good shot. Instead, he stood with his right side to Hunter.

When the shooter didn't move, the guy gave a harder kick and swore. He glared at the girl as if she had caused the shooter's death. "What happened?" He kicked her in the ribs. She cried out.

"I don't know! I didn't see it."

"*Bitch!*" He kicked her again, but turned, apparently searching with his back to Hunter. If only he weren't wearing a pack. Hunter noted the direction the grass blew and made mental adjustments as he pictured the arrow hitting its target. It was an exercise he did before every competition. Only this time there was no circular target, but he didn't need an actual bullseye to pretend one was painted on the guy's shirt.

The man slowly turned full-circle, and Hunter felt his gaze rake over the air pump, sliding past, but then returning. He must have seen something. Hunter took a deep breath and straightened for an instant to get a better look. He saw the bullseye and took his shot.

The arrow hit the man high on the left side of his chest. He staggered back but didn't go down, firing at Hunter.

The bullet pinged off the air pump, and Hunter cringed even as he notched another arrow.

"Come out where I can see you, you asshole! Why don't you show yourself like a real man?"

Hunter's eyes narrowed, anger burning away the fear and he stood. "A real man? What would you know about *a real man*? You beat on helpless girls!"

"*Screw you!*" He lifted his gun and Hunter loosed the arrow at the same time a gunshot rang out. His arrow missed high.

Flinching, Hunter braced for the bullet, but it never came. The man dropped.

The girl held a gun in her hands, her arms still outstretched and pointed at the man.

It took a few seconds for Hunter to process what had happened. She must have picked up the first shooter's gun. Hunter hadn't paid attention to where it might have landed when the man fell, but he didn't see it on the ground anywhere. He started towards her, but she steadied the weapon. "Don't!"

He raised his hands. "Whoa."

"Don't come any closer!"

Red snorted, and Hunter tore his gaze from the girl to the horses. Both were literally at the end of their ropes, tugging hard and in danger of breaking them.

"Look, I'm not going to hurt you. Let me see to the horses, okay?" He also wanted to see how the man Red had kicked was doing. Was he dead? What if he woke up and started shooting? He wanted to get to him and disarm him before he came to.

She bit her lip and then nodded.

Hunter held his arms wide, the bow in one hand, the other empty as he edged towards the horses, maintaining eye contact with her until he had to turn his full attention to the animals. Buddy followed Hunter, but his ears were pricked forward, and his tail wagged a few times as he looked at the girl.

As he passed the guy who'd been kicked, Hunter took one look and averted his eyes. Red's hoof had caught the man in the temple, crushing the side of his head. This guy wasn't going to bother them anymore.

"Easy, Red," Hunter spoke softly. Soothingly. He caught the halter and stroked the horse's neck. "It's okay. It's all over." The poor horse was soaked in sweat, and the mare wasn't any better. Her eyes rolled in fear. He moved over to her, stroking her muzzle until her breathing slowed. She dipped her head, pressing it against his chest. He chuckled. "I know. It was pretty scary." He pressed his forehead against hers until Red nudged him, seeking more attention. "Hey, Red. Don't worry. I haven't forgotten you." He scratched the spot at the top of Red's neck; the spot he knew the horse loved having scratched. After a few more moments, he had the horses calmed down. Turning, he looked for Buddy, but the dog wasn't there.

He twisted, and then shook his head, a wry smile on his face. Buddy was getting all the attention he wanted from the girl. She'd looped her still bound arms over Buddy's head, her face buried in the dog's fur.

ELLY CREPT onto the other bench seat in the cabin and peered through the smoked glass. A man burst into sight and raced onto the dock. He wasn't heading right towards them, but towards a smaller boat docked a few slips down and on the other side of the pier. The pounding of his feet shook the whole dock, and she could feel the vibration transmitted through the hull where the boat was tied off.

When the man scrambled into the boat, and she cringed at the fear twisting his face. He kept shooting looks in the direction from which he'd just come. Who was he running from? And why was he so afraid?

A few seconds later, two men emerged from behind a yacht club and strolled onto the pier. They laughed and shared a bottle of vodka.

"Tony! Come on, man. We have a lot more booze." The men snorted with laughter, bumping into each other, obviously sharing what they thought was a hilarious joke. One guy raised the bottle and waved it around. "We got all the booze in the world!" He tilted the bottle, guzzling it before the other snatched it from him, upending it in his own mouth.

Tony ignored them, his hands darting out, probably flipping switches she couldn't see. Elly didn't know if it was his boat or if he was trying to do what they had done. The men got closer, trapping him in the boat as they stood on the pier, swapping the bottle back and forth.

"What's the matter, Tony? You act like you don't want us around?" The jovial tone was gone.

"Look, I don't want no trouble. Just let me get the boat started and we can go for a cruise on the lake, okay? That'll be fun, won't it, Kevin?" Tony pleaded as he moved to shut the glass window between the front and the back as if the tiny barrier could protect him.

Kevin jumped into the front of the boat. "You think we got it, don't you? But we don't." Then his threatening manner slipped as he broke into a fit of giggles. "At least, I don't think we do. What do you think, Dante?"

The other guy didn't answer. He stared at Tony then looked at Kevin, his expression confused. Without a word, he collapsed and fell into the lake.

Tony pressed back into the boat, trying to put as much distance between himself and the remaining man.

Kevin broke into another fit of giggles and Elly shuddered. She longed to help Tony, but she didn't know what they could do.

Jake slipped the gun from the back of his waistband, and Elly whispered, "What are you doing?" She'd forgotten he had the gun.

Jake edged off the seat. "I'm going out there and shooting that guy—Kevin."

"What? You can't do that. He's clearly infected with the virus."

"Yeah, I know and I'd just be putting him out of his misery and maybe saving Tony before he gets infected too." Jake easygoing demeanor was gone.

Elly wanted to help too, but it was too risky. "You can't. You could catch it from him."

"Not if I shoot him from here."

Elly narrowed her eyes. "Are you some kind of marksman, because I don't think it's going to be easy to hit a target a hundred feet away while you're both on rocking boats."

"But we can't just let that guy die. I don't think Tony has it yet. He seemed too scared." His head dropped for a second. "Too many have already died. We got to save whoever we can." It was a solemn pronouncement coming from a teenager, but the circumstances forced early maturation.

She sighed. "I agree." She peeked through the window again. For the time being, Kevin seemed to be relaxing at one end of the small speedboat while Tony was at the tip of the boat leaning back over the water and appeared ready to jump in the lake. The water was still pretty cold, but it was the least of his problems. It would solve Tony's problem, but it would still leave Kevin too close for comfort. What if he started exploring all the boats? He was mere feet away. All it would take was one of them to sneeze for him to hear them. Then what? It was better to be proactive.

"I've got an idea…what if I distract him? He might follow me and then you could sneak up and shoot him from behind." She couldn't believe she was advocating cold-blooded murder, but Kevin was sick, and he'd die anyway. They were just going to make sure he didn't infect anyone else before he succumbed to the disease.

Jake nodded. "Yeah, okay."

"Wait…have you ever used that before?" She gestured to the gun, concerned at the way he handled it. He didn't seem comfortable at all.

At first, Jake put up an air of confidence, but as she stared at him, her arms crossed, his shoulders sagged. "I never fired a gun before in my life." He gave a short, wry laugh. "I only found this piece this morning." His head shot up when Elly, who had been ready to examine the gun, snatched her hand back. "Don't worry— I wiped it down real good, so it shouldn't be contaminated or anything. And it's loaded. I know that much. I'm awesome at shooting in video games, but, yeah, never shot anything more than a water pistol."

Elly reached again. "I know how to use it. I go to the firing range all the time back home."

After a brief hesitation, he handed over the gun.

The first thing she did was make sure the safety was engaged. She didn't want to shoot herself as she climbed out of the boat. "Come on. You get to be the diversion now."

Jake nodded. "Yeah. Okay."

They created a brief plan. She would wait in the cabin until the man followed Jake—if he did. That was the tricky part. She gave him the bottle of scotch as bait. "Here, we know he likes booze. Just don't let him have it if you can help it. Oh, and make sure you're not standing right behind him. Get off to the side so I have a clear shot."

As quietly as possible, Jake exited the cabin, leaving the door open only an inch so she could get out quickly, and he leaped lightly onto the dock. Already, she was glad he was the bait because there was no way she was that agile.

Jake took a few steps towards Kevin, pretending to stagger. "Hey, dude! Look! I have this bottle of primo booze!"

Elly leaned over the bench seat and watched through the window.

Kevin lounged in the front of the boat while Tony sat on the edge as far away as he could without falling in the lake. His head lolled towards Jake. Then he sat up, a grin splitting his face.

"Whaddya got there? Whiskey?"

Jake shook his head. "Nope. Scotch. Top shelf stuff."

"Well now," Kevin tossed the now empty vodka bottle into the water and staggered to his feet. On his first attempt to step out of the boat, he almost fell into the harbor, and Elly wished he would. "I'm up for scotch...what about you, Tony?"

Tony shook his head, but he kept a wary eye on both Jake and Kevin.

Kevin made it onto the dock, swaying for a few seconds.

Then Jake laughed. "You gotta catch me first!" He took off down the pier towards shore.

The second Kevin passed their boat, Elly bolted from the cabin and climbed up onto the pier. She banged her shin on the edge of the pier but ignored the pain as she ran behind Kevin. She hoped Jake didn't run too far. She wasn't sure she could keep up with him. Luckily, Kevin couldn't keep up with him either, and as soon as he reached the shore, he stopped and bent, his hands on his knees.

"Wait up, kid!"

Elly stopped about fifteen feet from him, released the safety, and raised the gun. Jake had moved to the side, out of the line of fire. "Hey!"

Kevin straightened and turned at the sound of her voice. He smirked. "Well, hello there!"

He didn't seem to notice the gun, and Elly tried to pull the trigger but froze. She took three steps back. Maybe she could get him to leave. "Go away! Or I'll shoot!"

"I don't think so. Not now when things just got interesting." He leered at her.

"Shoot him, Elly!" Jake danced on the balls of his feet in her periphery. She wanted to shoot but hadn't counted on how hard it was to pull the trigger when the gun was aimed at another person. If he was attacking her, she knew she could, but this guy made no move towards her, probably because he was still out of breath.

She drew a deep breath and steadied her aim. "I'm sorry." She pulled the trigger.

Kevin dropped in a boneless heap. There was no look of surprise or any last words. Just one second, he was leering, the next, he was on the ground.

"Great shot, Elly!" Jake skirted around Kevin.

Elly reengaged the safety and lowered the gun. She felt sick, and her hands shook. What if he was still alive? Oh God. There was no way she was going to be able to finish him off if he was still alive. "Is...is he dead? We should make sure." Her voice sounded funny in her ears.

"I'm pretty sure. His eyes are open, and he's not moving or blinking." He stepped to Elly's side. "I don't want to get too close to him to check, but you hit him right in the chest."

She handed him the gun and, numb, headed back to the boat.

Tony had moved to the front of his boat and was standing on the seat, and leaning forward.

Elly nodded to him. "You're safe now."

Tony nodded. "Thank you." But then he eyed Jake. "What about him?"

Jake grinned. "I was just pretending to lure him away from you. We saw what was happening and decided we had to help."

"Not we...you. You were the one. I was ready to just lay low."

Jake's grin faltered. "Are you mad at me?"

Startled, Elly turned to him. "Mad at you? No! I was just giving you credit for wanting to help this guy. You're a good kid." She turned to Tony. "You should be thanking Jake. He's the one that risked his life to draw that guy away."

The wariness eased. "I owe you one, Jake." Then he looked at Elly. "And I owe you one too." His voice rose at the end, questioning.

"Elly. My name is Elly."

"Thanks, Elly." Then he tilted his head at the boat Elly and Jake had claimed. "Nice boat. All I have is this one, but I'm hoping I can take it out and maybe find an abandoned dock. Thought I'd try the North Shore."

Jake swept his arm out. "Dude, you have your pick of boats. Well, almost. Check them out. I bet you can find something more suited to living in. That's what we did. The keys were just sitting there."

"You're stealing a boat."

Elly dipped her head as her cheeks burned but Jake laughed. "Really? What are the chances that the owner is still alive? He's not here now, is he? And if he or she comes looking for their boat, they can just pick one of the others instead."

"True." Tony looked at some of the nearest vessels, his expression speculative.

"Oh, but we already checked most of the boats here, but this is the first pier we tried. I'll bet you find a good boat on the next one over."

"Thanks. I guess I owe you again." Tony stood with his hands shoved in his pockets. "Are you just planning on sticking around here? Things might get dicey." He tipped his head toward the bodies. "Those guys were my buddies at the fire station." His voice broke, and he paused before clearing his throat. "We were the last three. I don't think I caught anything, but I don't want to take a chance on contaminating either of you." He looked out over the city, took a deep breath, then met Elly's eyes. "Will you promise me that if you see me acting like those guys that you'll shoot me, too?"

Stunned, Elly could only nod. "But we're leaving tomorrow. I hope you're okay. I'd invite you along, being as this is pretty much the end of the world, but it's not my place..."

Tony waved away her offer. "That's okay. I want to stick around. I'm hoping I'll find some more people alive. With any luck, someone I know."

The conversation had given Elly a chance to bring her emotions under control, but her hands still shook as she entered the cabin of the boat and slumped back against the window.

Next thing she knew, Jake was handing her a shot glass brimming with scotch. "Here you go. I thought you could use one."

Elly took the shot. "Thanks." She downed it in one gulp.

Chapter Twenty-Two

Hunter checked the horses to make sure they hadn't hurt themselves in their panic. Both looked okay, just drenched in sweat. Murmuring assurances, he untied them and led them over to where the girl still hugged Buddy, only now she watched him over the top of the dog's head. Her hair, dirty blonde, hung over her eyes with leaves and twigs matted in the mess. One eye was blackened with a raw scrape beneath, while her bottom lip sported a split on one side. He guessed her to be about his age.

"Hi. I'm Hunter." He started to put his hand out, but not only were her hands still bound at the wrist with her arms wrapped around Buddy's neck, but the customary greeting wasn't a good idea these days. He hadn't spoken to anyone in about a week, and the last time he had, the world had yet to completely collapse. He was hungry for conversation. "Are you okay?"

She nodded, not meeting his gaze. Struggling to her feet, she released Buddy from her hug but still stroked his head. Buddy's tongue lolled as he stared at Hunter, his tail wagging.

When the girl didn't speak, Hunter asked, "What's your name?"

"Why?" She finally met his eyes, hers showing a wary defiance.

Taken aback at the question and the hostility, he shrugged. "Uh, because calling someone *'hey you'* gets awkward real fast." He cocked his head to the side, stroking his chin as if thinking hard. "My other option is choosing a name for you."

Her eyes narrowed, but she still didn't give up her name.

Hunter threw his hands up. "Fine. I'll call you Gertrude."

The girl's nose wrinkled even as the corners of her mouth turned up. "Eww! No way."

He hid a smile. "Sorry, but I think you happen to look like a Gertrude, and I'm getting good at this naming thing." He pointed to Buddy. "I named him Buddy and he seems to like it." He turned to the horses. "And this big guy here now goes by Red."

She studied the horses for a moment, then tipped her chin at the mare. "What's that one's name?"

"Oh...well, I just think of her as *the mare*. I was stumped. What can I say? I'm new to this naming game." As he'd hoped, she was losing some of her wariness.

She lifted an eyebrow at him and gave a slight roll of her eyes. "She's beautiful. I'd call her Princess." The hostility was gone and in its place was a note of wistfulness as she looked at the mare.

Hunter didn't know if he could ride a horse named Princess but if naming her that would make the girl happy, he'd do it. He nodded. "Great. Then that's her name from now on."

Her eyes flew to his. "Really?"

"Sure. Why not?" He tugged on Princess's rope. "Do you want to pet her?" He was keenly aware that her coming close would put him at risk if she had the virus, but so far, she had just seemed like a normal, scared girl.

She nodded, her eyes lighting. As she reached for the horse, Hunter saw the ropes around her wrists, and without thinking, withdrew the knife in his belt.

She recoiled with a strangled cry, tripping over Buddy, and landed on her side. The gun she'd taken from the gunman clattered across the pavement, sliding several feet in front of her, literally at Hunter's feet. Her eyes flew to it, and then to his face. Seeing her fear, he used his toe to slid the weapon over to her, then turned his attention to the horses—praying she didn't put a bullet in his back.

The horses, still skittish, pawed the ground, snorted and tried to retreat. It took him a few seconds to calm them again before he could turn to the girl. She'd turned to sit, scooting even farther away from him. "I am so sorry. I was only going to cut your bindings. I should have asked you first."

Her breathing ragged, she clenched the gun in her hands, but he was thankful that she kept it pointed down. He held the knife, holding it like one would to cut a piece of meat, not to stab anyone. He raised his eyebrows, asking permission.

She studied his face for a long moment, then extended her hands to him.

He sawed through the thick bindings, his jaw clenching when he noted the raw skin beneath. She had to let go of the gun with one hand as the rope parted and he could have taken the weapon from her then if he'd wanted. He hoped she realized that. Then again, she could have shot him at any time since she had acquired the gun, but hadn't.

As the bindings fell away, she snatched her hands away, rubbing her wrists. Seconds later, she scrambled to her feet.

Hunter sheathed the knife, and turned to the dead men and choked down the bile in the back of his throat. He'd always loved action movies with plenty of shootings, but facing real-life results of such a scene didn't give him a thrill. It sickened him.

He needed his arrows back though, and didn't know if he had the stomach to remove them from the bodies. Circling the guy Gertrude had shot, he reached down and tugged the arrow. It was more diffi-cult to remove than he anticipated. He cringed when it made a squelching sound and released the arrow. He'd make do with what he had.

Gertrude strode over, reached down, yanked the arrow free, wiped it on the thigh of the dead man, and handed it to Hunter. "Here. It's not super clean, but I don't think any of them had the virus —they were just mean."

Hunter nodded and slid the arrow back into the quiver, making a mental note to wipe it with bleach when he got a chance.

She moved to the first man Hunter had shot and put a foot on his chest, tearing out that arrow, too. She cast about for a place to wipe it, finally settling on the lower leg of the man. She extended it to Hunter. "Sophie."

He took it with a thank you on the tip of his tongue but did a double take when it registered what she'd said. "Excuse me?"

"Sophie. That's my name."

Her eyes were blue. Dark blue. He didn't know why he noticed that now, maybe because they fit the name. "I guess that's a little better than Gertrude."

"Just a little?" Her voice held a hint of amusement.

Hunter shrugged, glancing over his shoulder as he secured the bow to the saddle. "I'm heading to Green Bay. If you want to come with me, you can." He hadn't even thought about the idea until the words flew out of his mouth. He was almost as surprised as she appeared.

"Green Bay...in Wisconsin?"

Was there another one? He didn't say that, but his look must have conveyed the feeling because she made a face at him. Hunter nodded. "Yeah, that one. My dad was heading there. Not the city, but the actual bay. He owns a little island in it with cabins and stuff. He thought it would be a safe place to avoid the virus."

Sophie glanced at the dead men with pure loathing in her eyes, but she let out a deep breath. "I guess. I don't have anywhere else to go." Tears welled before she bent her head. "My family all died."

"I'm sorry."

She scuffed a high-topped rainbow colored sneaker along the blacktop and shrugged. "They're probably the lucky ones."

ELLY DOZED IN THE SEAT, listening to the splash of the water, the hum of the engine, and music Jake played through an mp3 player connected via a Bluetooth. It was strange that cellphones were no longer usable, electricity was gone, but Bluetooth still worked as long as the player got charged up via the boat battery.

The sun warmed her, and it didn't take much to pretend this was a pleasure cruise. Even the scent of the sunscreen she'd found in a drawer inside the cabin added to the illusion.

"We're going to need more gas soon."

She opened her eyes and sat up. "What? So soon?" The tank had been full when they'd left after Jake had siphoned several gallons from neighboring boats and, topped off their boat.

"This is one thirsty baby." Jake patted the helm and grinned at her. They had abandoned the masks, in her case, the bandana in his, as soon as they'd left the harbor, not even wearing them around their necks anymore.

"How far do we have to go?" She stood, and shading her eyes with her hand, scanned the shore on her left. They were out a good mile or so to avoid any shallows, but still close enough to head for shore if they had to. So far, they hadn't seen any other boats, but that didn't mean they wouldn't.

"Oh, we still have a long ways to go. We're not even to the border between Illinois and Wisconsin yet. But there are several of harbors coming up. We can tie up at one and see about getting more gas."

"Damn. I hate going anywhere there might be people."

Jake shrugged. "We can try some private homes. There are mansions with slips on the lake. We could go in closer and see if we can find gas there, but that means we'll use more gas as we follow the shoreline. We won't be going in a straight line."

She sighed. "Yeah. I guess that's not smart, especially since the chances of finding a boat all gassed up is slim compared to finding one in a harbor full of boats."

Jake pointed to smoke stacks rising in the distance. "I think that's Waukegan. They have a pretty big harbor. We could try there, or keep going. We could probably make..." he traced a line on a map he'd taped to the side of the windshield, "...Winthrop Harbor, but we'll be running a risk of running out by then."

"That wouldn't be good. It's not like we can just call up the Coast Guard."

Jake glanced at her, frowning. "I tried the radio a little bit ago when you were sleeping. I hoped somebody might be out there, but nobody answered. I didn't even hear any chatter."

She wished she hadn't made the comment about the Coast Guard. References like that weren't necessary and just reminded them of the horror of the last week. She almost wished she could forget her past life. It wouldn't be so painful then. There would be nothing to miss.

"Well, we already saw one survivor, so I'm sure there are others.

And there's you and me. We made it. If we did, others did too. Things won't ever be the same, but there's a lot left that we can work with."

He gave her a skeptical look. "You think so? A lot of people died. You saw all the bodies too."

She crossed her arms and watched the smoke stacks get larger as they neared them. "Yes, I saw the bodies, but most things will work if they have power."

He snorted. "Yeah, but what are the chances that the people left alive know how to run a power plant? Or can mine coal? What about the power lines? A few good storms snapping lines with nobody to fix them is going to add up."

Elly hadn't even thought about the infrastructure required and felt chagrined that this teen had thought of it first. "I guess it'll take a lot of work, but it'll happen. People like you will make it happen." That was one thing she was sure of.

"People like me?"

"Most of those who will have survived will be resourceful and smart. And you'll have a head start since you don't have to imagine these things. You just have to get them working again."

Jake's gaze drifted to the horizon. "I'd work on electricity first. Maybe get some solar panels. Then try to get some kind of internet going again so people can find each other. Communication is going to be key."

"See? You're already thinking like a visionary." She was only half-joking.

He gave her a sheepish grin, obviously pleased at her comment. Then he lifted one shoulder. "I'm no visionary. I'm just not sure how I'll survive long-term without my cellphone. I'm mean, I'm pretty sure I'm rocking the pirate look, and I can't even post a selfie. *Priorities.*"

She laughed, shaking her head, and pointed. "Is that the opening to the harbor up there?" It was still a good distance away, and she wasn't sure if it was a harbor or something else. She wished she had binoculars.

Jake consulted the map. "Yeah. I think so. I'm hoping we can make it to Milwaukee or just north of there if we can fill up here."

"Now I know why I never had a boat—I couldn't afford one!" Elly shook her head as she circled behind Jake and peered at the map. She tapped it. "I hope we can get enough fuel here, but if not, do you think we can make it to Winthrop Harbor?"

Jake glanced at the gas gauge. "Probably. It can be our back-up."

"Sounds good. Besides, look at all those boats. Some of them must have enough gas to siphon."

Jake turned the boat slightly so it was heading closer to shore. "I don't know this area at all. I know the coast near my dad's house in Florida, but this is totally different."

Elly tensed as they entered with the engine as low as possible. If anyone was around, they didn't want to attract their attention.

Jake pointed to an empty slip not too close to shore. They'd decided to try to stay as close to open water as they could.

Elly nodded and readied the tie rope. Jake cut the engine as soon as they were near enough, letting their momentum carry them the rest of the way. Elly caught a post on the pier, and looped the rope over, making a knot she could undo quickly if she had to.

Using gestures only, they agreed on a boat to check first. It was bigger than theirs, and Jake had two five gallon gas cans, and Elly had two more. They would have to fill them several times to get to Milwaukee. It wasn't going to be a quick job.

"How are you going to know if it's diesel or gasoline?" Elly whispered.

"The opening for the tank should be a little different—and smell." Jake unscrewed the cap for the boat, inserted the hose he'd used back in Chicago, and took a deep breath, exhaled, and then put the hose in his mouth, his cheeks drawing in as he sucked in. He suddenly pulled his mouth away, spitting and the acrid scent of gasoline filled the air.

Elly grabbed the hose from him and shoved it in one of the cans she held. When it was full, she passed it to Jake. They were able to get ten gallons from the boat before the stream of gasoline turned to a trickle.

It took them almost two hours to get enough gas to fill up the tank, and both of them felt a little sick from the fumes, and in Jake's case, from probably swallowing trace amounts. After the first time, Elly ran back to their boat and retrieved a water bottle for Jake so he could rinse his mouth after siphoning. She was kicking herself for not bringing it along to begin with. She hoped he didn't suffer any ill effects. She had tried to take over for him, but he insisted on doing it and pointed out that his germs were already all over the end of the hose.

"We did it! It wasn't as hard as I expected." Jake put the boat in reverse and left the dock, heading back out to open water. About half way to the opening, he blanched, leaned over the side of the boat and puked.

Elly jumped to his side, taking over the wheel and the stick. "Are you okay?"

Jake vomited one more time, then coughed, and spit into the water. "Yeah." He didn't sound fine, but after a few more coughs, he said, "That was nasty." He grabbed a water bottle and rinsed his mouth, shaking his head and shuddering. "Ugh. Whew."

"You're sure you're okay?"

Jake took a long swallow of the water, then cocked his head with a grin. "What would you do if I wasn't? Call nine-one-one?"

She returned his smile. "Point taken. You want me to drive this thing for a while? I think I have the hang of it."

"Sure. Just head north." He pointed as he sat on the back seat, lifting his feet to rest on the seat opposite him, his ankles crossed. "I'm going to take a little nap." His eyes were already closed, but then he opened one. "Just do me a favor, okay? Don't light a match anywhere near me for a while."

SOPHIE HAD NEVER RIDDEN BEFORE, but Hunter thought she had done well so far. He had given her the mare, or rather, Princess, while he now rode Red. The exercise had calmed the big horse down, and he was much easier to deal with now than he had been at the farm where Hunter had found him.

Hunter and Sophie had taken all of the supplies the men had been carrying. Some of it was too bulky, but they had packs of meals ready to eat, dried beef, and dried fruit. Those would come in handy to munch on while traveling. It had taken some repacking to get as much as they could on the horses and Sophie wore a pack on her back too. They also both now had handguns and enough ammo to protect them all the way to the island.

After leaving the gas station yesterday, they had ridden a few miles before finding an empty house. It appeared as if it had been abandoned long before the virus hit so there were no supplies, but it was also less risky. The chance of the house being contaminated was low, and Hunter looked forward to sleeping under a roof. They had enough supplies anyway. In fact, Hunter worried the horses were carrying too much, but they seemed to be doing okay.

After settling the horses in the fenced backyard, with the side door to the detached garage left open in case the horses wanted to seek shelter of their own, Hunter went into the house. Something smelled great.

"I heated up some beans and made biscuits." She jabbed a thumb over her shoulder. "There's an old grill out there, and I found almost a full bag of charcoal in the shed on the side of the house."

Hunter looked where she had laid a piece of newspaper on the counter and set the biscuits to cool. They were lumpy, scorched, and absolutely beautiful. In awe of Sophie, he turned to her. "We had the ingredients for biscuits?" He never would have thought to make any. Didn't even know he could.

"Yeah. You had flour and salt, while I had a can of shortening—or, well the guys did."

"That's all you need?"

She laughed. "Sure. And some water. I would have rather had buttermilk and a biscuit cutter, but I just patted them out and used that cast iron pan. I baked them on the grill so they might be cooked a little unevenly."

Hunter picked up one of the biscuits, inhaling the aroma as he closed his eyes. "They smell amazing." He was about to take a bite when Sophie put her hand over his, stopping him.

"Wait. I have more." She produced a small jar of strawberry jam. It was a name brand. His favorite. "Ta-da!"

"Here. We don't have a butter knife, but a spoon will work."

She had spooned beans onto the only two plates he owned, and when he poked around in the beans, he discovered some of the dried meat. It made the beans more filling and added a smoky flavor. It reminded him of pork and beans.

"I fed Buddy while everything was heating."

Hunter glanced at Buddy, who lay stretched out on the floor, his head on his paws as he watched them. His tail thumped on the wooden floor when he saw Hunter looking at him. "I wondered where he went. He probably heard his food hit his dish."

There wasn't much dog food left. He'd only brought a small bag, trying to save weight. He worried the canned beef stew and dried beef might be too salty for the dog, but he'd figure something out. Maybe he could catch the dog some fish or shoot a rabbit, now that he had a gun.

He ate four of the ten biscuits and felt guilty because she only had two, saying she'd save the rest for breakfast in the morning. He should have given her one of his so it would be even, but she waved off that suggestion. "I'm full. Those guys weren't too good about sharing their food with me."

"All the more reason to give you one of mine. It's not like you have any extra weight to lose." He eyed her slim figure, then felt his cheeks heat when she caught him.

While she had splashed her face with water and washed her hands, her clothes were still dirty and her hair matted.

"How much water do we have?"

Hunter thought about it. "I have a couple of two-liter bottles outside, and I think there was still one in your stuff. Plus, about a half-dozen smaller bottles. Why?"

"I would love to heat up some of it and wash. I feel so dirty." She shuddered, and he had a feeling she meant more than just physically dirty.

"Yeah. Go ahead. I'll run out and get two of the big bottles. I was looking on a map, and there are several lakes and streams coming up. Refilling shouldn't be a problem." He left and returned to the house. He found her on the far side of the house, outside beside the grill. She had every pot and pan he had, cleaned and ready to be filled.

She smiled. "Thanks. One more thing...and I hate to ask, but I don't suppose you have any clean t-shirts I could borrow, do you? And maybe a towel, or even just an old rag I can use to dry off?"

"Yeah, hold on, I have other stuff, too. Be right back." He dashed out to the garage again and dug through his supplies. He'd bought extra toothbrushes, deodorants, and other items from the dollar bins at the store. He found a toothbrush, a stick of deodorant—it was guy-scented, but he didn't think she'd mind—and a trial-sized shampoo plus conditioner.

He wasn't sure if he had an extra towel because he couldn't remember what he'd taken from the backseat of his car, but he found one of his old towels from college in the bottom of one saddle bag. He raised it to his nose. It didn't smell too funky, so he set it beside the other supplies.

As he searched through his bags for a t-shirt, he looked down at himself. His own shirt was dirty and stained. He hadn't bothered to change it in days. He was sure he wasn't all that fresh smelling either. Why bother with deodorant when there was nobody around to smell you? He grabbed a couple of his T-shirts. They were clean. Probably. He knew none of his jeans would fit her, but he had an old pair of sweatpants. They had a drawstring, and she could probably get them to fit that way. He rolled everything for her up in the towel, keeping one of the shirts out for himself.

When he returned, she had cleaned the plates and was stoking the grill with a few more briquettes of charcoal. He handed her the towel. "I left the rest of the things inside. I had an extra toothbrush—new—and just other stuff you might want to use inside." He backed away, rubbing his hands on his jeans as she used the towel to remove one pan from the grill. "I was going to wash up out here, but the mosquitoes are getting bad."

The house had four rooms, but no doors on any of them and the bathroom was disgusting, as was the kitchen. Rodent droppings and dead bugs covered the floors and counters. The only decent room was the living room. The hardwood floor, while dusty and scattered with paper, was relatively clean. It was apparent the rodents had left it alone with nothing to eat and nowhere to nest. When Sophie carried the water into the living room, Hunter headed out the back door to give her some privacy. "I'll make sure the horses are okay and take a look around before it gets dark."

He wandered out into the yard to see if the horses needed

anything. He'd filled the one bucket he'd brought with water for them. The horses were grazing and content. The grass was long, and they had plenty to eat. Hunter gathered the two liter bottles he'd used to fill the bucket and returned them to the garage to take with them tomorrow. Behind the yard, the ground sloped up to a hill so he climbed it. The sun was setting, but it was still light enough to see the area.

When he reached the top, he looked east. It was more of the same. Lots of farmland, but it seemed like it was becoming a bit woodier. They had traveled due east, following roads for the most part. The wrecks he'd found on the big highways were fewer on the side roads, and he thought most of them he could navigate around if he had to, but getting across the river by car would probably be impossible on the bridges. He was pretty sure they would have been packed with vehicles—even worse than the regular highways.

For now, they'd stick with the horses, cross the river, and see about switching to a car, or better yet, a truck. There had to be some horse trailers they could find. He didn't want to abandon Red or Princess. He had never pulled a horse trailer before, or loaded horses, but they could figure that out. Otherwise, he'd have to turn them loose, and he worried about them surviving. Winter would be harsh, and these horses weren't used to being on their own. He knew some horses would survive and become wild, but others would starve or freeze, and the thought of that happening to either of the horses worried him. He didn't know what he'd do with them on the island, but that was also a problem for another day.

When he felt enough time had passed, he went back into the house, knocking on the door as he did. "Am I good to come in?"

"Yeah, all clear."

Hunter entered the living room and stopped dead in his tracks. Sophie sat cross-legged on the floor wearing his sweats and t-shirt that had some comic book hero on the front, dragging his brush through her wet hair. Her face, marred only by a few scratches and a fading bruise on her cheek, shone clean and fresh. Her hair hung wet, but brushed off her face, falling on either side. Even wet, it was lighter than he expected. It felt as if his tongue knotted as he gaped. She was beautiful.

When she looked up at him, she got a tiny crease in her brow. "What's wrong?"

Trying to shake out the knot, he managed, "Nothing. It's just…you look…different." He wanted to say gorgeous, beautiful, or fantastic but didn't want to freak her out. She'd hinted at how the men had treated her and had been skittish anytime he came too close. She bit her lip, her expression unsure so he clarified, "You look nice. And the bruise around your eye looks like it's fading."

Her expression relaxed, and she smiled at him. "Thanks for letting me use all of this." Sophie waved at the bottle of shampoo, and other personal items. She ran her tongue over her teeth. "Especially the toothbrush. My teeth felt so fuzzy, I couldn't stand it anymore."

"Yeah, you're welcome."

She pointed with the brush towards the side of the house. "I left some clean water for you if you want to wash up. It's still on the grill staying warm."

"Thanks. I do."

After Hunter had cleaned up and returned to the living room, he dropped to sit cross-legged on his sleeping bag she must have unrolled for him. He stretched. "That did feel great. Thanks for heating the water and for getting my bag out."

"It's the least I could do." She eyed him, her mouth quirking.

"What?"

"You look…different…too." Then she averted her eyes and lay with her head on her arm and pulled her blanket up. "Goodnight."

Chapter Twenty-Three

Elly gripped the wheel, her knuckles white as the waves hammered the boat. "*Jake!*"

About a half-hour ago, she'd sent Jake down into the cabin to take a break from the sun and get a nap. The kid had been at the helm all morning, except for a brief respite when they had to refuel around Milwaukee, and that couldn't be considered a true break. Their gas siphoning skills were improving so it hadn't taken as long as it had, but it still wasn't a quick fill-up.

They had spent the evening before moored in Kenosha harbor and had found some unopened bags of chips, a box of energy bars, and a six pack of beer in nearby boats, along with a good, sharp, fillet knife. Better still, they caught two nice-sized walleyes and fried them up on the stove in the cabin, so food hadn't been an issue and water was all around them. Before docking, they had been far enough in the lake that Elly felt it was safe to drink the water with just a t-shirt to filter it.

The main worry was running out of fuel. Looking on the map, there would be a stretch where it might be more difficult to find a harbor. They'd have to keep their eyes peeled. There was always the chance of a private dock with a boat already fueled up.

Driving the boat wasn't difficult, especially in calm waters, and Elly had enjoyed it once Jake had given her a quick rundown of how this boat operated. She maintained an even speed and kept her eye on fuel gauges, but also on the engine temperature. It had run a little hot for a while, and neither of them knew why. However, it had cooled off now, and the boat skimmed along the lake.

Sitting behind the wheel cruising the lake took her back to her college days and boating in the Gulf. It looked different up here—the water was a deeper blue, and colder. A lot colder, but the air was warm and the motion of the boat over the waves the same. Jake had assured her the water warmed by the end of the summer

She lifted her face to the sun, basking in the warmth, feeling almost guilty about the pleasure the simple act gave her. She was alive and healthy and despite her sorrow about the deaths of so many, she couldn't help feeling thankful that she was still alive.

A shiver shook her when the warm breeze turned into a cool wind. She turned around, scanned the sky and swore. The sun, so warm and gentle a moment before, dimmed when an ominous black thunderhead swallowed it.

Their general direction was northwest as she followed the shoreline but kept about a mile out to avoid any shoals. The storm bored down on them from the southwest. It had come out of nowhere, and it came fast.

A blast of wind pitched the boat to the right. Elly put a hand out, catching the rail circling the boat as the craft then rocked to the left. It felt as if the lake had become alive and reached up to slam against the hull and toss waves over the bow. Drenched, and shivering, Elly tried to keep the boat from capsizing.

The door to the cabin flew open, and Jake paused, his eyes widening at the roiling water. "What the hell?" He grabbed the wheel, and Elly was happy to relinquish it.

Jake scanned the shore as he turned the wheel to the left. "We're going in. Look for a place we can tie up and ride out the storm!"

He angled the boat towards shore as Elly clung to the rail and sought a place they could seek protection. They had already passed Milwaukee earlier in the morning and for the last hour, the western shore had been short rocky beaches and trees. Not a single dock in sight.

A bolt of lightning crackled through the air, only a second ahead of the booming thunder. Elly jumped and turned to Jake. "Go faster!"

"I've got it full throttle now. We're burning through our gas like crazy!"

When one wave threatened to send her over the side as the boat pitched, she ducked into the cabin and grabbed a life jacket for each of them. She clipped hers on and then helped Jake with his, clipping it for him so he could keep both hands on the wheel.

She returned to the side of the boat, searching the shore. Rain pelted them, coming down in sheets and she swiped at her eyes. For a minute, she wasn't sure if what she saw was just white caps on the water, but after another swipe at her eyes, she made out a breakwall not far ahead. Beyond it, sailboat masts tipped in the gale, bobbing from the massive waves.

"There! A harbor!" She didn't know what harbor it was, but it didn't matter. Any harbor in a storm, wasn't that the saying?

"I see it!" Jake struggled to keep the boat on course. "The waves keep trying to push us the other way!"

Elly turned to see if he needed help when the boat pitched to the left then dived into a swell. Her hand slipped off the wet railing, her head cracking on something on the way down. Light burst in her vison, then darkness engulfed her.

HUNTER DREW BACK on the reins at the top of a hill, pulling Red to a halt.

Sophie and Princess stopped beside him. "What's wrong?"

"Nothing. I'm just trying to decide where to cross." He reached into the bag he'd attached to the saddle horn and pulled out a bottle of water, tilting it. It tasted warm and flat. A month ago, he would have spit it out, but today, he just made a face and swallowed it. The water had come from a water barrel they'd found on the side of a farmhouse. He'd added purification tablets, but it still tasted funky. He hoped it didn't make him sick, but there hadn't been another option. The streams they'd crossed had been murky and smelled bad. They had tried the taps in a few homes where the occupants were deceased, but with no electricity, water didn't pump. After they had left the third home, they found the rain barrel, but later, Hunter remembered that there might still be clean water in the hot water tanks of a lot of homes, stored before the electricity cut off.

Buddy and the horses didn't seem to mind drinking from the streams, but he and Sophie waited, hoping to find something better. They had enough to drink today if they were careful. He saw farm homes in the distance, but he'd wanted to make it to the river as soon as possible. He itched to get back into Wisconsin, even if the journey to find the island was far from over. Just being in his home state would be a relief. It was just wishful thinking, but he felt as if things would be better when he was on home territory even though as far as he knew, this virus had swept the whole country and beyond.

"There's the bridge right there." Sophie swept a few locks of hair out of her face and pointed. The sun highlighted the golden strands. She hadn't ever ridden a horse before two days ago, but she was doing well. Granted, Princess was an easy horse to ride, but she hadn't complained of being sore, even though Hunter knew she had to be feeling the effects of hours of riding. He was, and he at least had experience.

Red danced to the left, stomping a leg, and swishing his tail to get rid of a persistent horse fly. Hunter shooed another one circling his own head. "Yeah, I know."

He almost gave her a 'duh' look but held back. Her observation was more of a question than a statement. Instead of sarcasm, he explained his hesitation, "But look at all the cars. We'll have to pass close to some of them to get through." He sighed "There's no telling how many corpses we'll come across." After seeing so many, he should be immune to his gut-reaction of wanting to vomit every time he saw one, but he still had to avert his eyes and try not to think about the putrid state of the bodies he'd come across.

Below them stretched a long span of bridge over the Mississippi. Like he'd feared, cars jammed the bridge. They'd have to use precautions against the virus the whole crossing. He glanced north, tempted to find another less crowded bridge, but chances were, all were just as bad. It didn't make sense to add miles when the horses showed signs of fatigue. He was certain they had never been ridden so many miles a day for days on end. Just like people, horses had to work to get fit. With proper food and rest, Red and Princess would be great trail horses in a month or two, but right now, they plodded forward. It didn't make sense to add distance only to have to deal with the same problem twenty miles up the river.

In Hunter's trek across southern Minnesota, he'd given a wide berth to most of the roads, staying at least a hundred yards away. However, he had to cross some no matter what, and when he did, he couldn't believe how many cars he saw in ditches, crashed into trees, pile-ups and other cars just abandoned. The dead bodies littering the roads showed where those who had abandoned their cars had ended up. A few managed to make it into the brush and corn fields before succumbing to the disease. More than once, Buddy had given them warning of a body. His nose would hit the ground, and he'd whine. Hunter would have to call him close and make him stay near, or the dog would try to investigate the body.

One thing that struck Hunter was how many people had been on the move when the illness hit, either trying to flee to safety, as he had done, or driven by an apparently irresistible urge to be around other people. He shuddered, wondering how he'd managed to avoid catching the virus so far. He guessed he could thank his education struggles for saving him. In his determination to pass his classes, he hadn't had time to socialize for the last month. He'd also had a bad cold that had kept him in his dorm room except for classes. He wondered if some of the victims of the accidents had been healthy, but killed when a sick person crashed into them. The chances were pretty good. Or they were killed in food stampedes. He'd heard about some of them on the radio the day after he left. Everyone had tried to stock up on food, but the stores didn't have enough stocked. Thank god his dad had given him an early warning. What a shitty way to die.

Hunter pulled his face mask from the bag and realized that Sophie didn't have one. He had a few extras packed with his other gear. "Hold on." He dismounted and rummaged through his gear until he found the box of respirator masks. "Here." When she looked perplexed, he showed her how to get the bands placed on her head. "This mask will filter everything. So far, it's worked."

"I never had one of these, and I didn't get sick." Her voice emerged muffled from the mask. She slid one of the elastic bands higher on her head and squeezed the metal bridge against her nose.

"I guess you're lucky. Or maybe you're just immune. My dad said that some people have some kind of genetic mutation that resists HIV. Maybe you have something like that to resist this virus."

"Are you calling me a mutant? Like a teenage turtle?"

He shrugged. "If it means surviving this, I say turn me green, slap a shell on my back, and mutate me."

As he remounted, he heard a muffled chuckle, but she had already moved ahead of him down the hill. He took a deep breath and urged Red forward.

It hadn't rained since Hunter had left the farm, and each day had been warmer than the last. The stench of decay mixed with the smell of swamp and mud saturated the air. The mask helped a little, but he didn't have masks for the horses, and they balked at crossing the bridge.

Hunter dismounted and, ignoring the unrecognizable corpse fifteen feet away, stroked Red's neck and murmured reassurances to the animal. He hoped that if he coaxed Red forward, Princess would follow his lead, so he motioned for Sophie to remain mounted.

Buddy trotted towards the corpse and Hunter had to interrupt his soothing of Red to issue a sharp command to the dog to get away from the body. He obeyed but turned towards another victim lying half out of a car. Hunter whistled and called Buddy over. "Stay." He wondered if the dog knew how to 'heel'. It would be hard enough coaxing the horses forward without having to keep a constant eye on a curious dog.

"Hey, Buddy! Come!" Sophie held out a small piece of beef jerky. The dog darted over, and Sophie had him sit before giving him the treat.

With her distracting the dog, Hunter led Red forward, his voice low as he spoke in a soothing tone. Princess followed Red, and Hunter was relieved to see Buddy staying right beside Sophie and the horse and not darting off to investigate the bodies. Vaguely, he heard Sophie praising the dog.

"Watch out, Hunter!"

His heart thundered with an instant adrenaline surge at her warning, and he spun, keeping a tight grip on the bridle. He'd expected an attack from some unknown foe, but instead, he found a pile of corpses. A few more steps backward and he'd have tripped over them. *Ugh.* Time to get back in the saddle. Keeping up his soothing litany, he re-mounted.

Red skittered a few steps sideways before Hunter had him under control, but then he skirted the pile and continued across the bridge. The horses had no more desire to remain on the bridge than Hunter and Sophie did. Red picked up his pace on his own accord.

By the time they reached the last third of the bridge, the horse was in a near panic, his coat drenched, and Hunter had to fight to keep him to a fast walk. If there weren't so many obstacles in the way, he probably would have let the horse have its head, but cars, motorcycles, a camper, and several semi-trucks created almost a complete barricade at this end. He was glad they hadn't switched to a car because there was no way one would have made it through, but the horses had just enough room to pick their way around. Even Buddy was no longer interested in the corpses and raced ahead of them to the eastern side of the river.

Hunter turned in the saddle. "You okay?" Sophie's eyes were wide as she stared straight ahead.

She nodded but didn't speak. Princess was generally calmer than Red, but she had picked up her speed as well and snorted, tossing her head.

"Are you doing okay?" Hunter wondered if he should take Princess's reins and lead her, except he wasn't certain he could lead her while keeping Red under control as well. The last few days had improved his riding skills, but he was far from an expert horseman.

"No. I'm good. She's just a little spooked. Can you really blame her?" Sophie stroked Princess's neck. She leaned forward, her face near the horse's ear. "I don't like any of this either, girl, but we'll get through it together."

He scanned the wrecks wondering if anyone had survived, and if they had, where they had gone. Before the virus hit he'd never seen a dead person, but now he had seen enough corpses to last him the rest of his life. Even his own mother had been hidden by a closed casket, which was a good thing because he had only been a little kid. Would he have tried to wake her? His memory of what his mom looked like was hazy, and he suspected the mental image he had of her was composed of photographs he'd seen his whole life, along with a few precious videos.

He glanced at Sophie, wondering what her story was, but he hadn't broached the subject yet. He'd tried to ask her about the men who had her captive, but she ignored the question, said nature was calling, and headed behind a bush. Hunter hadn't mentioned it again.

His gaze caught on a car seat in the vehicle they were passing. The remains of a baby lay strapped into the seat. The only clue it had been a human was the tuft of blonde hair. Blood dripped down the window. At first, he thought maybe the person inside had just recently died, but then he noticed the condensation on the inside of the windows, and he knew what caused it. He swallowed hard to keep his stomach in check and averted his eyes.

It wasn't fair. What had that little baby done to deserve death when his life had barely begun? As he rode on, he imagined how the last day had played out. The parents would have strapped him or her into the seat, never aware that it would be the last time they would ever hold their child. What had the child had for a last meal? A bottle? Chicken nuggets from a drive-thru or had restaurants already closed?

His knowledge about babies could be written on a postage stamp with room left over, but he knew there would have been a last diaper change, a last time the mother had guided a little hand through a miniature sleeve, and a final time she would have tied tiny shoes onto baby feet. Or maybe the dad had done those things. He knew first-hand that dads were capable of doing all the things mothers did for their kids. That train of thought led him to his father, and his chest tightened with longing to see him again. What if he got to the island and they were all dead?

"Hey, Hunter. Hold up a second."

He twisted in the saddle, drawing Red to a halt. "Something wrong?"

"I think so. Princess is walking funny."

He observed the mare, noting she was favoring her left rear leg. Shit. They couldn't stop here for long. He'd have to look her over once they were clear of the bridge. He had one foot out of the stirrup to dismount, but then had an idea. "Here, you can ride behind me. Maybe Princess is just tired."

He took Princess's reins from Sophie and removed his foot from the stirrup so she could wedge her foot in. With a firm grip of her hand, he helped her swing up behind him. "Do you have enough room back there?" He had saddle bags, but the bow was behind the saddle, almost on Red's rump so that should be out of the way.

"Yeah, I can deal with it for a little while." She wiggled a bit.

Trying to ignore her movement as she tried to get comfortable, he handed Princess's reins to her and decided that as soon as he found a good location, they'd stop and rest. Let the horses graze and check both of them over. He worried about the cause of Princess's irregular gait

Sophie wrapped her arms around his waist, and he didn't mind that it was hot out, and she was pressed up against his back.

Chapter Twenty-Four

"I'll do it." Cole blocked Sean from leaving the kitchen. "You shouldn't have to see Trent like that, Sean. I'll go. I'll take care of…his body. Joe said he'd help me."

Trent had become silent in the middle of the night, and this morning, they opened the door of the quarantine and found his body in a puddle of blood. Jenna had to be physically restrained by Sean from going to her son's side.

The commotion had drawn Joe from his cabin, and he'd offered a couple of codeine pills left over from a dental procedure and insisted he no longer needed them. Sean had managed to get Jenna to take them, and she now slept, with Piper curled beside her.

Sean's eyes closed and his throat worked. "He's my son. I should be the one to bury him."

"I'm sorry, Sean. It's too dangerous. You've never had to handle contagious bodies before." Unfortunately, Cole had become proficient at the task in Africa.

Sean pushed at Cole's chest in an attempt to get past. "I don't give a shit if I get sick, don't you understand?"

Cole grunted as he struggled to keep his brother from getting by. "Listen to me! I get it. You don't care what happens to you now. I feel the same way, but we have to think about Piper and Jenna. What if we die? What's going to happen to them? For *any* of us to survive, we all have to do our best to stay alive—even if we don't want to."

"*What the hell do you know about how I feel?* It's not *your* son lying out there in," he made finger quotes, "'quarantine'! It's not your son's blood staining the floor and swirling down the drain!"

"You're right." Anger and his own fears about Hunter fueled Cole's strength as he shoved Sean, sending him staggering back a few steps. Cole advanced, stabbing two fingers against Sean's chest. "I know how you feel because the chances that Hunter is still alive are pretty much zero."

Cole stood nose to nose with Sean, his chest heaving as he fought to control his emotions. He was losing the fight and losing it fast. "Hunter is out there somewhere," Cole flung an arm wide, "and I don't know if he's dead or alive. *That's* how I know how it feels. I want to keep hoping, but..." He swallowed hard and retreated, allowing his brother to pass if he chose. "You still have a wife and child who need you." He drew in a deep breath and met Sean's eyes. "I don't."

Sean held Cole's gaze for a long moment before he shifted it, looking beyond Cole towards the beach. Finally, he nodded, his shoulders slumped.

"We'll have a funeral, Sean. We can do that much."

"But you said you have to burn his body." There was a hitch in Sean's voice.

"We do, but afterward, we can bury his ashes and make a marker. Joe says he can do a little bit of stone work if he has the right tools. We'll get him those tools, somehow."

Cole's heart ached for his brother, and when tears pooled in Sean's eyes, he felt helpless to comfort him. After several hard blinks and a swipe at his eyes, Sean turned and plodded back to the room he shared with Jenna. "I'm going to see how Piper and Jenna are doing."

Sighing, Cole gathered the supplies he'd need and then knocked on the door to Joe's cabin. "If you're still willing to help..."

"Of course." Joe took one step out but then reached down to lift the mask he kept around his neck up and over his nose. "Sorry. I should have put it on as soon as I saw you at the door."

"Don't bother. Just wear it when we're taking care of Trent. If you haven't shown symptoms of the disease by now, I don't think you're going to. Not unless you have a new exposure and all of us are at the same risk for that." Cole didn't think they had become contaminated this morning because he hadn't allowed anyone into the room nor to touch anything. They had all worn their masks as well.

Joe fell into step beside him as they headed for the work shed where the gardening tools were kept. "What about the exposure while we take care of your nephew?"

"I have some gear for that, and I'll be doing most of the risky stuff. What I need you to do is help me dig a pit and build a really big, hot fire and keep it going. Once we have Tre—the body burning, we can make another fire to burn all the gear that can't be decontaminated. Basically, all the paper or disposable stuff, and everything that was in the quarantine with him like blankets and pillows."

Cole handed Joe a shovel and ax and took the same for himself. He headed for the beach, intending to build the fire there because of the proximity to the quarantine, but Joe put a hand on his shoulder.

"The wind is blowing from the southwest."

Puzzled, Cole shrugged. "Yeah? So?"

"Right into the house."

Then it dawned on him what Joe was getting at. "Oh. Shit."

Sean's family didn't need to smell that. Not if they could help it. He took an abrupt left turn towards a small, rocky beach on the east side of the island and north of the house. "We'll have to move him farther, but you're right. Thanks. I don't know what I was thinking."

"It's a wonder you're able to think at all. You've done a great job keeping us all safe, Cole."

Surprised, Cole stopped and looked at Joe. The last thing he thought he'd done was keep everyone safe. Trent was dead, and it was partially his fault. "I wish I could accept that praise, but it's kind of hard when my nephew died because of my decision."

"It wasn't your fault. Nobody could have predicted that boat would come out of nowhere."

"I should have predicted it. It was my job to predict scenarios like that."

Joe gave him a skeptical look. "Well, that's neither here nor there. It was a different world then. It's nobody's fault Trent got sick. Not yours, not his, not Sean's and not even the kids who infected him. You know none of them are in their right minds when the sickness hits."

Cole shrugged but didn't reply. If it helped Sean and Jenna deal with Trent's death, he'd take all the blame.

"I'm gonna miss the kid, though. He helped me in the work shed a few times—always with masks and gloves—I wouldn't risk contaminating anyone. Anyway, bright kid."

Cole made a sound of agreement, but he was surprised at the sentiment. Joe had kept mostly to himself, but had shared what he had, and in return, Cole and the others had also shared everything. Joe had turned into an asset with plenty of mechanical knowledge. He and Sean were close to getting a windmill working. However, with Joe somewhat segregated in a modified quarantine, the rest of them didn't get too many chances to speak to him.

Cole chose a location at the edge of the grass before the beach began. It was far enough away from the house, but not too far. There was a large boulder that must have been deposited eons ago, perhaps when glaciers receded. It would probably remain in the same place for eons more. There was something comforting about that idea, and he hoped Sean and Jenna felt the same. He envisioned them sitting on the boulder to be near Trent as they gazed out over the bay.

"This is a good spot." Joe looked at Cole, his weathered face solemn. He rested his hands on the shovel, leaning on it. "His folks can come and visit him."

Cole nodded, glad for the confirmation, but his tongue felt too thick to speak. He dipped his head and used all of his strength to jam the shovel into the sandy dirt.

It didn't take long for them to dig a deep enough hole. It didn't have to be deep enough to keep animals out since they were cremating Trent, but it had to be deep enough to start a fire, place Trent on top, and add more wood on top. Cole didn't know how he was going to be able to lay his nephew in the fire.

As if reading his mind, Joe said, "You know, after we get Trent here and everything…" He cleared his throat. "After we get the fire going, I'll stay and make sure it doesn't burn out. As bad as this is, it would be worse if the job was only partly done. Do you want me to cover the hole when it's done?"

Cole swiped his forearm across his brow. He hadn't given it that much thought. The epidemiologist side of him had taken over, wanting to stem the chances of contamination from the body. He didn't know how contagious victims of the disease were but opted to assume they were at least as contagious as Ebola victims had been after death.

"I'll have to ask Sean and Jenna. I'm not sure if they want to see him that way."

Joe nodded and started chopping up a dead tree near the hole. Cole went a little deeper into the woods and found another tree that had fallen long ago. As he swung the ax and it bit into the wood, he tried not to think of Hunter. It was so hard to cling to hope after so much death.

They set the wood and doused it with some precious gasoline. Cole piled more logs next to the dirt that had come out of the hole. He walked to the water line and squatted, rinsing his hands then scooping a handful of water to splash on his face. Joe did the same, then both men stood and looked out over the sun-kissed bay.

Cole entered the women's side of the changing room which was now the store room for protective gear. He had kept several complete suits, including the respirator masks that offered even better protection than the hepa filter masks they had been using. All of it was left over from his days of battling Ebola but wished he had even more.

He had stockpiled the gear, more to placate Hunter than because he thought it would be needed. When Cole had gone to Africa, Hunter hadn't taken his absence well. He'd been caught drinking and smoking some weed at a party. When Cole left, Hunter had to stay with Sean and Jenna with Sean having to take on the role of disciplinarian. It had strained the relationship between Sean and Hunter.

When he returned from Africa, Cole had a long talk with Hunter, expressing his disappointment and it was then that his son had confessed his fears that he'd had while Cole was gone. He worried about being left alone—about being left an orphan. Even though he was almost grown by then, he confessed he still needed his dad. And there was nothing Cole could say about that because there had been a risk and Hunter's fears weren't unfounded.

That was when he decided to retire. Hunter only had a few more years at home before college and Cole didn't want to miss any more of it. Now, he was thankful for that time they'd had and could only pray that he'd have more time still.

In addition to the full suits, as a precaution Cole had bought several boxes of large lawn-sized trash bags and multiple rolls of duct tape. When the protective suits ran out, if they ever did, they could make suits out of bags and duct tape. It wasn't ideal but miles better than no protection at all. They still had plenty of masks as well since Joe had added his to the stockpile. He only had two sizes of gloves, large and medium. Piper really needed small gloves, while Jenna could make do with medium, she really should have had small gloves to prevent them from slipping off.

He had already prepared several five-gallon buckets with mixtures of bleach and water. One bucket had a top and a pump with a short hose and sprayer. They'd use that bucket for spraying the ground anywhere they had walked. Another bucket was to throw the rubber boots and the heavy rubber gloves to decontaminate. They didn't have an endless supply of them and would have to re-use them if, god forbid, they ever had to do this again.

The suits, made of plastic that was about the thickness of a tarp, would go into a trash bag Cole had rigged to stay open. There had been a wheeled trashcan cart, and he'd used the frame of it to tape two trash bags, one inside the other. That was the burn bag. Disposable inner gloves would also go in there as well as all the tape used to seal the openings around wrists, neck, and ankles.

"Here, take off your shoes and step into this." He handed Joe a bright yellow suit with a zipper down the front. "Pull it up to your waist, but don't zip it all the way yet. You'll have to put on your boots and tape around them, and it's a pain in the ass to do it with the suit already zipped."

He showed Joe how to layer the protective gear and told him how they would remove it when they were finished. "We'll have to watch each other to make sure we never touch any unprotected part of ourselves with the contaminated gear." As he emphasized his points and explained the procedure, Joe crossed his arms, his expression bordering on boredom.

"Listen, Joe, you have to know how to do this, and how to do it correctly."

"I think I can manage. I've been dressing and undressing myself for a long time."

"It sounds obvious, but people screw up all the time without thinking. Their nose itches and they reach up and swipe their gloved hand across it," Cole pantomimed the action, "and, *boom.* They've just contaminated themselves. Even when they're paying attention, they might accidentally take the gear off in the wrong order."

Joe waved his hands. "I got it. Sorry. Just seems so obvious."

"Good, because not only will I be spotting you when you remove your gear, but you'll be watching me, too. Just because I've done this many times doesn't mean I don't need a second pair of eyes. More than once, I've had that second pair of eyes catch me just before I contaminated myself." In Africa, it had often been Elly who had been his buddy when he took off the gear. He hoped she was hunkered down safe somewhere.

———————

"ELLY! WAKE UP! *PLEASE* WAKE UP!"

Water poured on Elly's face, and she coughed and rolled over. "Stop it!" When she tried to get to her hands and knees, the floor pitched, and she landed hard on her side. Disoriented, nauseated, and her head pounding, she struggled to her feet. A bolt of lightning dropped from the sky a hundred yards away, the thunder instantaneous. It all came back to her. One hand clenched around the grip rail and the other pressed to the side of her head, she moved to Jake's side.

"How close are we to land?" She had to shout to make herself heard over the sound of the waves, wind, rain, and thunder. Looking left and right, she strained to see land. Just before the storm hit, it had been just off to their left. It had looked like an easy run to get back if they needed to. But now, it was impossible for her to determine in which direction the shore lay through the torrential rain. She wasn't even sure what direction they were heading.

"The storm hit too fast! I couldn't get the boat docked anywhere. I saw a dock up ahead, but lost it in the rain and had to head back out to open water." He pushed rain out of his eyes and shook his head. "I just hope there's no land dead ahead. I can't see a thing."

"What do you want me to do?"

"We're almost out of gas."

"Did you use the reserve?" At the last harbor, they had filled two of the gas cans to have in reserve. It was something Elly never would have recommended in normal times due to the risk and when a call to the Coast Guard was an option, but now, it was insurance against being left adrift in the middle of the lake. Or like now, with no power and dangerous conditions.

"No, I haven't been able to let go of the wheel. The water's too rough."

"After the storm." She motioned towards the cans. "So they don't spill." She wanted to explain how it would be futile even if she managed to get the gas into the tank because the waves were so high that they'd just waste gas trying to maintain their position. It would be better to wait and then head for shore when the water was calm again.

Letting go of the wheel for a second, he pointed left. "*Rocks!* I need to be able to get away if we get too close."

He had a point. They'd be helpless, and the boat would be pummeled against the rocks if they didn't get away from them. She held up a finger. "One can."

Jake nodded, his expression grim.

They had used bungee cords to strap the cans down, and she was glad for that because other gear had tumbled across the boat but the cans were still where they had been secured. She fumbled for one.

It took her several tries to get the nozzle into the tank, and she spilled some, but Elly managed to empty the can.

Jake tried the engine. At first it sputtered and died, but finally, it caught. "I'm just going to keep it slow and steady until we can see better." He looked at her, his eyes moving to her temple. "Are you okay?"

She felt her head, finding a lump, but the skin didn't seem to be broken, and no blood stained her hand. "Yes. I'm fine." That was mostly true.

He tilted his head towards the seats. "Sit down and hang on tight. I think the storm is dying down."

Elly sat, her legs shaking as the effects of fear and adrenaline took over. She wanted to close her eyes, but that made the nausea worse, so she tried to focus on the horizon. After a few minutes, she saw sliver of sunshine slash across the horizon. It was the end of the storm. She breathed a sigh of relief.

The storm took another twenty minutes to dissipate.

"Elly, I hate to ask you, but could you take over for a minute?"

Elly turned to find Jake, his face ashen. She scrambled to her feet and took the wheel. "What's wrong?" The danger was over, more or less.

"I just gotta sit." He flexed his fingers, his hands shaking. "I think I lost feeling in my fingers." He laughed, but it sounded shaky. "I've never done anything like that. I thought for sure we were gonna die. And then when you fell and were out of it, I thought you were dead." He propped his elbows on his splayed knees and dug his fingers through his hair. "I was scared shitless."

"Take all the time you need. I'm fine. Why don't you go have a shot of that scotch?"

His head shot up. "Really? But I'm only seventeen."

"Oh. I guess I forgot how young you are. You didn't act like a kid, and you certainly did the job of a man. How about settling for a few cookies and some soda? I think there are still a few left."

A grin split his face. "Aw, I was hoping for the whiskey." But he went into the cabin and returned with a package of cookies and two cans of soda. "Here's to storms and sugar overload." He popped the top and tapped it to hers.

"Cheers." She took a long drink. The stuff was terrible for her, but nothing had ever tasted so good.

They each ate a few cookies and then Jake put them away. "I can take over again."

Elly shook her head. "That's okay. I'm just tooling along here. I think there's a small harbor up ahead. Do you see it?"

It took them another twenty minutes to reach the harbor, and when they did, Jake pointed to the map, now ragged but still legible. "I think this is Algoma!"

"Yeah? And...?" She looked at what she could see of the small town. "Is that important for some reason?"

"Hell, yeah it is! It's the last small town we'll see until we hit the shipping channel across the peninsula. It's a shortcut to Green Bay."

"Really? How long until we get to the shipping channel?"

Jake trailed his finger up the map and shrugged. "Probably late this evening, but we should make it before it's too dark. It says there's a Coast Guard station there."

"I wonder if anyone is alive there." What she wouldn't give to find out what was happening across the country. Their days on the boat had been deceptively normal. They had a fridge and microwave in the cabin and even a little stove although they hadn't been using it. But the absence of other boaters and the eerie, empty harbors, drove the truth home. This went far beyond Chicago. If she hadn't met Jake and at least seen the one other guy in Chicago who had survived, she would have thought she was the only person still walking the face of the Earth.

Chapter Twenty-Five

Hunter and Sophie had to ride for over an hour before they found a suitable place to stop. The bridge had ended in a good-sized city, and they'd hurried through to avoid any contact with people. Finally, they came to a farm. There hadn't seemed any signs of life from the house, and they didn't need to get very close to either the barn or the house to learn that whoever and whatever had lived on the farm hadn't made it. The now-familiar stench told the story.

Sophie nudged him. "What about down there?" She pointed to the far end of a fenced pasture.

He regarded the tree and bushes. It would provide cover if anyone was around, especially once they built a fire. He looked near the house for a woodpile. Farmhouses always had a woodpile and this one was no different. Sure enough, stacked neatly by the side was a pile high enough for many nights if they had to stay for a few days to let Princess heal. Food could become an issue, though. "Yeah, that could work."

They had made camp under the tree and had let the horses free in the fenced area. It was nice to not have to have to stake them out and worry about the stakes coming out. They didn't find a stream, but there was a hand pump beside a trough at the other end of the pasture. He'd pumped until his arm was sore and had enough water for the horses, a bucket for Buddy, and one for him and Sophie.

Hunter ran his hand down Princess's leg. He'd already inspected her hoof and hadn't found anything alarming, but other than routine cleaning of hooves with a pick, he didn't know what to look for in the way of injuries. There had been no redness, swelling or discharge around the hoof, so he took that to be a good sign.

"Easy, girl." He wasn't certain, but it seemed like there was a slight swelling near the back of her leg. He checked the opposite leg in the same location. The side she was favoring was definitely swollen compared to the other side. He sighed and stroked her back, and moved to her head, untying the lead rope from around the fence and unclipping it from her halter. "Go, Princess. Eat up." He was out of the oats he'd brought, but the grass here was thick and still green.

He carried the bucket back to the camp, set it down, and flexed his hand. Sophie wasn't there, but she had taken out the cooking kit and some ingredients. He hoped she hadn't gone in the house. Then he spied her coming from behind the house, a bundle in her arms.

"Hunter, look what I found." She eased down to kneel, setting her bundle on the ground. It was a faded, green, towel. Inside were dozens of ripe strawberries.

His mouth flooded. "Where did those come from?"

"There's a garden back there. Nothing else is ripe yet, but there's a big patch of strawberries." She popped one in her mouth and closed her eyes for a moment, then opened them, smiling. "Oh my god, they taste so good. Better than candy."

He dropped to sit beside her and took a few. The sweet, tart, juice burst over his tongue in an explosion of goodness. "Did you see anything else?"

"Just a clothesline. That's where I got the towel."

Hunter froze in the act of popping a few more strawberries in his mouth. He opened his hand, examining the fruit. "What if the towel was contaminated?"

"What if it is? Then we die like everyone else, but at least we have a fabulous last meal." She took another and bit it in half. The juice stained her lips red, reminding him of the blood he'd seen on victims' faces.

He returned the berries to the towel and stood, wiping his hands on his jeans. "I'm going to get wood for a fire."

He dug into his pack and pulled out a thick pair of leather gloves he'd found at the first farm and tucked them into his back pocket. They'd serve double duty—protect his hands from the sharp edge of the wood and from the virus if it still lurked on any surfaces near the house.

As he took care of the chore, he couldn't get Sophie's fatalistic reply out of his mind. Did she really not care if she lived or died? He wondered how he would feel if his dad wasn't waiting like a beacon of hope out on an island. Would he just give up and not care if he lived or died? Would he become careless? Did it mean he would take risks?

He reached the woodpile and looked for a way to carry enough wood for the night. Tugging his mask up over his nose, he put the gloves on and poked around in a shed near the house. The stench was no worse near the door of the small, aluminum building and there was no lock on the door. He opened it and discovered the shed was the equivalent of a giant junk drawer.

A shelving unit on one side was stuffed full of greasy engine parts, although what model of engines they were from, Hunter had no clue. The other side of the shed contained a large red metal tool cart. Mugs on top of the cart overflowed with rusted nails, screws, washers, and drill bits. At the back of the shed was a hand-truck.

Taking the hand-truck over to the wood pile, he slipped on the gloves and loaded it with as much wood as he could. He had to go slow and pull it behind him, nearly horizontal to the ground to keep the wood from tumbling off. As he passed the house, he noted a flower garden with a rock border. He took eight of the rocks and added them to the pile of wood. They were all about the same size and would be perfect to lay beneath the grill.

When he reached the campsite, he parked the hand-truck beside the tree and set up the rocks, arranging the kindling flat as he'd learned in Boy Scouts. He stuffed torn paper into spaces between and under the kindling and lit them. As the kindling caught, he glanced at Sophie. "Did you mean it when you said that?" He didn't explain what he meant. He could see in her face that she knew.

She sorted through the packets of food they had, setting aside rice and beans. Drawing a deep breath and tucking a lock of hair behind her ear, she shrugged. "I guess. I mean, what's the difference? We're all gonna die soon anyway. Either from the disease now or starve to death in the next year."

"Starve to death? What makes you think that?"

She spread her hands, gesturing at the farm. "Who's left to plant the food? Who's going to truck the produce to the grocery stores?" Her eyes opened wide as she tilted her head. "Are you really this naïve, Hunter?"

He didn't reply, just added a small log to the fire. Of course, he worried about the things she brought up, but people survived long before Walmart came into existence and he was pretty sure they'd survive long after it disappeared.

"Face it, Hunter—the world as we knew it is gone. From now on, people are going to take what they can and to hell with the rest. That's what happened in my little town." She pulled her knees up to her chest and wrapped her arms around them.

Her tone alerted him that she'd hinted at something important. He slanted her a look. Maybe this was when she'd open up to him. "What happened?"

Sophie didn't speak for a long time. Long enough that he had time to set the rack over the fire, fill the pot with water, and set it to boil.

She handed him the beans, dried beef, and a couple of cubes of chicken bouillon he'd taken from the farmhouse. He dumped it all in the water. He'd add the rice later. He wasn't the best of cooks, but after a long day, he and Sophie would eat just about anything.

"My parents were both at work when they got sick. I guess I missed out because I was mad at my mom and had gone up to my room the night before."

"What were you mad about?"

Her lip quivered as she lifted one shoulder. "It's so stupid now. I wanted to go with my friend's family to their summer cabin over Memorial Day weekend, but my mom said no, that I had to go to my brother's eighth grade graduation instead. I was so angry. I called my brother a spoiled brat and stormed up to my room. It was the last I ever saw any of them alive. I was supposed to go to school and pretended to, but skipped instead and hung out by a lake near my house. I didn't go home until late at night because I met a guy there. He had beer, and we ate a couple of hot dogs."

He wanted to ask if the man she'd met had been one of the guys they had killed, but didn't interrupt for fear she would clam up again. This was the first time she'd said anything about her family.

"Obviously, I couldn't go home drunk, so I called and left a message that I was spending the night at my friend's house." Her hands were clenched in her lap and every few seconds, she twisted them a tiny bit. "I thought it was strange that nobody answered their phone. Not my mom. Not my dad. Not even my brother. I guess I passed out from the beer because next thing I remember was the guy trying to get my jeans off me."

She paused, her hands twisting tighter. He feared for her wrists, but she cleared her throat and continued, "I freaked and hit him with a beer bottle, and I thought I killed him, but then I saw he was breathing so I jumped on my bike and went home as fast as I could pedal. I think it was about one in the morning by then, and I was still kind of drunk and freaked out about the guy. I never even realized nobody was home. I was just relieved I didn't get caught."

"Were you okay? The guy didn't...he didn't..." Hunter stumbled over the word, not knowing if he should ask, but she seemed to trust him. "He didn't hurt you, did he?"

She shook her head. "No, but I was pretty shaken. The next day was a Saturday, and I slept late. It was about noon when I woke up."

Her hands stilled, and she stared at them for a long moment. "The house was so quiet. I'll never forget that. I jumped out of bed. I just knew something was wrong, but I didn't know what. My parents' room was empty, the bed made. I couldn't tell if my brother had been there because his room is always a mess, but I didn't see him, and his computer was off, and he only did that when he was leaving for school—I think." She gave a soft laugh. "Anyway, my mom left a rambling message on our voicemail, and there was a message from a hospital about my brother. I didn't know what to do because my mom still didn't answer her cell and none of my friends did either. I turned on the TV just to hear another voice, and that's when I learned about the virus. I waited at home for days, but never heard from my family again."

A knot formed in Hunter's throat. He tried to speak through it. "I'm sorry, Sophie."

"Yeah. Me too. My mom had left a message on my cellphone earlier on the day I skipped school. I never heard my phone ring when she left it." Tears streamed down her face, tracing around her nose and dripped onto her hands. "My mom sounded normal then—not like in the rambling message. I listened to it over and over until the phones stopped working. Anyway, she apologized and had offered a compromise on the weekend. If I went to the graduation ceremony on the Friday night, I could skip the party on Saturday and go to the lake house."

She brought her hand up, using the back of her wrist to swipe at her nose as she shrugged. "So, you see, everyone I love is dead, and I should be too. I would be if I hadn't been a terrible daughter. I'd be with my family."

He wanted to tell her that he was glad she wasn't with her family, but he couldn't squeeze the words out. Instead, he reached for her hand, not caring about the tears or anything else that might be on it. He rubbed his thumb gently across the back of it.

Her breathing shaky, she added, "I guess I'm lucky in some ways."

"How's that?" He couldn't see how she could consider herself lucky.

She gave his hand a return squeeze. "Because you found me before the guys who had me could... *do* anything. They were waiting to see if I would get the virus first. They didn't care if they had it and could give it to me, of course." She shook her head.

COLE CLEANED TRENT'S BODY, arranging his limbs, so he appeared to be sleeping. They couldn't wait too long to dispose of the body and not just from a contamination aspect. The weather had been hot for so early in the summer. He left Trent in the clothes he'd been wearing and just wiped his face free of blood as much as he could, but his lips were torn, and the cracks contained dried blood that wouldn't wipe away—not unless he wiped harder than he dared.

He rolled his nephew onto a large, clean sheet, leaving a space for his head. As he performed the heartbreaking task, a memory popped into his head of how when Hunter had been born, the nurse had wrapped him like a mummy. It was a precious memory that he tried to push away to keep from tarnishing it, but it played out in his mind and it helped get him through the horrible job.

When he had learned the art of mummy-wrapping his son, it had given him joy. Often it was after giving his son a bath, drying, powdering, and diapering the baby. It was their special time, and it gave Brenda a solid hour to sit and relax in the evening. He'd present his wife with the sweet smelling, sleepy bundle who needed just one more feeding before going to sleep.

The memory gave him a brief mental respite, but dealing with Trent's remains was an exhausting job, especially while dressed in a full biohazard suit. He sat back on his haunches to catch his breath after getting the sheet tucked in. He had a plastic tarp to take the body to the funeral pyre, but he couldn't bring it in until he had disinfected the room. He spent the next hour spraying the room down with a mixture of bleach and water. It meant moving Trent yet again once he had the tarp in place. Grunting, he rolled Trent one more time, then stood bent at the waist as he caught his breath.

Dammit. Trent's eyes wouldn't stay closed. He'd tried to close them to make him appear to be sleeping so Sean, Jenna and Piper could see Trent one last time, ideally looking peaceful. Reaching down, he tried again, gently closing the eyelids, but gave up after a few attempts. He wasn't a mortician and didn't know the tricks to keep the lids shut for open casket funerals.

"Joe!" Sweat ran into his eyes, but he couldn't wipe it away since the suit had a full hood—not that he would have touched his eyes anyway, but the sweat burned, and he blinked hard to clear his vision. "I'm ready for your help now!"

"Coming in." Joe opened the door and glanced around the room before his gaze landed on Trent. He made the sign of the cross, his eyes closing briefly as his mouth moved. Cole waited, touched by the other man's behavior.

"Are the others getting gear on?" Cole sat on the bench for a moment, the heat from the suit and his exertion making him light-headed for a few seconds. He longed for a drink of water.

"Yep. I told them a few minutes ago that it was almost time. They're waiting by the spot."

"We'll light the fire after they get a look and say their goodbyes, but tomorrow we're having a more formal ceremony when we don't have to wear all this protection." He gestured to the suit. He was finding it difficult to mourn his nephew while also playing the role of undertaker.

"Good idea." Joe knelt, taking the head of the tarp. "I'll take this end. You look a little shaky."

"It's the heat." Cole drew a deep breath. It had to be over a hundred degrees in the suit.

"I feel like a piece of cod in a fish boil myself."

Cole gave a wan smile and nodded. "Okay. Let's get this over with."

Chapter Twenty-Six

Elly jumped onto the dock and looped the rope around a cleat. They were at the end of the shipping channel in Sturgeon Bay, according to the map. After this, they would be in open water in Green Bay so they had to make sure to top up their gas tanks before they crossed the bay. She hoped she could find the island. Cole had told her the name of the town the island was offshore from, but the town was on the other side of the bay. He said it wasn't more than a mile or so out, so at least they could get to the other side. Then, they could follow that coast and check whatever islands they came to.

They had passed a few boats and were both wary and hopeful, but the boats had turned out to be drifting. Jake had tossed a can of soda into one to get the attention of anyone who might be in the cabin, but their shouts didn't get a response, and a cloud of flies rose in the air.

After that, they just watched the other boats float by, neither of them speaking. Even the Coast Guard station at the entrance of the channel had shown no signs of life. They had blasted their horn a few times to no avail.

They had decided one of them would stay with the boat while the other ventured on shore a little way to see if there were any supplies to be had. They had enough, but she thought they shouldn't show up at Cole's island without something to contribute.

"I'll be back in twenty minutes, if not sooner."

"I'm going to see about getting gas from these other boats."

"Be careful."

"Okay… *Mom.*" Jake grinned.

She narrowed her eyes at him before chuckling and heading towards shore. Technically, she was old enough to be his mother if she'd been a teen mom, but she didn't feel old enough to have a child in his late teens. Still, she couldn't help uttering the directive. It just came naturally. She wiped her sunglasses on her shirt and put them on, scanning the shore as she strode down the dock. A bridge was on her left, but on the other side was a large, red boat. Stenciled on the side, it claimed to be a fireboat that offered rides. It looked cool and any other time she would have been drawn to it, but she didn't have time to explore. A café on shore drew her. She hoped there would be stores of food inside.

At a couple of other harbors she had explored and found most places ransacked, but with the rate at which people died, there had to be a few places that hadn't been touched.

She had both her own backpack and carried Jake's, both empty now. She hoped she could fill them with something. She pulled her mask on and donned gloves, stretching the blue material over her hands, inspecting them for any holes. With her supply limited, she couldn't afford to toss them out and had been washing them in soapy water with a touch of bleach. She worried the bleach would weaken the rubber.

The café had a broken front door, and she peeked in, nudging the door wider with her toe. A glass bakery case at the front was broken and a cooler that probably normally contained cans or bottles of soft drinks for purchase, was empty, the door hanging by one hinge. On a positive note, she didn't see any bodies, and while her mask blocked mild odors, she didn't detect the heavy stench of death.

Venturing farther in, she paused at a door that she hoped led to the kitchen. Listening for anything, but all she heard was the faint sound of the boats outside bumping against the docks as the waves lapped at their hulls, and seagulls. Inside, there was nothing except a few papers blowing across the floor.

She pushed the swinging door into a kitchen that, while not in great shape, didn't look totally trashed. A bag of flour lay on its side on a stainless steel table, the contents spilling out onto the table and the floor. Rodent droppings and little footprints let her know that bag of flour was contaminated, but she spied large plastic bins on the lower shelf of a metal shelving unit. Crossing to it, she pulled the first bin out and found a couple of twenty-five pound sacks of flour. That would make a lot of bread. She wouldn't be able to carry it herself, but one of the smaller worktables had wheels. She was going to load the table in the kitchen but thought of the threshold of the door to the outside. The wheels were small and probably wouldn't handle the bump well when it was fully loaded. Instead, she wheeled the table outside, lifting it slightly to get it over the bump. Returning to the kitchen, she lugged the sacks of flour.

One bin held three sacks of sugar, but two had been gnawed into by rodents, the contents leaking out, but the third hadn't been touched yet.

On the top shelf of the unit, she found a container holding three two-pound bags of dry yeast. It was untouched, and she considered it her best find. Thrilled, she put those in her backpack along with a five-pound bag of bread flour and a small box of salt. Glancing at her watch, she realized her time was almost up.

She wrangled the make-shift cart down the sidewalk and across the street. There was a ramp down to the harbor, but with nothing holding the sacks on the slippery metal, she worried about everything sliding off, the bags breaking open on the concrete. Deciding to stand in front of the cart and reaching her hands around to grasp the legs of the table, she could keep the cart from going too fast.

"Hey!"

Elly whirled, catching the cart before it could send her crashing down the ramp. The voice was too deep to be Jake's. A large man carrying a shotgun strode down the sidewalk towards her. She froze at the sight of the weapon.

"That belongs to me!"

"I'm sorry. I thought everyone was... gone."

"You thought wrong. Everything in this town is now mine. Get the hell out of here. And leave the table."

If she walked away from the table now, it would careen down the ramp. "I can't."

She didn't mean she wasn't going to leave, just that if she abandoned the cart, the flour, sugar, and yeast would probably break open when it fell from the cart.

The man hitched the gun up, bringing it to bear on her. "Step away right now."

Shrugging, she raised her hands and stepped to the side. She hated to see food going to waste, but there wasn't anything she could do about it. It would have been comical watching him chase after the cart, his mouth open in surprise, but Elly bolted the second he was past her. She had come up via steps farther down and found them. Praying Jake had all the gas they needed, she raced down the pier and spied Jake, his back to her, a gas can tilted as he filled the tank.

"*Jake*! Start the boat!"

He turned, confused at first, but then he set the can down and jumped to start the boat. As she raced down the pier, she felt the vibration of another set of feet pounding after her. She was never going to make it.

When she reached the cabin cruiser, she leaped in and reached for the rope in the same motion. Glad she had tied a quick-release knot, she yanked on the end just as the boat lurched in reverse.

"Get down!" Jake ducked.

Elly didn't ask why, but before she could follow the command, she tumbled backward, landing on the yeast and flour in her bag when the boat jerked forward. Stunned, she flinched at the sound of a shot, instinctively covering her face when she saw something falling on her like confetti.

Turning over, she crawled to Jake, who was trying to maneuver the boat from a crouching position. Blood ran down his face. "Are you okay?"

"Yeah. Not sure what hit me, but it was small. Probably a piece of plastic from the boat." He nodded towards the railing in front of him. A good-sized chunk of fiberglass was missing, and the railing hung loose. Another shot made them both duck, but this one didn't hit the boat.

"Did you get enough gas?"

"I was just topping it off when you hollered. I have the other can full, so yeah, I think so."

As the harbor receded, Elly eased up to stand, slinging off the backpack as she watched the man on the pier. He shook the weapon and shouted something, but between the distance and the boat's engine, she couldn't make out what he said.

Jake swiped a streak of blood from his face and wiped his hand on his cargo shorts. "So what happened?"

Elly sat on the seat next to the captain's seat and unzipped the backpack, hoping the bags hadn't exploded when she landed on them. "I found a café with a bakery. The front was trashed, but the kitchen wasn't in bad shape and I had bags of flour and sugar loaded up to bring back to the boat when that guy showed up."

The yeast looked okay, but the bag of flour had a tear in it. She left it in the backpack. They could deal with it later. "All I ended up getting were a few bags of yeast and a small bag of bread flour." She lifted one of the bags of yeast.

"The yeast is a good thing, right? I mean, you don't need much to make bread."

She raised an eyebrow. "How do you know that?"

"Hey, just because I'm a cool guy doesn't mean I don't know how to bake." He grinned. "Okay, I'm not exactly a baker, but my mom used to bake a lot, and I'd help her when I was little." His smile faded, and he turned away from her. "My mom always gave me a bit of dough to knead." He didn't speak for a few minutes, just stared ahead. "I don't remember the last time I baked with her." His voice twisted on the last bit, and he cleared his throat.

Elly patted his shoulder as she carried the backpack and yeast into the cabin. When she returned, Jake had schooled his face into his normal grin, asking if they could make beer with the yeast, but his eyes still held a hint of sadness.

"When we get to the island, we'll suggest it. If I remember right, Cole liked a cold beer now and again. He'd probably like that idea. I'm sure his son will go for it."

"His son?"

"Didn't I tell you about Hunter?"

"Not that I remember. Maybe you did when we first met. That seems like a long time ago now, doesn't it?"

She agreed that it did and told Jake as much as she could recall about Cole's son which wasn't much since she'd never met the young man. "I hope he'll be there too."

"Yeah. Who knows? We could get there and find it deserted."

Elly sighed, afraid to voice the same fear as if acknowledging the fear would make it come true. Instead, she reached around Jake for the map, sat down and spread it across her lap. "We should reach the other side of the bay in a few hours, right?"

He nodded. "I think so. The island should be a little south of where the channel opens up."

Elly stood. She couldn't see across the bay yet, but they still had a few miles before they reached the end of the channel. Her stomach twisted with a combination of anticipation, excitement, and apprehension.

HUNTER AWOKE EARLY and checked on the horses. He breathed a sigh of relief that the swelling was down on Princess's leg but worried it would come back. She still favored it a little, and that was without carrying a burden. What they needed was a horse trailer and a truck. He stroked the mare and checked to make sure they still had enough water.

Chances of eventually finding both a truck and trailer were good as there were farms all around this area, but they could zig zag across the county stopping at random farms without finding one. He wondered if there was a riding stable nearby.

To his left was a good-sized hill. He glanced back at the camp site wondering if he should let Sophie know where he was going, but decided against it. She'd been sleeping soundly when he'd left. They had a long day ahead of them.

He hopped the fence and jogged to the base of the hill, climbing it in a few minutes. The view was even better than he'd hoped. Below lay a beautiful green valley stretching for miles east. Roads crossed the land breaking it into roughly rectangular sections, and at least every third section had a farm. If they followed the road going due east, they would pass at least five farms, three on the north side of the road and two on the south. Compared to other roads, the one heading east didn't have too many wrecks, although he saw a few dotting the roadway, there looked to be room on pass them without going too close. The shoulder of the road would be easy on the horses too.

When he returned to the campsite, he found Sophie had built a small fire and was stirring a pot of oatmeal.

"I thought this would be a good way to use up the strawberries before they get soft and mushy."

"That sounds great and smells even better." He put aside his misgivings about the strawberries. There were so many chances to get the virus, other than taking sensible precautions, they couldn't let fear rule all their decisions. He rolled their bedding into a neat bedroll and gathered up everything that Sophie wasn't using, packing it away. They'd be ready to go as soon as they were done eating.

By mid-morning, they had passed eight farms, and the hill he had scouted from was well out of sight behind them. Sophie rode Princess but had packed almost all the gear on Red to lighten the mare's load.

So far, they hadn't found any trailers, but they had found another strawberry patch and had picked a quarter bucketful and had found another farm with a hand pump that worked. They let the horses drink while they picked the strawberries. A few chickens clucked around that farm and at first, Hunter had held out hope that someone was alive at the farm, but the house had the familiar smell, although not as strong as others. Either the bodies had been dead so long that they were mostly decomposed, or they were still somewhat fresh. Either way, neither of them wanted to explore the house to find out and stuck to the outbuildings. Whoever lived here had freed their animals before succumbing, and Hunter had new respect for the deceased owners of the farm.

Hunter pumped more water to wash the sticky juice from his hands and splashed his face while he was at it.

"Hey, look!"

He swiped his face on his shoulder, he reached for the gun he'd taken from Sophie's attacker, his hand resting on the handle as he spun.

Sophie stared at him for a second before shaking her head. "Down boy, I was talking about them."

He followed where she pointed and saw two goats. They approached the trough, and one butted Hunter's thigh, not the least bit shy with him.

Laughing, he reached down and ran his hand over the coarse coat. "Are you thirsty? I can pump some for you too." The trough was too high for them, but Hunter spied a battered metal bucket in the weeds by the back door of the farmhouse. He jogged to it, trailed by the goats, and returned to the pump, filling the bucket. Both animals dipped their heads in at the same time although only one could fit. "Hey there, I'll pump enough for both of you."

Sophie laughed and took the shoulders of one of the goats and pulled him away. After a minute, Hunter did the same with the other goat while Sophie released hers to get his turn.

"They're so cute!"

"Yeah, but we can't keep them." Hunter felt as if he was channeling his father.

"I wasn't going to ask, but why not?" She shot him a petulant look.

"I don't think they can keep up with the horses."

"Maybe they can, maybe they can't, but look how skinny they are."

Hunter looked and shrugged. While not robust, he couldn't see their ribs. They seemed okay to him. "I'm going to check out the barn over there." The driveway led straight to it, and he hoped it doubled as a garage. Braced for disappointment, he stood back in shock when he found a large silver pickup truck. He ran to the back. And it had a trailer hitch. Perfect. Keys. He glanced at the house. It would be worth it to risk going inside if he could get the keys. They had to be here somewhere.

Leaving the doors open, he jogged back to Sophie. "There's a truck, a good one. But I need to go inside to look for keys."

She glanced at the house, then to the barn, her lips pursed to the side as though weighing the risk. "Okay, but be careful."

"I will. I've done it before at the first farm I was at." He ran to Red and dug a mask and gloves out of his pack. "I'm going to try not to touch anything except keys if I can find them."

Hunter braced for what he'd see inside the home. He tried the doorknob, but it was locked. He grabbed a stone lining the flower bed and broke one of the small square panes. He worried about putting a hole in his glove so he turned to Sophie, "Can you grab that towel out of the pack—the one you gathered the strawberries in."

She nodded and raced across the yard to where the horses were hitched and found the towel. Before he could take the towel, she elbowed him out of the way. "Let me. If you slice your gloves without knowing it, you could get sick." She shook out the towel, folded it, and set it inside the window frame, then made a motion to say it was all his now.

He nodded, and reached inside, found the deadbolt and gave it a twist. The lock on the doorknob was still engaged, and he leaned on it, just able to grab it and give it a twist. The door opened. It had been easier than he expected and even though he knew the people inside were dead, he felt guilty for breaking into their house.

The kitchen was neat. Much neater than he expected. He paused. Maybe the owners weren't dead. What if they had just abandoned their home to escape their virus, just like his dad had done? What if someone was breaking into their home right now?

The counters were clear, and he looked beside the door to see if there was a key hook, but there was nothing. Just a plaque that said, "This Home is Built on Love and Shenanigans."

Hunter closed his eyes briefly. He hadn't been raised to be particularly religious, but if he knew a prayer, he'd say one for this family. Drawing a deep breath, he moved into the dining room. A layer of dust coated the dark table. It felt wrong, like the dust shouldn't be there and he would bet anything that it never had been before.

The well-kept home made it easy to search for the keys, but making his way through the first floor, he came up empty. Hunter stood at the base of the stairs, willing himself to climb to the second floor. The smell of death became stronger with each step, and he stopped on the landing. Dread flooded him, but he took the rest of the steps quickly, just to get it over with.

He opened the first door on his left. It had a single bed tucked under the eaves. Monster truck posters decorated the walls, and a few dusty football trophies stood on the dresser. A red and blue tassel hung from the arm of one of the little plastic football players on top of a trophy. The bed was made, and the room empty. He guessed the usual occupant of the room was away college. Or had been.

The next room was white, with a yellow canopy over the bed that billowed when he opened the door. This room was also empty, the owner of the room probably a teenage girl from all the makeup littering the dresser.

Two more rooms to go. He stepped across the hall and found a plain room. Clean, but no personality. Probably a guest room. That left one more, and as he opened the door, the stench almost knocked him out. He found the family. They were all in the room. Three were laid out neatly on the bed, their hands clasped as though they had died taking a nap on the sofa. Except for the holes in their foreheads, they might have been.

The prescription bottles on the dresser told the story. Sleeping pills. The other bottle had pain killers.

The fourth body was sprawled on the floor, a dark stain beneath the head. The wall opposite the bed had a matching stain sprayed across it. It appeared the family had chosen to take their own lives, with the husband and father making sure they all went painlessly, while he died last, at his own hand. The gun lay beside the body.

He started to back out when a glint of metal caught his eye. There, on the night table on the far side, was a set of keys. Shit. He picked his way around the father and grabbed the keys.

Sprinting from the room, he flew down the stairs, gorge rising in his throat. He tried to swallow it, knowing he couldn't take his mask off inside the house.

Hunter burst through the door onto the porch, tore his glove off and was about to reach for his mask when Sophie stopped him. "Wait!" She squirted hand sanitizer into his palm, rubbing it all around with her glove clad hands.

The scent of alcohol when he ripped his mask off made the nausea he'd tried to hold back impossible to contain. He turned away from Sophie and retched until his stomach was empty and sore.

While he stood bent, waiting for the dry heaves to stop, Sophie took his other hand and repeated the process of sanitizing it, taking the keys he held and dropping them onto the grass.

She gave him a water bottle. "Rinse, and then just take small sips."

He followed her suggestions and felt better in a few minutes. "Sorry."

"It's okay." She retrieved the keys and doused them in hand sanitizer.

If the keys hadn't been for the truck, Hunter didn't know what they would do. He didn't think he could go through something like that at another house, but the keys worked, and even better, the truck had almost a full tank. The cab had a second seat, and they piled the gear inside. "We'll go to a few more farms near here and see if we can find a trailer. If we can't, we have to go."

Sophie looked out the window at the horses, now unsaddled and grazing in a small paddock. "We have to come back and free them first."

Hunter agreed. He couldn't let them die of thirst.

Their luck stayed with them, and the second farm down had a small horse trailer. Hunter and Sophie had to take a few minutes to figure out how to hitch it to the truck, but once they did, they laughed and gave each other a high five.

It was already noon by the time they arrived back at the farm and managed to get the horses into the trailer. Hunter checked the empty barn and found several bales of hay. There were only three bales and a few sacks of sawdust. He grabbed the bags along with the hay. They could use the sawdust if they found a stable for the horses.

The farmer must have been running low on hay or maybe they had set it out for the horses they had freed. He felt like he knew the family and that they probably would have done that. These bales were tucked way in the back of the loft.

Red and Princess must have been in a trailer before because they didn't balk when Hunter led them in to the trailer. He got them settled and lifted the gate, unable to believe they could be at the island by evening.

As they drove down the winding drive, the goats raced alongside them, and Hunter stopped. "I'll be right back."

He didn't know if they would stay in the truck, but he threw one of his blankets in the area between the bales and spread it over the bed. He hoped they didn't eat all the hay, but then shrugged. If they did, they did. It wasn't enough to last the horses anyway.

Sophie came out to see what he was doing. She grinned and coaxed the goats into the bed.

Hunter closed the tailgate. "What if they jump out?"

"We can't help it if they do, but I think they're smarter than that."

Chapter Twenty-Seven

Cole lay in bed. When he remembered what day it was, he didn't want to get up. Every morning, his first thought was of Hunter and where he might be. Part of him clung to hope, but the other part, the realistic part, knew chances were slim. Every day, the realistic side took another bite from the hopeful side, and now, there was just a tiny crumb left. When that was gone, what would be his reason to get up in the morning?

"Cole?"

He rolled his head. Sean. Draping his arm across his eyes, he wished he could pretend he was still asleep. It would delay the stab of guilt he felt when he looked at his brother. "Yeah?"

"I know you wanted to have the... the funeral first thing, but I wondered if we could do it this evening instead?"

Cole sat and swung his feet off the bed. "We can do it whenever you like. I only said morning because I thought that would be easiest for your family, but it's your decision." He stood and drew on the t-shirt he'd draped over the chair in the room. He'd planned to take a swim this morning to get clean for the funeral, but now he'd swim later.

Sean leaned against the doorjamb and nodded. "Okay, then later this evening. Jenna wants to bake a cake, and we're not sure how it'll turn out using the grill as an oven."

"How can she make a cake without eggs?" Cole hoped to venture onshore and see if they could round up any chickens. While they had some powdered milk, he hadn't thought to get powdered eggs. It was surprising how many dishes required them.

"We had a couple of cans of soda in the car. They must have rolled out during a grocery run sometime. Anyway, Jenna knows a recipe that uses soda instead of eggs."

"Interesting." When Sean remained in the threshold with the silence growing awkward, he asked the first thing that came to his mind, just to break the silence. "What kind of cake?"

"Chocolate. It was Trent's favorite."

"Hunter loved… loves chocolate, too." He stumbled over the tense and Sean picked up on it.

"Cole, I didn't know how to bring this up, but Jenna thought it might do you good if you laid Hunter to rest today, too."

His gut reaction was anger. "No!" His hands clenched and his jaw tightened.

"Think about it, Cole. I know it's hard—God knows, I *know*—but I've been watching you. You're working yourself to death around here. We have enough wood stacked to last two winters."

"No—" Sean exaggerated. Besides, they needed as much as possible to get through the winter for heating and cooking.

"Yes! We do. Joe even said so, and he knows more about that. He lived in a little cabin up north for a few years. Anyway, that's not my point. You're trying to keep your mind from worrying about Hunter and, as much as it hurts, admitting he's not coming. He tried his best, but the world went crazy. Accepting it can help you move on."

"Move on? To what? What do I have to move on to, Sean?" Cole's voice sounded strangled even to his own ears. "I have no wife and if I give up on Hunter, no child." He waved towards the mainland. "And with no hope of ever having either again. What's the point?"

"The point is, we need you, Cole. I need you, and I'm going to need you a whole helluva lot more after today. I still have a daughter to protect and a wife. I can't let anything happen to them, but I'm not sure I can protect them all by myself."

Cole tried to hang on to the anger because as long as he had that, he could hang on to hope too.

"Piper is like a daughter to you. You've said that before."

Cole nodded, his throat working, but no sound came out when he tried to acknowledge Sean's point. He loved Piper, but that didn't mean he had to give up on his son. He wouldn't do it. He straightened and drew a deep breath. "I can't give up on Hunter. I may never give up unless I see his body, but I'll be okay. I promise to be here for you and your family. They're my family too."

Sean sighed. "I understand. I'd feel the same if there was any way I could deny Trent's death."

He had to bite his tongue to hold back and insist it wasn't denial. Today wasn't the day to have this conversation.

"Are you sure this is the place?" Sophie leaned against the passenger door, her arms crossed. "Nobody's here."

Hunter shook his head. "Hell no, I'm not sure, but why would anyone be here? They'll be on the island."

"Where's the island, and how do we get there?"

Kicking a rock, he watched it bounce down to the pier and drop into the river. "I thought there'd be a boat or something."

"How do we get the animals onto a boat?"

"I don't know! I didn't expect to be here with horses and goats." He turned to scan the area, hoping for a solution, but instead, he spotted his dad's vehicle. "Look! There's his car." He jogged over to it, feeling vindicated.

Sophie followed him and spied the note before he did. She opened the door and handed it over to him.

"He says that they'll be checking the docks every morning."

"But it's afternoon now."

"Yeah. I guess we'll have to camp out one more night." He tried to swallow the disappointment. He'd been so sure he'd see his dad tonight. "It'll give us time to find a place for the animals. One of these garages might work as a temporary stable. Let's look around."

They ended up deciding on the old one-car garage at the back of the property. There was a large fenced yard, and while there wasn't a pump, the river was close enough to haul water. They'd just have to make sure they got back every day.

They threw down the sawdust and a pile of hay in the corner. The garage was big enough for the goats too, and Hunter tossed the blanket in a corner for them.

A bucket hung on a peg on the wall, and he grabbed it. Two buckets of water would be better for all four animals. He shut the door, grabbed the other bucket they'd been using and headed for the river. Sophie stood on the edge of the river and pointed left. "Did you know that Lake Michigan is right there?"

"Yeah, I figured from the map. I don't think you can see the island from here, with the way the shore bends." He thought his dad had said that, but their last few phone calls had broken up so he wasn't positive.

Sophie didn't reply but instead, headed left, intent on something. Hunter looked at both buckets. He'd hoped she'd carry one, but then again, the buckets probably weighed almost as much as she did. Shrugging, he grabbed the handles.

"Hunter! Look!" She jumped up and down, jabbing her finger out towards the lake.

He released the handles and raced to her. "What?"

"A boat!"

"Maybe it's my dad!"

"I know! That's what I thought!"

They ran out as far as they could, waving their hands and shouting. "Dad!"

At first, it looked as though the boat was going to pass the entrance to the river, but suddenly it veered towards them.

Sophie threw her arms around him. "I wasn't sure there really was an island."

Hunter laughed. "I know, right?"

As the boat came closer, a boy Hunter didn't recognize drove the boat. His smile faded. Then a woman appeared beside the boy. Hunter scanned the boat, searching for his dad or even Uncle Sean.

"Is that your aunt and cousin?"

He shook his head. "No, I don't know who they are." His first feeling was crushing disappointment, but then he became wary and looked around. They were completely in the open, and he felt exposed. "Let's get back."

Sophie nodded.

As they retreated, they kept their eyes on the boat. So far, nobody had seemed threatening, but they hadn't smiled either. He rested his hand on the butt of the gun.

When the boat was almost even with them, the operator cut back on the throttle and the woman said, "Is this Oconto?"

That wasn't the question Hunter expected. He didn't know what he expected, but it wasn't something as normal as asking directions. Disconcerted, he simply nodded.

The woman waved, then leaned forward, peering at him. He squirmed under her scrutiny.

"What's she doing?" Sophie whispered.

"I don't know, but it's creeping me out." He took Sophie's hand. "Let's go."

"Hunter? Is that you?"

He stopped dead in his tracks and slowly turned. "Who are you?"

"Are you Hunter Evans?"

It seemed silly to deny it. "Yeah. Why do you want to know?" He walked towards the dock where the boat was inching in.

"Oh my god! I can't believe it! You've grown a lot since the last set of pictures I'd seen."

Hunter cocked his head feeling he should know her, but he didn't recognize her at all. His first thought was that she must be a teacher he'd had at some point, but he couldn't pinpoint her to a grade. He asked again, "Who *are* you?"

She smiled. "I'm your dad's friend, Elly Jackson. We worked together in Africa."

He knew the name, and now that she said it, he recalled pictures his dad had sent him on his phone in a few of the lighter moments of his work there. This woman might be the same one who had been in them. She got out of the boat and crossed the pier towards them. "It's so great to finally meet you."

"Where's my dad?" He didn't intend to sound rude, but he had expected to see his dad when he arrived. What if something had happened to him?

Her smile disappeared. "You mean he's not here with you?"

"We just got here an hour or so ago. We thought your boat was him coming to get us."

The guy who had driven the boat hopped out, and Hunter saw he was younger, probably still in high school, or he would have been.

"Hey, Hunter. I'm Jake. Elly has told me almost nothing about you." He put out a fist.

Hunter bumped it. "Hi, Jake. Is Elly your mom?" He hadn't known she had kids, but then again, he hadn't paid much attention to what his dad said about people he worked with. They were just names to him other than to remember the look on his dad's face when he spoke of her. He'd totally been crushing the lady. "This is Sophie. We met on the way here."

Sophie nodded at the boy but hung back and Jake, to his credit, just smiled and lifted his chin. "Hey, Sophie."

Elly had a mask, but it was around her neck. Hunter had left his packed since he hadn't seen signs of anyone. Sophie carried hers in her back pocket. Jake had slid his up his arm, and it wrapped around his left biceps.

Hunter felt almost naked without his on. He glanced towards the truck, and stepped back. "We should probably..." he made the motions of a mask.

Elly nodded and slipped hers up, indicating that Jake should do the same. "I'm sorry. I should know better."

Jake rolled his eyes but put the mask on. "Kind of pointless now since we've already breathed around each other."

Hunter explained how he had just arrived and how they had horses and goats with them, but that he expected his dad to come in the morning. Or he hoped he would. "I'm so much later than he thought I would be, he probably thinks I screwed up along the way."

"I don't know about you, but I know I've made a ton of mistakes the last few weeks, but somehow, I survived. So did you. We couldn't have screwed up too badly." She offered him a smile. "We could take the boat out there. We're getting low on gas, though, so wanted to stop and find some."

"I don't know how you got gas. I got lucky, and the truck was almost full, but it's close to empty now."

"We've been siphoning from other boats, but there aren't any here."

"How much do you have left in the boat? I know my dad said it was only about a fifteen minute boat ride south of the river."

Jake and Elly exchanged a look then Elly nodded. "We have enough for that. Your dad told me about the island and invited me up here, but I thought I was going to get back home to Atlanta. That didn't happen as you can see, but I hope his offer is still standing."

"Can we go with you?"

"Of course!" Elly laughed. "Can you imagine the look on your dad's face if I showed up and said I left you back on the mainland?"

Hunter grinned. He liked Elly. She was nice. He could see why his dad was friends with her. "We just have to take water to the horses."

Jake helped him, and it took only a few minutes. Then they grabbed all of their gear from the truck and stowed it in the boat.

Before he knew it, they were on their way. Excitement churned through his stomach, and he waved away the granola bar Jake offered him. "Thanks, but I'm not hungry."

Sophie took one and looked a little more relaxed as she sat in the back of the boat, laughing as the wind blew her hair.

Just like his father had said, once they rounded a bend, the island came into view. It wasn't big, but a large house and a row of smaller cabins spread out along a beach. A dock with a couple of boats was south of the beach. Was his dad watching them even now?

Hunter waved, just in case, but he didn't see any return movement. He thought of the virus, unable to shake the nagging fear that it had reached the island, but he did his best to ignore the worry. He refused to consider that they might all be dead.

COLE BUTTONED HIS WHITE SHIRT. It was one he used to wear to the office when he worked, and he wasn't even sure why he had packed it, but it seemed appropriate today. He didn't have a tie, but he wore a clean pair of khaki pants. His last clean pair. Laundry had been far down on the list of things for any of them to do.

Both the shirt and the pants were loose on him, and he had to draw his belt in two notches. Maybe Sean was right, and he was working too hard, but on the other hand, he had never been more fit.

Piper sat in the kitchen, her eyes still red, but she had combed her hair and wore what would normally be considered regular school clothes, but now seemed like formal wear.

"Are your mom and dad still dressing?"

She nodded. "I heard you and Dad arguing this morning."

Cole started to look out at the bay. It was habit to check for more boats, especially after what had happened to Trent, but he froze at her comment and faced her. "I'm sorry you had to hear that."

She shrugged. "My dad's probably right, but I'm glad you still believe. Hunter would like that."

He didn't know how to respond so he turned back to the bay. Her words touched him. He stared at the sparkling water, not really registering the sound until it was so close, he couldn't ignore it. "A boat! It's heading right for the island."

Piper jumped up from the table and headed for the door.

"No, Piper. Stay here!" He took the rifle they had mounted above the door. It was always loaded. "Stay inside and lock the door behind me. Then let your parents know we seem to have visitors."

The last thing he wanted to do was show whoever it was that there was a pretty young girl here. He strode down to the dock, gripping the rifle across his body. He raised it when he reached the dock, not pointing it, but anyone would recognize the threat. Then he saw someone waving at him. Two people, actually. As they came closer, one appeared to be a tall young man, and the other, a short, slim woman. Two others were in the boat that he could see, but they didn't wave. He wished he had brought binoculars. It was one thing they were missing. He squinted at the boat, ignoring the slam of the screen door behind him.

"Who is it?" Sean jogged up to him, shading his eyes with his hand. He had a gun tucked in his waistband.

"I don't know. They'll be close enough in a minute."

"I think you should fire that rifle and scare them away before they come any closer."

"We have time."

"If you won't, I will." Sean started to reach for the rifle, but Cole jerked it out of his reach.

"I said, I'll do it if I feel we have to. We don't even know what they want yet. Maybe they have good news from the mainland."

"Yeah, right," Sean grumbled, but he didn't make another grab for the rifle.

Cole blinked. Then he rubbed his eyes. It was just wishful thinking, but the tall guy, the way he stood…

Then the guy waved at him, and Cole almost dropped the rifle. "No way… can it be? Sean? Is that… tell me that's Hunter." His voice held a pleading note.

Sean shot a look at Cole, then back to the boat. "*Holy shit.*"

"Dad! *Dad!*"

Cole shoved the rifle at Sean and raced to the slip the boat headed for. "Hunter!" He laughed and his knees went weak, but he refused to collapse. He couldn't wipe the grin from his face. The closer the boat came, the bigger his grin became. All the anxiety and worry over the last month flowed out of him and left his limbs feeling like they were made of rubber.

Sean joined him on the pier, smiling, but sadness tinted the smile. "I'm happy for you, Cole. I am, but I can't deal with this right now. I'll go tell the girls that Hunter is here."

Cole's joy diminished a fraction, but he refused to feel guilty that his son was alive, and he believed Sean was happy for him.

A boy Cole didn't know drove the boat, and it was only then that he recognized Elly. She grinned and waved. "Hey, Cole!"

He didn't know the young girl with them either, but he didn't care. As soon as the boat docked, Hunter leaped out. He wore a mask, as did all of the others. Cole pulled his mask from his pocket. He hadn't planned on wearing it today, but had pocketed it out of habit.

Cole met him with the biggest, hardest hug he'd ever given his son. Hunter returned it.

"Dad…" Hunter buried his face against his shoulder, And Cole reached up, holding the nape of son's neck, giving it a gentle squeeze. All of his fears melted away.

They stepped apart and Hunter swiped at his eyes. Cole didn't care if he had tears on his face. What did it matter? "You look good!"

"You too, Dad." Then Hunter laughed. "You're like, all buff! The apocalypse must be agreeing with you."

"Shut up and get in here for another hug." He grabbed Hunter, the hug more playful this time. "You're not so soft in the middle yourself."

Finally, Cole released him, and just grinned like an idiot. He had so many questions he wanted to ask, but they could wait.

Elly stepped forward, he pulled her in for a warm embrace. "It's great to see you, Elly. I'm so relieved you made it."

"I hope your invitation stands. I didn't have anywhere else to go." There was a bit of hesitation in her eyes.

"Of course it stands. You're welcome here." Then he turned to the other two, the boy and the girl. Both hung back. "Hi. I'm Cole. Hunter's dad."

The boy, really a young man, stepped forward, his hand extended. "Nice to meet you, Cole. I'm Jake. Me and Elly met in Chicago."

Cole liked the confidence in his voice. He raised his eyebrows at Elly, curious about how she had come to team up with the teen. Her eyes crinkled. "It's a long story."

Hunter beckoned to the girl, and she slipped up to his son, wrapping her arms around his waist. "Dad, I'd like you to meet Sophie. There was an incident days ago, I guess—I kind of lost track of the days, but we've been traveling together." He put his arm around her shoulders and pulled her close.

Cole gave the girl a speculative look before he held out his hand. "Welcome, Sophie."

Introductions made, they all seemed to be speaking at once as they headed towards the beach and Cole tried to follow all the conversations coming at him. There was something about horses, and arrows, and a storm. He just let them talk. They'd sort it all out later. The only thing he cared about was that his son was home.

When they reached the beach, Hunter stopped and turned to Cole. "Where's Uncle Sean? He was with you, but then he left. Doesn't he want to see me?" He looked around. "And where's Trent? And Aunt Jenna? Piper?"

Cole drew in a deep breath. "Aunt Jenna and Piper are fine. They're in the big house."

Fear entered Hunter's eyes. "And Trent?"

Cole felt everyone's eyes on him. "Come on up to the house. I'll tell you everything."

Afterword

If you have a moment, a review of this book would be fantastic and greatly appreciated. It would help other readers decide if this book is something they might enjoy.

Infection on Amazon

Join MP McDonald's Newsletter list and get a free copy of Mark Taylor: Genesis (The Mark Taylor Series: Prequel)

I came up with the idea for *Infection* and the disease, Sympatico Syndrome by playing the *What if* game. I have been fascinated by diseases since I was a child and used to read the Family Home Medical Guide for fun. In college, one of my favorite classes was microbiology, and if I hadn't already been enrolled in a respiratory therapy program, I would have gone into something involving microbiology.

When I came across an article recently about how toxoplasmosis, the disease that can be spread via contaminated cat litter boxes, changes victims' behavior, I had to read about it. The short version is that it makes primates who are infected less wary of leopards compared to those who are not infected. Scientists think it is because those less wary are more likely to become a jaguar's next meal, and that would put toxoplasmosis into the leopard—which is exactly where the toxoplasmosis wants to live.

I know that many extremely infectious diseases such as Ebola have one thing that limits their spread, and that is that victims are usually so sick at the most infectious stage that they are unable to circulate and spread the disease. In outbreaks, it is usually only those in close contact, i.e., family members and other caregivers, that are at the most risk.

My thought was, what if a disease that had a similar mortality rate, but the infected victims feel great—at first. Beyond great. The disease floods their brain with feel-good endorphins and everyone becomes a friend. That makes the spread of the disease much more likely.

Sympatico Syndrome was the result. I hope it made as much sense in this book as it did in my head.

Aislado Island is completely fictional. There is no such place, nor is there a naval base that deals with biological weapons. Geneva Convention prohibits biological warfare.

The second book of this series, *Isolation,* is in the works and I hope to publish it in early 2017. To be notified of the release, please join my mailing list. (Don't worry, your privacy is important to me and I would never sell or distribute your address to any third parties.)

Also by M.P. McDonald

The Mark Taylor Series

Mark Taylor: Genesis

No Good Deed: Book One

March Into Hell: Book Two

Deeds of Mercy: Book Three

March Into Madness: Book Four

CJ Sheridan Thrillers

Shoot: Book One

Capture: Book Two

Suspense

Seeking Vengeance

I'd like to invite you to receive a free copy of Mark Taylor: Genesis when you join my book info list. Get the free book here:

M.P. McDonald Book Info

No Good Deed: Sample First Chapter

Description:

Seeing the future comes at a price. What price would you be willing to pay to save thousands of lives?

Mark Taylor knows his actions scream *guilty*—but he was only trying to stop the horrible terrorist attack. Instead of a thank you, the government labels him an enemy combatant and throws him in the brig with no rights, no trial, and no way to prove his innocence. He learns first hand that the CIA can do anything they want to him—anything at all.

Mark's just a regular guy—a photographer—who finds himself in an extraordinary situation when an antique camera he buys at a dusty Afghanistan bazaar produces photographs of future tragedies. Tragedies he's driven to prevent.

His frantic warnings about September 11th are ignored but put him in the government cross-hairs where he learns what being labeled an 'enemy combatant' *really* means...

Chapter One

The baby floated face down in the tub. The image hadn't changed, not that Mark Taylor expected it to—not yet anyway. He tucked the photo in his back pocket and trotted down the steps from the 'L' platform. With any luck at all, the next time he looked, the baby would be fine. He skirted around an old lady tottering in his path and glanced at his watch.

All he had to do was find the apartment, convince the mom that he wasn't a nut case, or worse—a peeping tom—just because he knew that her phone would ring and distract her from bathing her daughter. Yep. Nothing complicated. Just get in, alert the mom, and get out. Five minutes. Tops. Mark jogged, cursing under his breath at the rush of people heading towards the train station. The crowd thinned, and he broke into a sprint, his breath exploding out in a cloud of white.

Cars blocked the crosswalk, trapped there when the light turned red. *Shit*. He paced left, then right, willing the light to change. To hell with it. He darted into the street, ignoring the blasting horns. It wasn't like the cars could advance anyway. He stumbled when one bumped his thigh, or he bumped it. He wasn't sure which and didn't have time to find out. Limping, he raced on.

Mid-block, he slowed to read the address numbers set above the entrance of an apartment building. This was the one. He pivoted and took the short flight of concrete steps two at a time and tugged at the door. Locked. *Of course.*

Bracing his hands on the door, he panted. *Think.* There had to be a way in. He wouldn't fail. Not this time.

He swiped his hand down a panel of numbered call buttons, not caring who answered as long as someone let him in. "Come on...*come on.*"

"Who is it?"

"Hey buddy, I forgot my key." It was the first thing that came to him and it didn't work. The next lie didn't either. Unable to think up a plausible story, he resorted to the truth on the fourth response. "It's an emergency! Life or death."

Maybe his voice sounded as desperate as he felt, or maybe the person didn't give a damn—whatever the reason, the guy let him in.

He blinked as his eyes adjusted to the dimness. It was the second floor. He was sure of that. The dream played in his head like a movie, showing him the silver number twenty-two nailed to the door.

There was an elevator, but it was on the fifth floor. He spotted the stairs and flew up them, grabbing the railing to make the tight turn up to the second flight. It occurred to him that the door to the hallway might be locked, but luck was on his side this time, and it opened. Bent in a runner's stance, hands on knees, he huffed and glanced at the number on the door nearest him. Twenty-three. He guessed left and turned in that direction. He raised his hand to knock, but froze when an anguished scream raised the hairs on the back of his neck.

"Christy!"

Startled, he stumbled back, bumping against the wall opposite the door. He was too late. He spun and slammed the side of his fist against the wall, a curse ready to explode off his tongue, when he heard fumbling at the door behind him.

"Help me! Someone!"

At the desperate plea, he lunged to the closed door. "Hello? You okay?" He knew it was a stupid question. Of course things weren't okay.

The door cracked open before a young women clutching a limp, gray baby, elbowed it wide." My baby." Wild, desperate eyes met Mark's. "Please..."

Mark swallowed the acid in his throat and instinctively reached for the infant. "What happened?" He couldn't let on that he already knew. That led to questions he couldn't answer.

"I forgot her in the tub!" She clutched the baby and gave her a shake. "Oh god! Christy! She's not breathing!"

"I know CPR—give her to me." His sharp tone sliced through the mother's shock and she released her daughter with a wail of grief.

Mark positioned the baby with her head in his hand, her bottom in the crook of his arm.

The mother keened with her hands balled in front of her mouth. "Help her!"

The poor woman was teetering on the edge of hysteria, not that Mark could blame her. He was toeing the line himself, but he couldn't cross it. Not if there was a chance of saving the baby. With his free hand, he caught the mother's arm and gave it a firm squeeze. "I'm gonna help her, but you gotta listen to me. You need to call 9-1-1. Got it?"

She tore her gaze from her daughter, nodded, and raced back into her apartment. Mark wracked his brain, searching for a scrap of CPR knowledge that he knew was there. He cringed at the baby's glassy stare and blue-tinged lips. Her legs dangled lifelessly over his arm.

ABCs. That was it. Airway, breathing and circulation. He didn't see any water in her mouth, so her airway seemed okay. He covered her miniature nose and mouth with his own, feeling like a big clumsy oaf. Her scent filled his nose—so clean and innocent. Like baby shampoo and powder. A damp, silky tuft of her hair tickled his cheek. If she died, it'd be his fault. He could have prevented this. He blew again. There wasn't time to worry about guilt now.

Her chest rose with the breaths and he felt it move against his arm. Out of the corner of his eye, he saw doors down the hall opening, and a small crowd gathered around him. Some shouted instructions, and a deep voice ordered someone to the lobby to let the paramedics in when they arrived.

There was no change in Christy's color. Shit. Those paramedics better get here pronto. Why didn't someone else step forward to do the CPR? Hell, there had to be someone more qualified. There was supposed to be a pulse point near the elbow, but damned if he could find it. It wasn't like he'd ever searched for one on a healthy kid before let alone one who might not have one. Was that it? He prodded the inside of her arm, but between his shaking hands and the pudgy cushion at the bend of her elbow, he couldn't feel a beat.

Go to the source. He put his ear to her chest. Nothing. He swallowed hard as he placed two fingers on her breastbone and pushed down. The feel of her tiny chest caving in with each compression made his stomach churn.

He lost count of the cycles of breaths and compressions. It seemed like forever before someone suggested he stop and check for a pulse again. The mom had returned to his side at some point, but his vision had narrowed to Christy's little body cradled in his arms. Mom stroked Christy's forehead and pleaded with her to breathe.

Listen to your mama, sweetie. *Breathe, dammit.* Wait...was she pinker? Or was it wishful thinking? He paused the compressions, but gave another breath.

As he lifted her to listen for a heartbeat, Christy blinked.

Startled, he jerked his head back and glanced at the mom to see if she'd noticed it too. Her eyes full of anguish and fear, lit with a spark of hope as she met his look. It hadn't been his imagination.

Christy shuddered, and then coughed. Mark sat her up as she gagged, worried she was choking. She rewarded his efforts by puking sour milk down the front of him. She cried then, the sound as soft as a newborn kitten's. Impulsively, he kissed the top of her head.

A cheer rose in the hallway, and Mark glanced around, astonished to see so many people. A grin tugged at the corners of his mouth. The mother took her daughter from Mark, but planted a kiss on his cheek. The elevator at the far end of the hall opened, and paramedics stepped out.

Sure. Now they show up. Mark laughed, unable to suppress the giddiness. He took a deep breath, and leaned against the wall, his knees wobbling like Jello. He swiped his arm across his forehead. It was like a damn sauna in here. People crowded around, slapping Mark's shoulders and pumping his hand. Someone handed him a towel and he used it to mop up the mess on the front of his leather jacket, but there wasn't much he could do for the bit that leaked inside.

"Good job, man!" The speaker looked to be early to mid-thirties, close to Mark's own age. "That was awesome!"

"Thanks." Mark opened his mouth to ask if he could use a bathroom to wash up, when his stomach lurched and the bitter taste of bile filled his mouth. Panic surged through him and he rushed into the nearest apartment with an open door. He spotted a hallway and found the bathroom just in time for his lunch to make a return visit.

Spitting out the vile taste, he flushed the toilet and moved to the sink to wash, scooping some water into his mouth and swished it around. He dried his hands on a towel hanging over the shower curtain. He reached for the doorknob, but stopped and pulled the photo out of his back pocket, just to make sure. The picture had only one similarity with the one he'd put in his pocket only minutes before. The baby was still Christy, but now, she was grinning at the camera, showing off two pearly white bottom teeth. It was official. He'd erased another photo.

There was a knock on the door a second before Mark opened it.

"You okay?" It was the guy from the hall. He leaned against the doorway, arms crossed.

Mark nodded and motioned towards the toilet "Yeah. Just feeling the nerves. Sorry for barging in."

The man laughed and stuck out a hand. "No problem. I'm Jason."

"Mark." He clasped the man's hand and gave it a shake.

Jason gave Mark a speculative look. "A few minutes before that happened," he pointed his chin towards the hall, "someone buzzed my apartment, saying they had to get in—that it was an emergency."

Mark tried to play it cool as he edged towards the hallway. "Yeah?"

"That was you, wasn't it?" It was a statement.

"I...uh—"

Jason waved a hand and cut him off. "No worries, dude. I was just curious. I had a grandfather who used to get premonitions. It was spooky. Never thought I'd meet someone else like that. Glad I let you in."

Rattled and still shaking from the flood of adrenaline, Mark could only nod. He breathed a sigh of relief when Jason motioned for him to go first as they went out to the hall.

They watched as the paramedics started an IV on the protesting Christy, and he winced at the blood oozing around the IV site. Poor little thing. He felt a tap on his shoulder and turned to find a Chicago police officer behind him.

"Sir, can I ask you a few questions?"

Mark shoved his hands into his pockets to hide the shaking and shrugged. "Sure."

He asked Mark's name and for some ID. After speaking some cop code into his shoulder radio, he glanced at Mark's driver's license. "You don't live here, so why were you in the building?"

Mark pulled at the collar of his shirt under his coat. Necessity forced him to lie in these situations and he hated it, but the truth was far too complicated. Experience allowed his story to slip easily off his tongue. "I intended to visit a friend, and when I got to the building, someone was coming out, so rather than buzz, I just caught the door. When I got up here, I realized I had the wrong building." He forced a laugh. "My buddy's building looks a lot like this one and I guess I got them mixed up." Mark shook his head and rubbed the back of his neck. He was rambling and decided to cut the explanation short. "It's about time my faulty memory came in handy."

Luck was with him and the officer chuckled. "It sure did. You did a great job."

Mark dipped his head as heat rushed up his cheeks. "Thanks."

The cop's radio squawked, and in the midst of indecipherable code, Mark heard his own name.

The officer cocked his head, his gaze fixed on Mark as he reached up to key the mic. "10-9?"

The message was repeated and the officer tensed, his eyes cold as he acknowledged it and requested back-up. With one hand hovering over his weapon, he pointed at Mark with the other. "Turn around and place your hands on the wall."

Confused, Mark hesitated. "What...why?"

"Hands on the wall. Now!"

The commanding tone jolted Mark into action and he nearly tripped in his haste to comply. "Listen, sir, can I just ask—"

"We can do this the easy way or the hard way. The officer grabbed Mark's arm. "I've been told to bring you in for questioning."

"Who wants to talk to me? Why?"

The few people still milling in the hallway fell silent.

The cop glanced at the watching crowd and hesitated. "Unpaid parking tickets."

Parking tickets? Since when did they go to this much trouble for parking tickets? What the hell was going on? He twisted to see the cop's face. "I don't owe on any tickets. What's this really about?"

Jason stepped forward and pulled out his wallet. "Look, officer, the dude just saved a baby. What does he owe? I'll pay it."

"Step aside; this isn't any of your affair."

"Come on, man, don't be a hard-ass." Jason smiled at the cop, and gestured towards Mark. "I mean, this guy doesn't exactly look like Charles Manson."

Jason's attempt at humor backfired when the cop offered to let Jason accompany Mark.

Jason glared at the cop before casting an apologetic look at Mark. "Sorry. I tried."

Mark nodded. His face burned as the bystanders—the same people who'd cheered him just a few minutes before—now pointed fingers, and whispered to each other.

The cop's fingers dug into Mark's bicep. "Come on. You got some people waiting to meet you."

"Who?" This was going way too far for a few tickets that he couldn't even remember getting. "You sure you got the right Mark Taylor?"

The fingers tightened again as the cop frog-marched him towards the elevator. Mark balked. This was crazy. When the cop pressed him forward, he didn't think, he just reacted, jerking his arm free. "Quit pushing me!" The second the words left his mouth, he wanted to suck them back in.

"Get down! Right now. On your knees." The cop pulled his baton and prodded Mark with it.

"Whoa! Calm down. I just want to know the truth. I have that right, don't I?"

"I'm not going to tell you again." The radio blasted a sharp tone, and Mark started at the sudden noise.

The cop mistook Mark's reflex and swung the baton. Mark ducked his head and the blow landed with a thud against his shoulder. Pain rocketed down his arm like he'd touched a live wire. He sank to his knees. Two more blows landed on his back. He bit his lip to keep from crying out as he fell face-down on the floor, his nose buried in the dank, musty carpet.

The bystanders yelled at the cop while the cop shouted for them to shut up. Without pausing, the officer ordered Mark to lie down. Confused, Mark attempted to lift his face away from the nasty floor to tell him he was already lying down, but a sudden sharp pressure in the middle of his back pinned him to the floor.

He fought to breathe as his arms were wrenched behind him and cuffed. He managed to turn his head, the skin on his face pulling painfully taut as he sucked in air.

The door from the stairwell burst open and three more officers ran towards them, pulling their batons as they charged down the hall. Two men in suits followed, their manner and attitude exuded an aura of power and authority.

The first to reach Mark flashed a badge at him, but Mark couldn't get a clear look from his angle on the floor.

"I'm Special Agent Johnson and this is Special Agent Monroe. We have a warrant for your arrest as material witness to terrorist acts against the United States."

* * *

End of Sample.

Find the book on Amazon:
No Good Deed: Book One

Acknowledgments

I'd like to thank my amazing beta readers, Vickie Boehnlein, Allirea Brumley, Win Johnson, Lala Price, and Pam Moore. I couldn't have published this without them. They gave me valuable feedback on what worked and what didn't work from a readers' point of view.

Special thanks to my writing buddy, J.R. Tate. She's an amazing author and I urge you all to check out her books.

Thanks also, to the Antioch Writer's Group, where I've received lots of encouragement and critique.

And finally, my daughter, Maggie, who helped me brainstorm several aspects of this novel, and who, as a teen herself, and budding writer, gave me feedback to make sure the teens in this novel sound like actual teens.

About the Author

M.P. McDonald is the author of supernatural thrillers and post-apocalyptic thrillers. With multiple stints on Amazon's top 100 list, her books have been well-received by readers. Always a fan of reluctant heroes, especially when there is a time travel or psychic twist, she fell in love with the television show Quantum Leap. Soon, she was reading and watching anything that had a similar concept. When that wasn't enough, she wrote her own stories with her unique spin.

If her writing takes your breath away, have no fear, as a respiratory therapist--she can give it back via a tube or two. She lives with her family in a frozen land full of ice, snow, and abominable snowmen.

On the days that she's not taking her car ice-skating, she sits huddled over a chilly computer, tapping out the story of a camera that can see the future. She hopes it can see summer approaching, too. If summer eventually arrives, she tries to get in a little fishing, swimming and biking between chapters.

www.mpmcdonald.com
mmcdonald64@gmail.com

Made in the USA
Las Vegas, NV
05 July 2022